The Magellan Chronicles

The Longest Voyage
(Book 3)

A biographical novel series of Ferdinand Magellan

By

Brett Stortroen

The Magellan Chronicles: The Longest Voyage
(Book 3)

Treasure Hill Publishing
Dunedin, Fl, USA

Library of Congress Cataloging-in-Publication Data

ISBN 978-1-957612-07-2

Cover art by Mark Daehlin

For inquiries, please email the author at
bstortroen@protonmail.com

By Brett Stortroen

Mecca, Muhammad & the Moon-God: A Candid Investigation into the Origins of Islam

Night of the Dragon: The Saga of Saint George

The Magellan Chronicles Series (Books 1-3)

Dedication

A special thanks to Thomas Nowaczyk for editorial assistance. His insightful comments were invaluable, much appreciated, and instrumental to the project.

Another thanks to my wife Iris for having patience during the many years of research for this book.

Maps

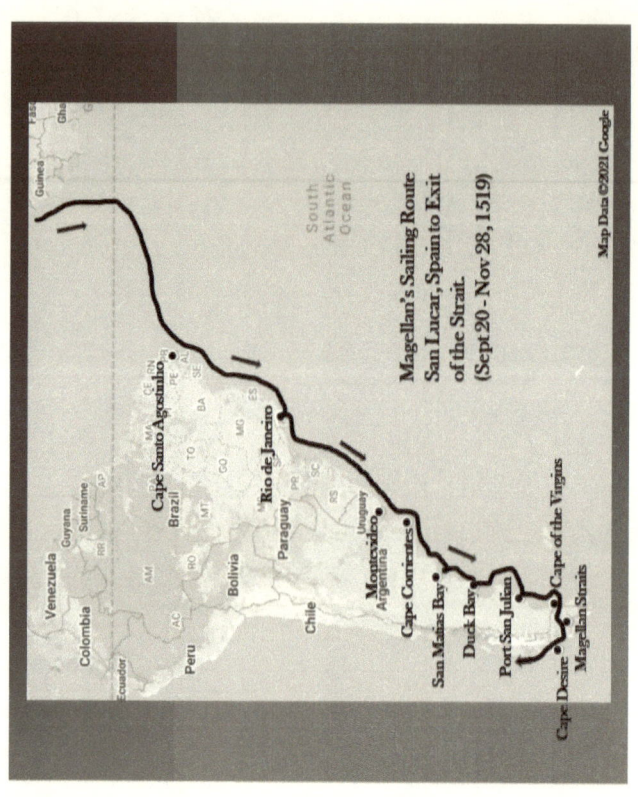

Magellan's Sailing Route: San Lucar, Spain to Exit of the Strait. (Sept 20 - Nov 28, 1519)

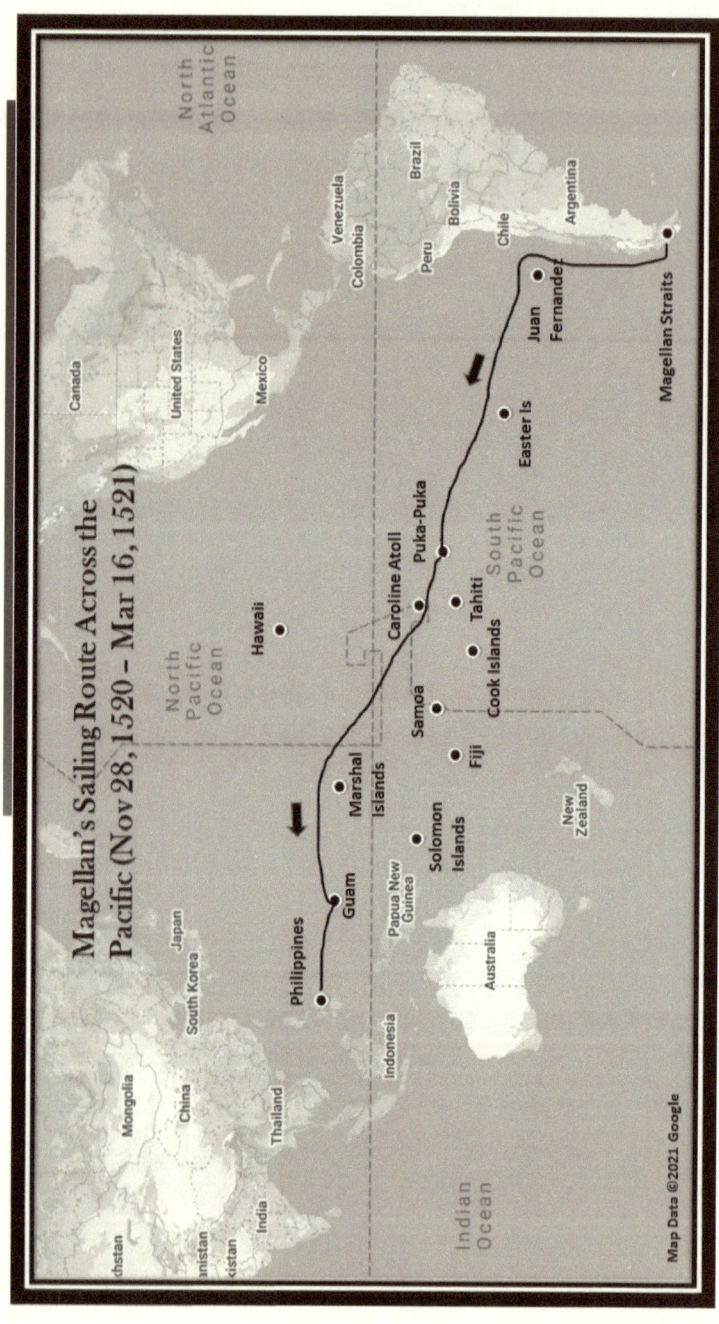

Magellan's Sailing Route Across the Pacific (Nov 28, 1520 – Mar 16, 1521)

Map Data ©2021 Google

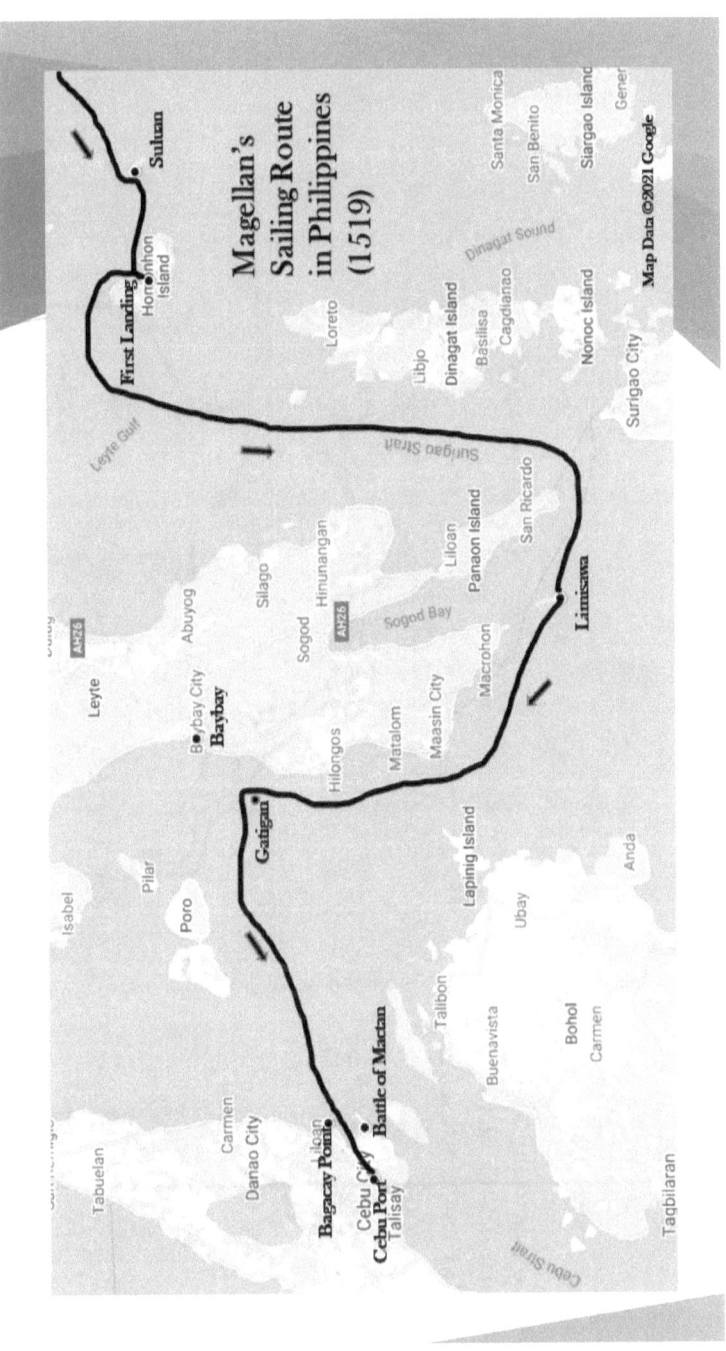

Magellan's
Sailing Route
in Philippines
(1519)

Map Data ©2021 Google

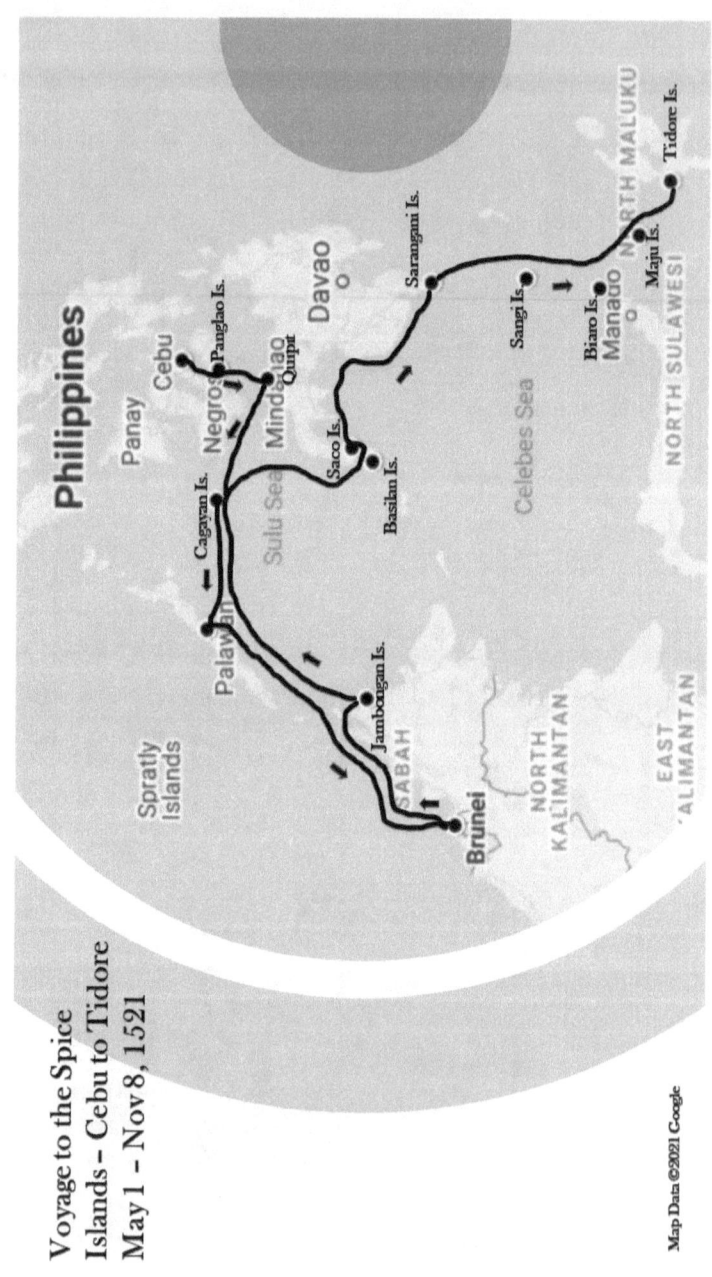

Voyage to the Spice
Islands – Cebu to Tidore
May 1 – Nov 8, 1521

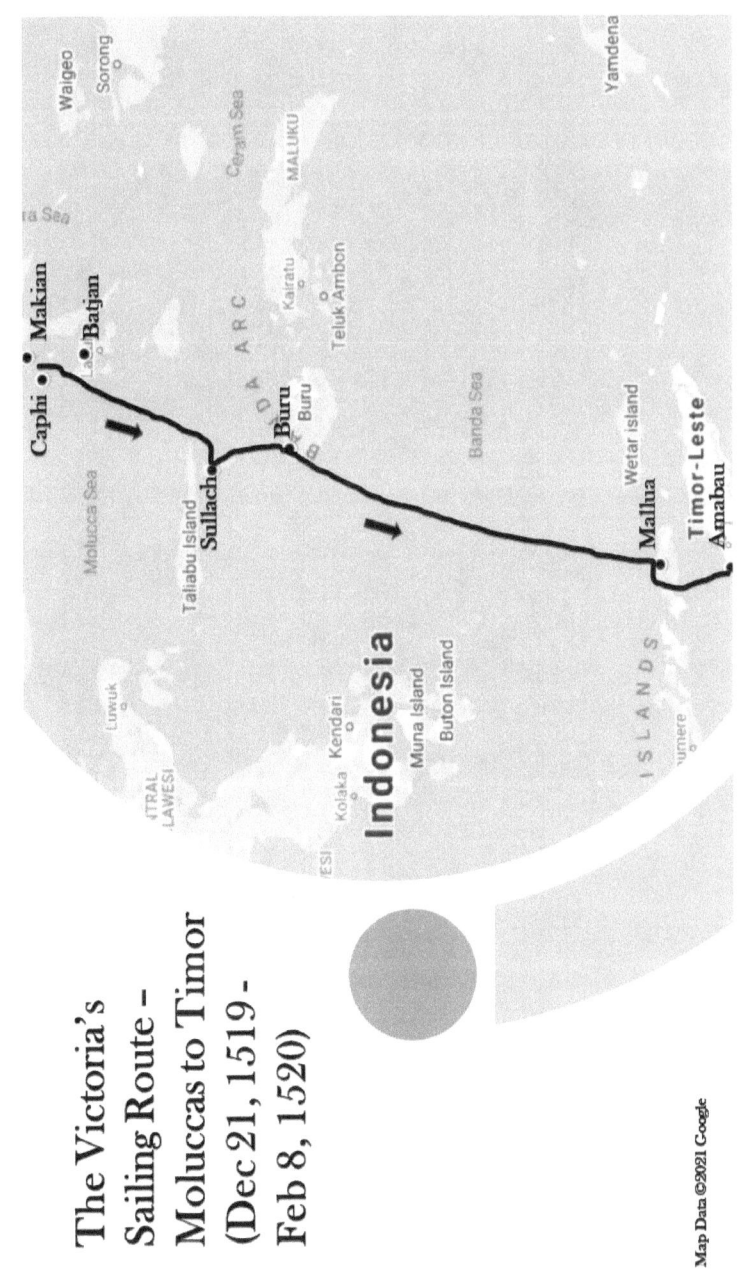

The Victoria's
Sailing Route –
Moluccas to Timor
(Dec 21, 1519 -
Feb 8, 1520)

Map Data ©2021 Google

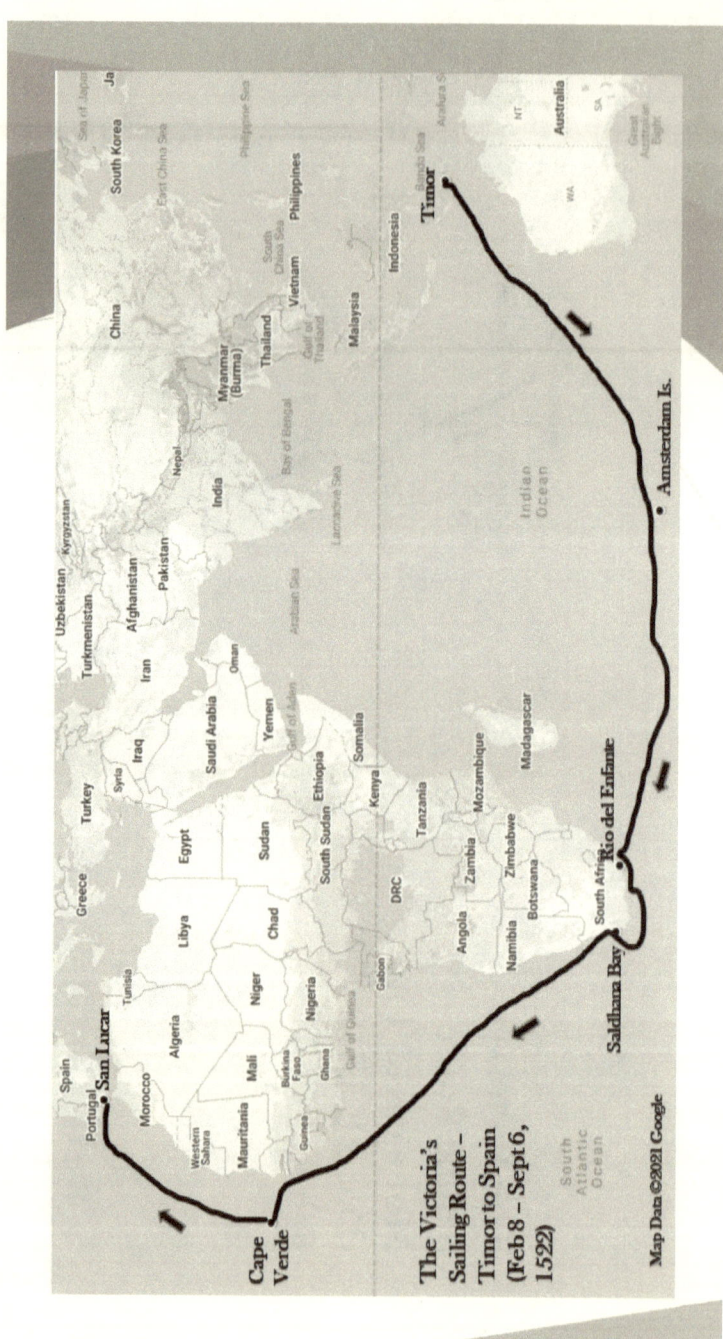

The Victoria's Sailing Route – Timor to Spain (Feb 8 – Sept 6, 1522)

1

Seville, Spain – October 20, 1517

The weather on the southern Iberian coast was sunny and pleasant and a fair wind filled the sails of a small caravel bounding toward the Spainish mainland. Fernão Magalhães stood on the main deck with his 24 year old servant, Enrique, and another young man of 18 years, Cristovão Rebêlo, his new page. Rebêlo was from Porto, not far from his own home.

Fernão's brother, Diogo, had previously sent the young man to Lisbon with a letter of high recommendation to serve in the proposed expedition to the Spice Islands. Fernão agreed with his brother's advice and considered the new responsibility to mentor Cristovão an honor and a privilege, for he had also served as a page in his youth.

But the court was never favorable to Fernão as he was to the court. Now, at the age of 37, he had the last humiliation he would tolerate, and left his homeland for good, his charges in tow.

At the mouth of the winding Guadalquivir River, the caravel stopped to unload cargo and take on a few more passengers, then headed upriver. From the port of San Lúcar they sailed north, then dropped anchor along the waterfront of Seville.

On their starboard side to the east loomed the Tower of Gold. It was situated on the riverbank as a defensive lookout point. Fernão stared past the tower at the massive fortress complex known as Alcazar. Adjacent to this edifice was another marvel—the magnificent Cathedral of Seville, its spires glistening in the sunlight. The city was one of Europe's most populated, with nearly 80,000 citizens, and bustling with commerce.

It was mid-afternoon when they disembarked. A man waved excitedly in their direction. 'Fernão Magalhães! Over here!'

'Duarte Barbosa!' Fernão exclaimed. 'Nice of you to greet us. Please meet Cristovão Rebêlo, my page, and Enrique from Sumatra.'

'They look like prime officer material,' Barbosa said with a grin.

'You know lads, I met Duarte in India,' Fernão said. 'I found him taking down notes for a new travel book. His detailed accounts of far-off lands are fascinating.'

'You are too flattering, my friend,' Duarte said. 'But thank you.'

Duarte then arranged a horse and cart to transport their luggage. Once it was loaded, they proceeded to the Alcazar. Fernão admired the imposing structure's stone and brick walls.

'An imposing fortress,' Fernão remarked, as they neared the front gate.

'It is,' Duarte said. 'The walls are 6 feet wide and 40 high. You see those towers dispersed along the walls. They are 15 feet wide and 60 high. Hard to assault.'

Fernão took in the magnitude of the structure, its walls and towers were topped with diamond-pointed crenellations which also served as another layer of fortification.

Just outside the main gate, the luggage was unloaded from the horse cart into small-wheeled hand carts and pulled by servants. The party entered through the main gate and found a long courtyard full of greenery and tall palm trees. They continued onward through a tall arched gate and into a wide expansive courtyard. Fernão gaped at the marvelous architecture, a combination of Arabesque and Gothic.

'Magnificent is it not?' Duarte said. 'We are standing in the Hunting Courtyard and in front of you is the Royal Palace. It has undergone several renovations since liberation from Islamic rule. Queen Isabela doubled its size some years back, most of it on the second floor. It was here that she debriefed Admiral Cristoforo Colombo on his second voyage to the New World.

'An amazing bit of history,' Fernão said. 'You are correct. It is all magnificent.'

From the center of the courtyard, Duarte pointed to his right. 'This is the *Casa de la Contratacíon de las Indias* or House of Trade of the Indies. We just call it *Casa de la Contratacíon* or the Casa. I am sure you know the details from your time at the India House in Lisbon.'

Fernão was indeed aware of the history and function of Spain's counterpart trading house from his encounters with the captains and pilots frequenting Lisbon. In 1503, Queen Isabela had established the Castilian trade headquarters in the Alcazar to oversee all trade and commerce. The crown imposed a 20 percent tariff on all precious metals entering Spain and called it the *quinto real* or royal fifth. The Casa was responsible to register cargoes and issue rules for outfitting ships. It also functioned as a maritime court for settling contract disputes, insurance claims, and for sentencing smugglers. Like the Portuguese, the Casa also maintained a secret map called the *Padrón Real* to be used as the master for all charts issued to captains leaving Spain. In Lisbon, Fernão had learned that Amerigo Vespucci was appointed as the first chief of navigation or *piloto-mayor* here. He had been responsible for training new pilots and seamen for outgoing voyages.

They entered a corridor through the Casa de Contratación and soon exited into a tiled courtyard with lush vegetation. Numerous windows overlooked the fountained patio.

'This will be your residence,' Duarte said. 'You are welcomed to stay for as long as you desire. The servants will show you to your quarters. I will come by in an hour and escort you to meet my father.'

'This is very good,' Fernão said. 'Thank you, my friend. See you soon.'

After leading them into the main residential corridor, the servant halted in front of one room. He unloaded the luggage of Enrique and Cristovão. 'Looks like you two share this one,' Fernão said before going off to his own room.

An hour later, Duarte knocked on Fernão's door. 'You ready?'

'Should Enrique and Cristovão attend?'

'I believe he wants you alone for this first meeting. Our servants will show them where to find dinner.'

Once Fernão had explained the situation to his young pupils, they retraced their steps back to the Hunting Courtyard for their own entertainment. Fernão departed alone with Duarte.

As an avid travel writer, Duarte vividly detailed the history and architecture of the Alcazar to his guest. The construction of the fortress had begun under the Abadi dynasty in the 11th century. Later, in the 12th and 13th centuries, the Almohads expanded the walls to their current perimeter. It was not until 1248, when Seville was finally wrested from Islamic rule by King Ferdinand III of Castile. His heir, Alfonso X, was so enamored by the grounds that he decided to setup a residence in the palace. He constructed a new palace with a Gothic theme during his tenure. Learned scholars from his court frequently gathered with the king in the Alcazar. From his palace, Alfonso X created his own poems and essays which eventually bequeathed him the title, *The Wise*. Later, in the 14th century, Alfonso XI and Pedro I rebuilt the Alcazar in the Mudejar architectural style, combining both Christian and Islamic themes. Pedro had spent much of his time as a youth in the Alcazar and was instilled with a tolerance towards Muslims and Jews. Thereafter, in 1364, he acquired the greatest craftsmen to construct his new dream palace; carpenters from Toledo, artists from Granada, and master builders from Seville—most all Muslims. In just two years, the new 38,000 square foot palace was completed.

They entered the main entrance of the palace and emerged into the rectangular Courtyard of the Maidens—a central point of social life in the Alcazar. In the center, a long reflecting pool was surrounded by a walkway and a Moorish sunken garden of orange trees and flower beds. Twenty-four lobed arches designed in Arabic ornamental stuccowork lined the entire perimeter, all were supported by white marble columns. They walked through the gallery towards the south until they entered through a semi-circular arched door, over 16 feet tall, carved with Christian and Islamic detailing, and full of inscriptions and starred latticework.

Fernão was impressed when they entered a square-shaped room nearly 1,100 square feet in size. The Ambassador's Hall was used for official receptions and was the highest profile room in the Alcazar. Three of the four sides opened to galleries via a triple series of arches, supported by exquisite columns of black and pink marble. Fernão's eyes followed the artistic themes upward. He admired the gold and blue arches above the columns. The chamber walls were fully covered with tiled skirting boards in the style of Granada, with polychrome plasterwork, and many inscriptions praising Allah. Every wall had a high theatrical balcony, and each was supported by three wrought iron dragons. Duarte pointed up to a grand wooden cupola, 30-foot in diameter. Both men stood in reverence upon the curved ceiling filled with geometric 12-pointed stars of gold and intended to invoke a sense of the cosmos. Servants began to file in with lounge chairs and a table was set with hot tea and dates.

A grey-bearded man in his 50s entered from a side gallery. 'Thank the Lord, our guest has arrived. I hope Duarte has accommodated you thus far.'

'Sir Diogo Barbosa!' Fernão said. 'Thank you for your hospitality. Duarte has given me an impressive tour.'

'Please, sit and take some tea,' Diogo Barbosa implored with a grin. 'It is good in these parts.' The three sat upon the cushioned seats located along the perimeter of the chamber and sipped fine Arabic tea and a compliment of fresh dates. 'I wanted to discuss a little business before dinner with the family.'

'Yes sir,' Fernão replied.

'Perfect. Duarte had informed me of your enterprise to the Moluccas. It is a sound plan and I have already made several propositions to the *Casa*. If Vespucci was still alive and serving as chief navigator, we would have greater cooperation. But now, Sebastian Cabot holds the position, and only interested in his own exploratory missions.'

'Vespucci was an honorable man,' Fernão said.

'You knew him?' Diogo asked.

'Yes. I was only 24-years-old when I met him at the India House in Lisbon.'

'I am sure that was an experience never to be forgotten.'

'It was indeed.'

'Fortunately, we have aroused the interest in one of the Casa representatives. The shipping agent, Juan de Aranda has been enthralled by the prospect for engaging in trade with the lucrative spice markets in the Moluccas. He accepts the possibility that the region lies within Spanish domain.' Diogo took a sip of tea and looked over Fernão. 'But Aranda needed confirmation of your reputation, and that of your partner Ruy Faleiro. So, he wrote to the Haros in Lisbon for a background check.' Diogo grinned. 'The Haros wrote in return and claimed your experienced careers were impeccable. Above all, they perceived your determination to see the project to its conclusion was solid. Once Aranda was satisfied of your credentials, he wrote to the vice-president of the Supreme Council—Bishop Fonseca. Ever since Fonseca's time as chaplain for Queen Isabela he has served the crown as chief advisor for all maritime and colonial affairs.'

'That is excellent news sir,' Fernão said. 'But I have one concern. Was it not Fonseca that opposed Admiral Cristoforo Colombo so many times? And against Balboa's expedition?'

'So, you know the history, good. It is true that Colombo often acted flamboyant and appeared reckless to Fonseca. But we all know it was simply a power struggle. Fonseca wished to reduce dependence upon independent entrepreneurs and secure all missions under crown authority, thus ensuring maximum profits for himself as guardian of the seas.'

'I heard Admiral Colombo was so vexed that he kicked and beat Fonseca's accountant,' Duarte commented with a smile.

The Barbosas laughed.

Fernão stared blankly.

'The accounts are true,' Duarte said. 'Colombo was not afraid of anyone, even Fonseca. Can you imagine he actually did that?'

Fernão began to chuckle, then all three burst out into laughter.

Diogo Barbosa straightened himself up in his chair, and with a sobering calm said to Fernão, 'If you have an audience with Fonseca, appeal to his business interests in logical precision. Appeal to his greed and you will win his mind. Be confident, but not boisterous, and you shall have your plans approved.'

Fernão nodded somberly. Duarte refilled his tea.

'Aranda has informed me that Fonseca leans in our direction,' Diogo said. 'He has informed the regent, Cardinal Ximenes—president of the Supreme Council. But first, I will introduce you to Aranda in the Casa.'

'Is it time for dinner?' Duarte asked.

'I believe so,' Diogo replied. 'Are you hungry Fernão?'

'Very much so.' Fernão could not believe the sudden turn of events and the new blessings suddenly reigning down from above. Now he had a family, but not just a family, a family of mariners.

Duarte had also been treated well, for he was born illegitimate, but always honored by Diogo Barbosa as a full-blooded and beloved son. Of course, among courtiers and nobles he was required to refer to Duarte as his nephew as was customary for such sons of the time born out of marriage.

The three exited the Admiral's Hall and climbed a stairway to the upper royal salons. Duarte took them on a short tour of the upper floor complex. Here were located the oratory of the Catholic Monarchs, Assembly Hall, Gala Dining Room, and the royal bed chambers. Auxiliary game rooms, offices and smaller dining areas were interspersed throughout. They entered one of the side dining rooms, already set with fine dishes and silver cutlery.

Diogo touched the arm of a servant girl. 'Please let my family know we are ready.'

In a matter of minutes more servants arrived carrying platters of appetizers: dates, oranges, sugar candies, and other assorted delicacies. Soon, Diogo's family began to arrive. First to enter was his beautiful wife, Maria Caldera. Her elegantly stitched white linen dress with black silk geometric patterned embroidery complemented her status as a high-born Andalusian. One-by-one the children entered. Diogo introduced them as they filed in and took their places. 'This is my other son, Jaime, and these are my daughter's Isabel, Guiomar, and Beatriz. The latter was a stunning young woman with flowing raven hair and dark eyes. She was attired like her mother, but with floral designs stitched in red and black silk. Fernão was mesmerized. She approached gracefully and took a seat near her mother. Duarte nudged him on the elbow, breaking his stare, as they took their seats near his father. The servants waited at attention along the perimeter of the dining room.

Diogo gave a short blessing over the meal including a thanks for the safe arrival of Fernão and the divine assistance in moving the project of the Moluccas forward. 'I hope you enjoy dinner in the royal palace,' Diogo said, after the blessing. 'Serving as the Alcaide of Alcazar does have its privileges. Please, enjoy a few treats before the main course.'

Everyone enjoyed the assorted delicacies. From ceramic jugs, servants poured fresh water in exquisitely designed goblets for the youngest, and red wine for the others.

Duarte turned to Fernão. 'You know my father was honored with the position of alcaide in gratitude for his service to Ferdinand and Isabela in their campaigns against the Moors. He fought in Granada and Navarre; and was even knighted Commander of the Order of Santiago.'

'Impressive,' Fernão replied. 'My ancestors have always been loyal to the Order of Santiago.'

'Indeed?' Diogo said with a raised eyebrow and a grin.

Diogo's son, Jaime, looked at Fernão and boasted, 'You know my father once returned to Portugal in 1501 and then captained a ship in the third armada under João de Nova to the Indies. Along the way they discovered the islands of Ascension and St. Helena.'

'I had heard about your mission while in Lisbon,' Fernão said to Diogo. 'I was only 22-years old at the time. Your fleet was outfitted primarily for trade and the vessels were lightly armed. But events suddenly changed. Your armada was forced to engage in the first significant naval battle of the Indies, a two-day affair. You faced the wrath of the Zamorin in a surprise attack. He blockaded your small armada of 4 vessels in the port of Cannanore. If my memory serves, the Zamorin had 40 large ships, 180 smaller craft and about 7,000 men.'

'That is correct,' Diogo commented. 'A fine memory.' Diogo then gathered some silverware and saltshakers to demonstrate the naval maneuvers. 'We charged their blockade in a column with cannons pounding and thus were able to evade all their grappling hooks. You know, we were the first to employ the tactic of a naval column.' Diogo sat up in his chair. 'The sound of cannons blaring and the smoke in the air. Such power and glory, is it not?'

'Yes sir!' Fernão exclaimed. 'Nothing can compare.'

They beamed in common bond. Diogo waved down a servant. 'Please bring the main course.' He then turned to Fernão. 'Duarte tells me you have spent much of your life in sea and land wars. Wounded three times; fought in Africa, India, and even remote Malacca. You served under Almeida and his valiant son, Lourenço. Then under Albuquerque. You know, Duarte once had a little run in with Albuquerque. Placed him in bonds.'

Fernão chuckled. 'He would not be alone. My friend, Francisco Serrão, also was locked up for some time for an undeserved punishment. But the viceroy often forgives after some time. I once stood up to him in a council of all the captains in Cochin. I expect it was the reason denied any opportunity to captain a vessel to the Moluccas.'

'You are a brave man to stand up to Albuquerque,' Diogo stated with a smile. 'Good for you.'

Servants brought in platters of meats and vegetables. They also brought in new goblets and poured fresh refills. Fernão signaled for a servant to pour only half. Diogo looked on curiously. 'Not a wine drinker?'

'Not so much, only in moderation. I like to keep focused. A habit I suppose but served me well over the years.'

'Understood,' Diogo said with approval.

The family commenced to eat dinner. About mid-meal, Beatriz dabbed her mouth with a handkerchief and spoke, 'You were in Malacca? I heard Albuquerque's vessel, the *Flor de la Mar*, had sunk off Sumatra with vast treasures.'

'Indeed. I lost all my personal treasure as reward for taking Malacca from the Sultan. A great loss.'

'A loss yes,' Diogo interjected. 'But the quest was worth it, was it not?'

'Yes sir,' Fernão replied with a smile 'Very much so.'

'Father says you plan to voyage to the Moluccas by a western route.' Beatriz said. 'Do you really think it is possible? Nobody has succeeded yet.'

'That may be true, but I know the way. I spent years in the India House in Lisbon poring over old maps and plotting routes. There is a strait, and I will find the way through it.'

'I wish you well, then, on your venture,' Beatriz replied, blushing. As the daughter of a captain and sister to a great adventurer, she was caught up in the excitement. She admired bold confidence, daring, and a self-determination.

Diogo noticed her interest and turned to Fernão. 'How is your Spanish?'

'I studied some as a youth in Lisbon but have not had need of it until now. So, not so good.'

'Perhaps Beatriz can tutor you over the next days. She speaks Portuguese and Spanish perfectly. She also knows the history of the Alcazar and Seville. This may be of interest to you?'

'Yes sir. I would be honored.' Fernão was absolutely enthralled. He glanced over to Beatriz. She blushed a deeper hue of red and looked away.

'Very well,' Diogo said. 'It will be so.'

The dinner concluded with sugared candy deserts. Fernão and Beatriz stole glances at one another.

Over the next weeks, Fernão walked the grounds of the Alcazar with Beatriz. She tutored him in Spanish and explained the history of the fortress architecture with astute expertise and feminine grace. Fernão was enticed by her charm as they frequented the elaborate courtyards; and the grottos interspersed with irrigated channels and pools. Labyrinths meandering through the lush gardens laden with fruit trees, palms, and flowers added to the romantic ambiance.

One sunny day they visited the two-leveled Dance Garden. Beatriz took Fernão's hand and led him into a tunnel which ended in a vaulted chamber. Galleries surrounded a long rectangular water tank. A grotto was situated on one end. Images from the arches above reflected upon the clear water inside the pool. They were both taken by its beauty. Light and air emanated from grills cut in the Crossing Courtyard above them. They sat on a bench adjacent to the pool.

'The mistress of Pedro the First had often bathed here, in private, and naked,' Beatriz said. Fernão felt a tightness across his belly and exhaled sharply. She turned from the pool and gazed into Fernão's eyes. He lurched forward and embraced her. Beatriz leaned into him and closed her eyes. He turned his head slightly. Their lips brushed together. The smell of her perfumed hair and the soft caress of her lips caused him to reel for a moment. He could not dishonor her, or his host. He thought of Francisco's sudden decision to marry his Javanese wife. He and Serrão both understood a mariner's life was spontaneous, and if one wanted to experience love in matrimony, it must occur as it unfolded. He pulled back. 'Beatriz. I have little money and I am almost a cripple. But I have great plans, and if you would be my wife, I would be greatly honored.'

Beatriz beamed at him. 'Do not worry. My father is rich. Besides, I admire battle wounds. It is a sign of courage. I will be honored to be your wife.'

'Then, with the grace of Our Lord, I will approach your father tomorrow.'

The next day, Fernão found Diogo in an agreeable mood and asked permission to marry Beatriz. It was a mere formality since Diogo, had already planned for their union and promised he would procure a suitable location.

On a chilly December morning, Fernão prepared to wed Beatriz in the Cathedral of Seville. Diogo Barbosa fulfilled his promise and had arranged the wedding in the magnificent church through the help of Dr. Sancho Matienzo. The revered doctor served as the treasurer of *Casa de Contratacíon de las Indies* and was also a canon in the cathedral. Dr. Matienzo was able to secure the date.

Fernão was anxious to conclude the ceremony. He decided to appear early. From the Alcazar, he crossed the street to the Cathedral of Seville. Fernão was dressed in his finest attire, a white linen shirt with long sleeves, and over this he wore a black satin vest. In the fashion of the day, he donned black hose to cover his legs. Like Da Gama, he wore a red cross in the shape of a dagger to represent the Order of Santiago. Fernão walked along the perimeter admiring its vast size. He remembered Beatriz explaining its architectural history. It was originally called the Aljama Mosque and built under the Almohad Caliph Abu Yacub in 1176. The mosque was converted into a church. It had been said that in 1401, the Cathedral canons had made a vow to build a church so beautiful and so grand that those who see it completed will take us for mad. The construction of the massive Gothic church did not begin until three decades later. It was nearly finished when Fernão had arrived in Seville. With dimensions approximately 440 feet long and 270 feet wide, it had surpassed the Hagia Sophia as the largest cathedral in the world.

Fernão entered an old double horseshoe archway called the Door of Forgiveness. The massive doors were covered with bronze panels designed with interlacing arches and Kufic inscriptions. It was formerly used as an access for ablutions in the Patio of the Orange Trees and the main entrance to the former mosque. He proceeded toward the center of the courtyard. A series of steps formed a polygonal floor plan. The lower steps were ceramic, and the upper step was whitewashed and painted in ochre. Fernão climbed to the top step, leaned forward, then cupped his hands to draw water from a fountain flowing within a large Visigoth marble bowl. He took a sip and then washed his hands. Fernão stared up at the Almohad tower, also known as the Giralda. Originally it had been topped with a minaret. Its height was approximately 340 feet and consisted of two parallel towers, one exterior and another smaller interior tower.

Fernão moved toward the perimeter gallery until he found an entrance to the cathedral and Dr. Matienzo waiting in front.

'Fernão,' Matienzo said. 'You are early.'

'Yes reverend,' he answered. 'I like to be early.'

'Well, maybe we have a look inside before the wedding guests arrive.'

They entered the cathedral. Fernão gaped in awe upon the enormity of the structure with its massive columns and high vaults. Matienzo informed him of its construction and dimensions as they walked. It had a central nave approximately 50 feet wide and 140 feet in height. The 4 aisles were 36 feet wide. There were 36 pillars and 68 ribbed vaults. Most of the vaults were four-sided. But the high chapel, choir and three central vaults of the transept took the form of a cross. They admired the choir located in the central section of the nave. It was 65 by 45 feet in size. The stalls were of ebony and styled in the Gothic-Mudéjar motif. There were 67 high level chairs done in baldachin, and 50 low seats. The king's seat bore the royal coat of arms. In the center-rear was the archbishop's seat and crowned with high Gothic pinnacles. Interspersed among the stalls were carvings of scenes from the Old and New testaments. They continued their tour, all the while taking in the marvelous artwork, stained-glass windows, and countless chapels.

The guests began to arrive and take their places near the main chapel.

'It is nearly time,' Matienzo said. 'We should join the others for your special day.'

The two walked toward the main chapel. Fernão noticed that above the altarpiece was an elaborate Gothic retablo of carved scenes of the life of Christ. It was nearing completion and already an impressive work of art.

There were nearly 50 guests, most were from the Barbosa family and close circle of friends. Enrique and Cristovão also attended. The closest relatives took their seats opposite the altar steps, the remainder were seated further away facing the main chapel. Dr. Matienzo nodded to Fernão to walk with him to a velvet bench of red and black. It faced the steps leading to the altar. Dr. Matienzo nodded and then moved to take a seat along the perimeter, and near the steps to the altar. After the guests had all taken their seats, Diogo Barbosa escorted Beatriz down the church hall and into the main chapel. She was stunning with her long dark hair contrasting against her white dress. Diogo Barbosa smiled and nodded at Fernão, then left her to stand with him in front of the velvet bench.

Diogo took a seat near the front, near his wife and children. Beatriz smiled and took Fernão's hand. Dr. Matienzo nodded to the priest to begin the ceremony. The priest gestured for the wedding couple to take their seat on the bench and then opened with three biblical readings. Fernão and Beatriz exchanged glances throughout the ceremony. It was nearly an hour before the service concluded and the vows were taken. The guests followed the newly wedded couple for the great reception in the Admiral's Hall of the Alcazar. Servants entered with small treats and glasses of wine. It was an exquisite affair. Later, they would feast in the upper dining rooms until late.

Fernão and Beatriz had greeted all their guests as they entered the great hall. Fernão's spirit was reviving. Suddenly his hard labors and disciplined life were bearing fruit. One by one, guests set their wedding gifts upon a table along the gallery wall. Duarte gave Fernão a signed copy of his book, *O Livro de Duarte Barbosa*—A *description of all the ports then visited in the Indian Ocean, and even beyond.* It was an honor, for books were a rare commodity in the infant age of printing. Diogo had honored him even greater with a hefty dowry to his daughter of 600,000 maravedis. Fernão was overwhelmed by such a blessed turn of events, for he had married a beautiful woman, no longer financially burdened, and with prospects for a glorious mission to the fabled Spice Islands. The next days with Beatriz were blissful and intimate as they frequented the vast grounds of the Alcazar.

After some days, Diogo invited Fernão to meet with the representatives of the Casa. Now, with a marital arrangement secured to the Barbosa family, approval for the enterprise seemed within Fernão's reach. From the Hunting Courtyard, they entered the

Admiral's Room of the *Casa de Contratacíon de las Indies*. Fernão estimated the rectangular chamber encompassed around 2,300 square feet. A wood ceiling matched the decorative furniture. A long desk with five chairs were located at the front, which faced numerous rows of chairs with a walkway in the middle. Five well-dressed gentlemen stood in the center of the room bantering about navigational matters. Fernão paused a moment to appreciate the magnitude of being present in such a place. So many of the great exploratory missions had been planned and executed within these walls.

Diogo Barbosa cleared his throat to announce their arrival.

'Ah, Barbosa. We have been expecting you.'

'Sir Cabot,' Diogo said. 'We are honored you have taken time to listen to our proposal.'

'Indeed, shall we proceed then?' Sebastian Cabot asked.

Barbossa nodded.

Cabot took the center high seat at the consular desk, flanked on both sides by the Casa administrators. Fernão sat next to Diogo in the front row facing them. He recognized the others in attendance from Diogo's descriptions, or by acquaintances prior to the meeting. These were the paymaster, Pedro Ochoa de Isásaga, Treasurer—Dr. Sancho de Matienzo, and the agent, Juan de Aranda. There was another person Fernão did not recognize, but whom he took to be a cleric in an administrative role.

'We have heard your initial proposal from our alcaide, Barbosa,' Cabot said. 'But we have not yet heard from you, Fernão Magalhães.' He gestured with his hand that Magalhães should rise. 'So please indulge us.'

Fernão stood up, unfurled a chart vertically and traced his finger across it. 'As you are aware, I plan to follow the southern continent, pass through a strait that exists near the tip and proceed onward to the Moluccas. My friend Francisco Serrão has already testified of the vast spice treasures in those islands and believes they are in Spanish domains. My partner, the esteemed cosmographer, Ruy Faleiro, has confirmed the feasibility of the mission with his calculations. He will soon join us here in Seville. I seek a fleet to journey to such islands, claim the lands for Spain, and secure a substantial bounty for the crown. But of course, I need the approval of the Casa—your approval specifically, and the support that would come from it.'

'How certain are you the Moluccas lie in our domains?' Cabot asked. 'Such a venture could easily damage relations with King Manuel. Furthermore, I, myself, had found a passage to the north, past Labrador. Unfortunately, winter had set in upon us before we could press onward. But it is worthy of another attempt. And, finally, how do you know a strait exists in the south? It is hearsay, is it not?'

Fernão traced his finger near the Dragon's Tail of the southern continent. 'It is here. Right here, at this place. As to how I might verify my certainty, I can only give you my word, it is so.'

Cabot turned to the other members.

All but Aranda shook their heads in distrust.

'We cannot support this enterprise based only on your word,' Cabot said. 'And the risk of offending our neighbor is too great. I am sorry we will not be able to accommodate you. Meeting adjourned, gentlemen.'

With another rejection, Fernão's heart pounded, and his head throbbed. Diogo put his arm around his shoulder as they departed.

But midway across the courtyard, Juan de Aranda came rushing toward them. 'Wait, wait! Please, let me hear more of your plans.'

The Casa representatives left the premises, so the three returned to a back office in the trading house. Fernão laid out the chart and detailed his plans, most fervently highlighting the lucrative rewards in undertaking such a journey. Aranda was so moved by his sincerity and prospective gains that the very next day he wrote a letter to High Chancellor Sauvage, for permission to bring Magalhães and Faleiro to the royal court.

In mid-December, the famed cosmographer, Ruy Faleiro, arrived in Seville. He was accompanied by his wife Eva, and his brother Francisco. Fernão and Enrique met them at the port. 'Magalhães! Ha-ha! I made it as promised.'

'It is good to see you, my friend. There have been many developments. Come with us Ruy. Diogo welcomes you to the Alcazar as his guest.'

An attractive young foreign girl followed. Enrique began to speak with her in a Sumatran dialect, questioning her, it seemed, gleaning information. She changed to several dialects, testing Enrique's linguistic skills. He was able to follow, until finally halting in confusion and unable to understand anymore.

Fernão raised an eyebrow. 'Is she with you Ruy?'

Ruy chuckled at him. 'Oh yes. Bought her in Lisbon from a captain. We will be able to use her as evidence for our mission.'

'But I already have Enrique for that.'

'Sure, but does he know as many dialects? It's all about the presentation my friend.'

Fernão smiled and looked at Enrique.

Enrique said, 'She is from Sumatra but has some knowledge of the languages further east, to the Moluccas and beyond. She claims to have been a slave for a Muslim merchant who frequented the eastern routes.

'Perhaps she may help,' Fernão said.

It was not long into their first meeting that Ruy discovered that Aranda had not only inserted himself into their affairs but had also written a letter to the chancellor without obtaining permission from the principal parties. Ruy flew into a rage and threatened to cease all proceedings. Aranda pleaded for him to wait for the chancellor's response since expectations for a positive outcome were in their favor. Ruy stubbornly refused to calm down and furthermore upbraided his partner for divulging too much information.

Fernão knew he had to tread carefully with such a volatile temperament and simply claimed it was to further the project, and that nobody would listen without some basic details. He further assured the touchy Faleiro that the location of the strait remained a secret. But it was not until Diogo stepped in as a mediator that a new agreement was reached between his new son-in-law and Ruy Faleiro. All they had to do at this point was wait for the chancellor's response.

2

Seville, Spain – January 20, 1518

Despite their practiced patience, Fernão Magalhães and Ruy Faleiro had not received any response from the chancellor regarding their proposal for an audience with the king. So, regardless of Aranda's pleas to wait for a royal dispatch, they decided to proceed with their own plans anyway and visit the royal court in Valladolid. The Faleiro brothers and their Sumatran slave girl would accompany Fernão and Enrique. To alleviate travel expenses, the wives of Fernão and Ruy would remain in the Alcazar, along with Cristovão. This helped in the expenses since only one horse drawn carriage would be needed. As a matter of honor, Fernão refused to touch any of his wife's dowry, especially for a risky enterprise such as this, and so funds were limited. Knowing their financial burden, Aranda had offered to assist with food and lodging for the lengthy journey to the court. Fernão thought it was a noble gesture, but Ruy was still hostile and refused any support. Aranda departed alone via a direct route on horseback, by way of Extremadura. Fernão's group joined a well-armed convoy of the duchess of Arcos. They took the route via Córdoba and Toledo. Just to the west of Madrid, as they were crossing the Sierra de Guadarrama at Herradon de Pinares, a courier arrived with a letter addressed to Fernão Magalhães and Ruy Faleiro.

'Enrique, your Spanish is better than mine,' Fernão said, holding the letter out to him. 'If you please?'

Enrique read over the content. 'Aranda says he received a dispatch containing two letters, just ten miles out of Seville. One letter was a reply from the chancellor granting permission for Fernão Magalhães and Ruy Faleiro to appear at court in Valladolid. The other was from the king himself and addressed to Sir Magalhães. He wants to meet you and grant you favor.' Enrique looked up with eyes wide in amazement. 'The king wants to see *you* sir!'

'Seriously?' Fernão asked.

'Yes, sir,' Enrique replied.

'What else does it say?' Ruy asked.

'Aranda will meet us at Medina del Campo, just outside Valladolid.'

When they arrived at Medina del Campo, Aranda provided them with lodging and food at a local inn. Ruy's dark eyebrows and brooding eyes stared over Aranda the entire evening, his choleric and suspicious mind always at the ready to burst out with a furious rage. This evening his brother, Francisco, kept him at bay. But, since Aranda had paid their bill, they both felt obligated and allowed him to join them for the remaining stretch. As they were about to cross a bridge over the Duero River, Aranda spoke to Ruy.

'Do not be angry that I have written to the chancellor, rather because of it, and for what I am about to do. I am to inform his highness about the information you brought to me from Portugal, and you should be willing to give me a part of what God may grant you.' Aranda paused for a moment, then continued, 'I believe a fifth of the profits from any expedition would be fair for my services in granting access.'

The Faleiro brother's faces reddened.

'You must think of us as fools,' Francisco Faleiro said.

Then, Ruy Faleiro exclaimed, 'Outrageous! You are mad Aranda! No recompense shall be paid.'

'Perhaps . . . I could be honored with an eighth.'

'Still excessive,' Fernão said, trying to mediate. 'A tenth seems more in line.'

'What?!' Ruy said so vehemently that his spittle hit Fernão's face. 'How dare you propose any counter-offer without consulting us.'

Aranda could see it was time to retreat. 'If you do not wish to give me anything, then I do not want anything. Nevertheless, I shall wholeheartedly endeavor to assist your project in service to the crown. I shall leave you all to decide for yourselves.' Before departing, Aranda's grin turned to a concerned frown. 'The Portuguese ambassador, Álvaro da Costa, is in town to arrange the marriage of Doña Leonor, sister of King Don Carlos to King Dom Manuel. You may want to delay your appearance some days. I hear rumors the ambassador has orders to circumvent your proposed mission.'

Fernão nodded in appreciation of the warning.

Fernão and the Faleiro brothers decided to settle in Simancas for three days, to discuss matters and delay their arrival at court, and thus avoid the Portuguese ambassador.

'I think we should give Aranda a cut,' Fernão said. 'He knows how to navigate the court intrigues and can further our cause.'

'I disagree,' Francisco replied. 'He should receive nothing.'

Ruy scratched his beard, looked at Fernão, then cleared his throat. 'Magalhães may have a point. Aranda was generous from his own purse and other goodwill gestures.'

'Are you sure about this brother?' Francisco asked.

'Yes. We should give him the eight shares of the profits as previously requested.'

'All right, then it is agreed upon,' Fernão said, surprised, but relieved by Ruy's sudden moment of clarity.

As they approached the highland city of Valladolid, a cold front was blowing in from the mountain range, and with it, snow. They donned fur-lined coats for protection against the sudden blizzard. From the carriage windows, Enrique and the Sumatran girl grasped at the flakes and marveled in wonder, for they had never seen snow. Aranda met the group as they approached and escorted them to his inn where they were treated to more of his hospitality. A fireplace blazed in the corner of the inn, and the party all dined on roasted lamb, spiced rice, and fresh asparagus. During the meal, the navigators pledged to give Aranda his eighth share. But the Faleiro brothers were still uncomfortable by the deal and moods eventually soured. The next day, they found other lodging, while Aranda proceeded to court. A few days later, Aranda met them at their inn. He had arranged appointments and requested they provide a precise estimate of the costs involved in their venture.

Finally, On February 23, 1518, they gathered at Aranda's inn and delivered their estimates. A notary stood by as they all signed a document promising Aranda's eighth share in recompense for his services with the court and the king. From this juncture of his life, Fernão would use the Spanish equivalent of his name in official matters and signed the document as *Fernando de Magallanes.*

Before departure to the palace, Fernão, Aranda, Enrique, and the Sumatran slave girl met outside the inn. The Faleiro brothers approached. Ruy was clothed in audacious attire. His long black beard was combed straight to a sharp point, and he donned a black cape embroidered with celestial spheres, all aligned in specific orbits.

'What?' Ruy asked in response to their gawking stares. 'Always remember. It is all about the presentation.'

The group entered the inn and sat at a long table to have some breakfast.

'You should know some details before we arrive at the Palace of the Viveros,' Aranda said. 'It is famous. Ferdinand and Isabela were married there. It joined the crowns of Aragon and Castile. The palace houses the Royal Audiencia and Chancellería of Valladolid with jurisdiction for all Castile. Did you know Admiral Colombo died in this city about 12 years ago?'

Fernão leaned in with interest.

'What about the king we are to meet?' Francisco asked.

'Ah yes, to the point my friend,' Aranda said. 'King Don Carlos descended from high nobility. His paternal grandfather was Maximilian I, the Holy Roman Emperor who had married Mary, the Duchess of Burgundy and bore an heir—Philip I (the Handsome), Archduke of Burgundy and father of Carlos.'

'Excuse me gentlemen, do you wish to order?' a middle-aged waitress asked.

'Just bread and tea,' Ruy replied. 'We will set out soon.'

Aranda continued. 'You see, Carlos' maternal grandfather was Ferdinand II, King of Aragon, who had married Isabella I, Queen of Castile and bore the eventual sole heir of Castile, Juana (the Mad).

'The mad?' Fernão asked.

'From what I have heard in the court circles she was indeed mad,' Aranda said. 'Her marriage to Philip drove her to extreme fits of jealously. She would fend off any woman who dared approach her handsome lover with such intensity that she was deemed crazy. When Philip died, her mental anguish further degraded her madness.'

'How so?' Ruy asked.

'It has been said that every night, Juana slept with her husband's embalmed corpse and was taken with her on every occasion of travel. No women were allowed in the bedchamber, not even midwives. She bore her fourth child alone, all the while next to the corpse of Philip. Her father, Ferdinand II, could no longer endure such lunacy and entrusted her future mental care under Fonseca, Bishop of Burgos.'

'So, you are saying the mother of King Don Carlos was mad?' Francisco asked.

'Very much so,' Aranda replied.

The Faleiro brothers and Fernão looked at one another, intrigued and amused. The waitress brought the group breakfast.

Aranda took sip of tea. 'In the year 1500, Juana's son, Carlos, resided in the city of Ghent, Flanders. His paternal aunt Margaret, Archduchess of Austria and Regent of the Netherlands raised him with the assistance of court tutors.'

'Why was he raised alone?' Fernão asked.

'Philip and Juana moved to Spain,' Aranda replied. 'They rarely visited their son. But he was raised by Flemish tutors. These are important men you will meet soon.'

'Who are they?' Ruy asked.'

'Cardinal Adrian of Utrecht, friend of Erasmus, and candidate for the papacy; Guillaume de Croÿ—Lord of Chièvres, Carlos' tutor,' and Chancellor Sauvage,' Aranda replied. 'But there is also his Spanish tutor—Juan Rodríguez de Fonseca, Bishop of Burgos, and president of the Casa de Contratación.'

'So how did Carlos become king?' Fernão asked.

'It is a long story,' Aranda replied. 'But in brief; when Ferdinand II died on January 23, 1516, Carlos inherited the Burgundian Netherlands. In 1516 he also became co-monarch of Spain with his mother Juana. But since his mother Juana was incapacitated, Cardinal Ximines, a pious and honest man, had assumed her command as regent. On March 14, 1516, in Brussels, Carlos was proclaimed as King of both Castile and Aragon. His Flemish court advisors accompanied the new king on the journey from their residence in Flanders to Spain. They finally arrived in Valladolid on November 18, 1517, just months before you arrived in Spain, Fernão.'

'Yes, an interesting history, thank you,' Fernão said. 'But what is he like?'

'Don Carlos was educated to the high ideals of the medieval knights.'

'Well, I shall wish to meet this king,' Fernão said.

'You will, soon,' Ruy interjected. 'We need to be off now.'

The group arrived in their carriage at the Palace of the Viveros. Once granted access inside the palace, Ruy and Fernão quickly realized Fonseca was the key person to persuade. Ruy pressed the prelate on the vast wealth that could be attained and the contributions to science which would inevitably result in their endeavor. He accentuated his expertise in matters of cosmography to bolster their credentials. Meanwhile,

Fernão presented his case upon his extensive navigational experience and straight-forward logic.

A series of interviews among the advisors ensued, with all evidence presented, but only met with a skeptical and tepid response. It was only by Fonseca's adamant approval that the others were assuaged, and subsequent permission given for an audience with the king on the following day.

Accordingly, Fernão and his group presented themselves again to the palace and were escorted to the royal court audience chamber. The leading court advisors and a few other figures took seats adjacent to the king's two-stepped dais. Aranda gestured for the team to sit in a row of benches near the entrance. Soon, an escort of German militia led the 18-year-old, King Don Carlos, to the dais. He was light skinned, with a prominent lower lip and lantern jaw, characteristic of the Habsburg lineage.

Fonseca rose from his seat and made a slight bow to the king. 'My lord, may I introduce Fernão Magalhães. He has noble Burgundian lineage such as your own kin and fought numerous wars against the infidel.'

Fernão stood and bowed.

Carlos smiled and sat forward in keen interest, for any knight fighting against the Islamic armies was of like mind to his own. The king admired chivalry and tenacious courage in his subjects. He gave a slow deliberate nod of approval to Fernão.

'May I also introduce our esteemed cosmographers, the Faleiro brothers—Ruy and Francisco.'

They arose and bowed.

'We have listened to their proposals and believe they are to be worthy of your audience,' Fonseco said, then gestured to Fernão to begin the presentation.

To the advisors, Fernão appeared slight of height, a face weathered from years at sea, and approached the throne with his noticeable limp. Nevertheless, Fernão stood tall, proud, and confident. 'Forgive me your highness for my Spanish is not yet fluent,' Fernão said in broken Spanish.

'You are not alone,' the young Carlos replied with a Flemish accented Spanish. 'As I have lived most of my life in Flanders, I am still learning myself.' He smiled. 'Do your best and my missionary to the New World, Bartolomé de las Casas, shall interpret the finer points to me. Please continue.'

Fernão felt relieved at the king's easy bearing and apparent interest. He continued, 'Twelve years ago, in Cochin, I met an Italian explorer named Ludovico di Varthema. He relayed, to our captains and viceroy, detailed accounts of his travels to the far east, including the Moluccas. I have his book here as evidence if you wish to see.'

'I have already read it,' Carlos replied with a grin. 'My tutors made sure I had a good education.' He nodded to Guillaume de Croÿ in gratitude for his years of mentorship.

'Excellent,' Fernão replied, a bit surprised. He sifted through some letters in his hands. 'I also have correspondence from my good friend and long-time comrade in arms, Francisco Serrão. He has reached the Moluccas and testifies of the great quantity of quality spices, especially cloves, nutmeg, and mace. He states here in writing: *I have found here a new world richer and greater than that of Vasco da Gama. I beg you to join me here, that you may sample for yourself the delights that surround me.* He further testifies the lands lie in the legal domains of Castile. We can elaborate on this further. But first I would like to present our guests from Sumatra. They speak the commercial language of Malay which is also understood by the Moluccan chiefs.'

Enrique and the girl approached the king. They spoke to one another in Malay and then shifted dialects, further impressing the court advisors and the king. They bowed and returned to their seats.

'I believe my servant, Enrique, is skilled enough to act as a translator if an armada should be requisitioned for a mission to the Spice Islands. We have calculated a complete voyage to the Moluccas would return within two years. It could also return loaded with a lucrative spice cargo.'

The priest, Bartolomé de las Casas, was seated next to the king and asked, 'What route do you intend to take?'

'By way of Cape Saint Mary or what you call *Rio de la Plata*,' Fernão replied. 'Then follow the coast until we find a strait that I know exists.'

'What if you cannot locate the strait leading to the other sea?'

'Then I would turn east and go the route of the Portuguese, past the Cape of Good Hope.'

The advisors and king were impressed by his boldness and tenacious refusal to give up.

'But I am confident the strait exists. Please let me demonstrate.'

Ruy handed Fernão a painted globe to illustrate his planned route. It was two feet in diameter with an iron axis protruding through the center and supported on an iron tripod. The globe was made of pasteboard covered over a wooden frame. A layer of gypsum covered the pasteboard and over this was secured a stretched parchment with all the painted drawings. The meridian was iron and the horizon brass. The sea was painted in ultra-marine, the land in brown and green, and the mountain tops of white. The names and inscriptions were in colors of silver, gold, white, and yellow. Fernão set the globe in front of the king and advisors, then spun it on the iron axis.

'This is a replica of Martin Behaim's globe,' Fernão said. 'He was my tutor in the India House of Portugal.'

'Behaim?' Fonseca asked. 'That name sounds familiar. Oh yes, I remember Vespucci had mentioned him several times with deep respect, considered him an excellent astronomer and cosmographer.'

'Vespucci was quite interested in Behaim's modified astrolabe,' Fernão responded. 'I was there when they discussed it.'

'You met Vespucci?' Chancellor Sauvage asked.

'Yes. As a young man in Lisbon just before I set out for the Indies. His calculations on longitude were precise.'

Others in the room murmured among themselves, amazed that he had been acquainted with such great men in his youth. Fernão turned the globe so they all could see the coastline of Brazil. 'As you can see here, the coastline turns westward as one travels south. Our domains begin in southern Brazil.' As he traced his finger southward of Brazil, the paint turned to all white, so as not to reveal the exact location of his proposed strait. 'I know the strait exists based on a chart I have seen. It is narrow, but it does exist. Once we have passed through, we shall emerge into the great ocean beyond.' He turned the globe to reveal the wide ocean gap and the Spice Islands marked clearly as their destination. 'We shall cross this expanse and eventually reach the Moluccas as you can see here.'

He then traced his finger up and down along the antemeridian line, running just to the west of the Moluccas. 'As you can also see, the line of demarcation shows the Moluccas are in the legal domain of Castile.' Fernão gestured for Ruy to come forward. 'Please allow Ruy to elaborate upon the astronomical calculations based on this planisphere.'

Ruy Faleiro's elaborate celestial, black-garbed cape, accentuated his role as astronomer par excellence. He displayed the planisphere; it revealed the astronomical spheres stretched out on a flat surface and designed to provide a visual aid to the audience with all the coordinates plotted. It was a result of the collaborative effort between the two Faleiro brothers, the Reinels—both father and son, Diogo Ribeiro, and Fernão Magalhães.

'Based on my calculations of longitude, the antimeridian lies in our jurisdiction as Magalhães has stated,' Ruy said. 'Allow me to illustrate with the astronomical charts.' He continued elaborating his mathematical analysis to the king and advisors for some time, further bolstering their conclusions.

Once the presentation concluded, the king looked over his advisors, expecting their opinion.

Fonseca stood up and spoke, 'I believe we have all the evidence needed. Magalhães has the navigational experience and is not afraid to lead an armada. Faleiro has provided ample scientific proofs to confirm.'

The king raised his arm. 'We shall conclude this audience. I will convene with my advisors and shall soon give my answer.' The participants all filed out.

After two days, the king responded with an official intent and request for demands. Magalhães and the Faleiro brothers offered their bold answer in two possible scenarios.

Their first option was based upon the crown incurring all the costs for the mission and proposed the following stipulations: No other expeditions were to be sent to the Spice Islands for a period of 10 years but if that could not be arranged, they should receive a 20th share of all resulting profits; and that all lands and islands discovered by them, a 20th share of annual profits will be theirs; and that in every following expedition they have the right to acquire goods up to 1,000 ducats for personal trade; and if more than 6 islands should be discovered, they would be granted 2 of them and held for their heirs in perpetuity; and in this first mission they should receive one-fifth of all net profits; and they would receive the titles of admirals.

Their second option was conditioned upon funding the armada at their own cost. Fernão had already met with the Haros and believed they would back up his move if required. Therefore, if the enterprise were privately funded the following demands were presented: The king would grant them ownership of all the lands they should discover and the exclusive rights to explore such lands for 10 years. In return, one-fifth of the profits would be paid to the crown. The would-be explorers sent up their proposals, and then proceeded to hold their breath.

A few days later, on March 22, 1518, the king sent a *capitulation*, an official letter of decree. Fernão was ecstatic upon the response. For the most part, the king had met their demands. In a separate royal decree issued the same day, they were given the titles captains-generals of the armada and a salary of 50,000 maravedis per year to be paid by the Casa de Contratación. The king ordered an immediate requisition for a fleet of five vessels; two of 130 *tons*, two of 90, and one of 60, all to be equipped with 234 crew and supplied with provisions and artillery for a period of two years.

In April, the king summoned the courts of the regions of Aragon to meet him in Zaragoza. Fernão's retinue was invited to follow along and continue planning for the expedition as they traveled. Along the way they stopped in Aranda de Duero to visit the king's brother, Prince Ferdinand, and to whom the two navigators were introduced. Further impressed with their knowledge and tenacious drive, the king decided to reward their efforts; on April 17, a cedula was issued for payment of 30,000 maravedis to offset their initial investments. Furthermore, he ordered a monthly increase salary of 8,000 for time served at sea. If the Casa de Contratación should approve, Fernão was to be given the title *pilot real*. Finally, in case of death, their heirs were to receive all due profits.

With the payment order, the two navigators immediately departed for Seville to collect their funds from the Casa, while the court proceeded to Zaragoza. All Fernão could think about was embracing his new wife. Upon arrival to the Alcazar, he rushed to their bedroom for a passionate reunion. Unclear how long he would remain, Fernão took every advantage to spend time with his beloved Beatriz. With the king's recent orders, the Casa reluctantly dispersed the 30,000 maravedis to the navigators. But every attempt to begin the outfitting of the fleet was rebuffed and delayed. Concerned, the king would lose their confidence, the two traveled to Zaragoza to meet with the court. Fernão pled their case and requested assistance in forcing the Casa to comply with the crown's orders to prepare the fleet on time.

Meanwhile, the Portuguese ambassador, Alvaro da Costa, had accompanied the court prelates to Zaragoza for negotiating the marriage alliance between King Dom Manuel and King Carlos' sister, Doña Leonor. During this period, he had acquired privy knowledge of the expedition and was alarmed by the implications.

Fernão Magalhães was alone in the palace courtyard meditating when Alvaro da Costa approached in haste.

'I have heard distressing news,' Alvaro said, with a frown. 'Have you no decency? If you pledge allegiance to another sovereign, over our dear lord Dom Manuel, it will be considered an act of treason. It will dishonor your name forever!' Fernão remained stoic as Alvaro continued his harangue, 'I am here to strengthen our two nations unity by the marriage treaty. But your hubris and brazen disrespect for your country endangers our alliance by this encroaching voyage.'

'The marriage will take place, Fernão replied. 'For Dom Manuel wishes it to be so.' He knew the king was almost 50 years of age and desired to have his young 19-year-old niece, Leonora. Manuel had previously been married to two of her maternal aunts, Isabella of Aragon, and Maria of Aragon, thus a family union would continue to bind the two nations. Fernão continued his rebuttal. 'The fleet will not trespass upon Portuguese domains. Furthermore, I have already pledged my word to King Carlos, and it would be a sin against my honor and conscience if I should break it.'

Frustrated by the logic, Alvaro changed tact. 'If you return to Portugal the king will recompense your efforts with a substantial reward.'

Fernão knew this was a ruse and answered with a glaring stare.

Thwarted again, Alvaro threatened, 'I shall write to your father-in-law's patron, the Duke of Braganza. Your entire family will be sent back to Portugal if you persist in this madness!'

'I do not believe the duke will side with you over Diogo Barbosa. My decision stands firm.'

'Very well. But this will not be the end of the matter,' Alvaro replied and then stormed off.

A few days later, in the afternoon, Ruy Faleiro met with Fernão outside their inn. His brooding suspicious eyes darted around. He was clearly agitated. 'Has Alvaro da Costa entreated you concerning our project?' Ruy asked.

'Yes,' Fernão replied. 'And he is not pleased with my refusal to acquiesce to his demands.'

'I have heard Alvaro was able to sway advisors Cardinal Utrecht and Guillaume de Croÿ. But Fonseco held firm and nullified his scheme.'

'Has the ambassador informed Dom Manuel of the mission?'

'I understand letters have been dispatched between them,' Ruy said, nervously scratching his neck. 'They are desperate to stop us. I have even heard assassination rumors. Do not take this lightly—we are targets.'

'That is possible. Let us then stay alert. But we shall continue with our planning.'

That evening, Ruy and Fernão concluded a lengthy procedural meeting with Fonseca in his house, and upon departure were surprised by the late hour, for it had become pitch dark. They stood in the front garden for a moment to let their eyes adjust to the light. Something moved and rustled the shadows. Fernão quietly unsheathed his sword, grabbed Ruy's shoulder, and nodded toward the tree line along the property border. Fernão thought he heard a bolt slipped into a crossbow, and shoved Ruy to the ground. The steel bolt whizzed past their heads and slammed into the front door. Losing the advantage of surprise, the assailant rushed off into the fields.

Hearing the noise, Fonseco emerged with an armed contingent. He looked at the metal shaft imbedded deep into the wood of his doorway. 'Gentlemen, please let my men escort you to your inn. The hour is late. We cannot afford to take risks.'

Fernão and Ruy both thanked him and the security detachment accompanied them to their lodging.

3

Zaragoza, Spain – July 20, 1518

King Carlos wrote a letter to the Casa ordering the latest funds received from the West Indies to be reserved for fitting out the fleet according to the plans laid out by Magalhães and Faleiro.

Soon afterward, the two navigators were summoned to the palace for a royal ceremony, to be knighted in the Order of Santiago. This was a strategic move by the king, for the Casa and royal advisors would be on notice to comply with their royal commission in the timely outfitting of the fleet. Furthermore, the Portuguese ambassador would now witness the crown's resolve to see the mission through to the end.

Fernão and Ruy approached the Aljafería Palace, a fortified structure built in the eleventh century by the Islamic Taifas. After the Reconquista it became the residence of the Christian kings of Aragon, and later the Catholic Monarchs. An imposing five-story tower loomed above. It appeared impenetrable. The entire complex was reminiscent of the Alcazar architecture in Seville. They climbed an elaborate staircase illuminated with Gothic-Mudéjar decorative artwork, then crossed a long gallery, and remained in one of the waiting rooms adjacent to the Throne Room. At the appointed hour, a guard escorted them to the royal chamber. The king's advisors turned to look at the pair as they cautiously entered the Throne Room.

'Please come forward,' King Don Carlos said. 'It is time to receive honors for your mission ahead.' He drew his ceremonial sword, inlaid with gold and jewels. A short reading was given by the cardinal, then Fernão and Ruy knelt before the king, offering their lives in service. King Carlos laid his sword on Fernão's shoulder, drew the blade toward his neck and raised it above his head, thus figuratively sparing him. The king laid the blade on his opposite shoulder, continuing the cut line. He repeated this gesture with Ruy, then pronounced them both Knights of the Order of Santiago. Fernão was emotional and fought back the tears welling behind his eyes, for this was the same order his family had pledged to support in Portugal, and in Spain it was considered the most prestigious of all military orders.

Soon after the ceremony, the two knighted navigators were sent back to Seville to continue outfitting the fleet. Upon arrival, Fernão rushed to his quarters where he found Beatriz on the patio, knitting.

'It is now official,' he said. 'I am knighted in the Order of Santiago!'

'This is wonderful news,' Beatriz replied, practically glowing at him. 'You have achieved so much. Two sovereigns of mighty nations, both vying for your services as captain-general, and now knighthood.'

'And now an expedited commission to prepare the fleet. Can the news be any greater?'

Beatriz smiled. 'Could that be possible?'

'What are you knitting?'

Beatriz held up what appeared to be a tiny sweater.

Fernão raised an eyebrow. 'Is this for me? I mean, is this for us? I mean, are you with child?'

She laughed and nodded.

'You are sure?'

'I am quite certain I am pregnant.'

He knelt beside the chair and embraced her. 'You are right. This is greater news.'

The latest shipment of goods from the West Indies was allocated for the Moluccas project but the money was quickly exhausted. In mid-August, the Casa informed the king of the situation, and mentioned a new shipment from the Caribbean had arrived, which they could allocate for the fleet, if permission was granted. The king complied and the endeavor moved forward. The agent, Juan de Aranda was tasked with the acquisition and transfer of the vessels. He journeyed to Cadiz and purchased four carracks and one caravel: *San Antonio*-120 tons, *Trinidad*-110 tons, *Conceptión*-90 tons, *Victoria*-85 tons, and *Santiago*-75 tons. In addition, a two-masted longboat and skiff were purchased. Duarte Barbosa was assigned to supply armaments, toward which he acquired a large arsenal in Bilbao.

The budding fleet anchored along the banks of the Guadalquivir River near the Tower of Gold. Fernão and Ruy looked aghast at the decrepit condition of the old vessels. 'What was Aranda thinking?' Ruy asked.

'Limited choices for the funds I suppose.'

'I never trusted that one.'

'Well, this is our fleet now. Best we get to rebuilding.'

Ruy's face contorted with a mad rage. 'Damn Aranda!' He stormed off while kicking and punching at the air.

During the following weeks, the ships were beached along the banks of the Guadalquivir River. The patching and careening process was initiated to bring the fleet in seaworthy condition. The sandy beach along the river led up to an ancient shipyard. It was a gothic-Mudéjar structure built from a brick factory and had 17 naves, all situated in front of the outer walls of the city. Caulkers, blacksmiths, carpenters, and other skilled craftsmen could work under the cover of the structure, all protected from inclement weather fronts, or the scathing heat of summer. In addition to working space, supplies and equipment were stored here for current projects. Fernão supervised the repairs and customizing of the vessels for the long voyage, including the installation of extra structural reinforcements and water-holding vats.

By October 22, 1518, the flagship *Trinidad* had been repaired and careened. It was ready to be refloated after dawn with the high tide. At 3 A.M. Fernão Magalhães was inspecting the hold for any possible leaks or structural deficiencies. A veteran pilot from the Columbus voyages, Rodríguez de Mafra, assisted by his side. A small crew prepared the rigging and other preparations, including the raising of the banners for the ceremonial floating of the king's flagship.

As the sun began to rise, a large crowd of onlookers had gathered to witness the spectacle. Suddenly, a man in the middle of the crowd began to shout: 'Look! What is the emblem of the King of Portugal doing there—the shields of Aviz?' He continued to incite the masses: 'Where is the banner of Castile?'

The crowd was quickly riled and hurled insults and threats at the workers on the *Trinidad*. The alarmed crew summoned the captain-general from the ship's hold. Fernão and Rodríguez emerged to face the tumultuous crowds and noticed the people pointing to the masts. Only four banners had been raised, all those of Magalhães, captain of the flagship.

Rodríguez grabbed the shoulder of a crewmate. 'Why are the royal banners of Castile missing on the main mast? And why are the *Trinidad's* colors missing on the foremast?'

'They are still at the shop for dye work,' the crewman replied. 'We raised the captain's colors as is customary.'

Fernão turned to Rodríguez. 'He is correct, the captain's colors are to be raised. They are my colors, not the King of Portugal's.' He squinted his eyes and stared at the raised colors. 'The problem arises because the five shields of Aviz on my family's coat of arms are small, virtually imperceptible from shore. The crowd cannot see the colors. I suspect an agent of Portugal incites the crowd.'

From his vantage point up on the deck, Fernão noticed an alcaide approaching. The alcaide stood near the gangway and bellowed, 'You must at once remove those banners!'

Fernão answered back, 'The royal arms are not those of the King of Portugal, they are mine—a captain and vassal of the King of Spain.' Unwilling to further entertain the whims of a minor official, he turned his back and returned below deck to prepare the vessel for its test float.

The alcaide, engaged, stormed off to summon a higher authority. Meanwhile, the crowd rushed toward the flagship as it lay perched at an angle upon wooden beams on the sandy beach near the river's edge. The mob demanded the banners to be removed and pushed forward up the gangway to enforce compliance. Alarmed, the crews blocked the entrance to the ship. A fight ensued to which pilot Rodríguez de Mafra was stabbed in the hand.

Taking notice of the chaos, Dr. Sancho de Matienzo arrived at the vessel. As the Canon of the

Cathedral of Seville and treasurer of the Casa, his authority was to be reckoned with. Fernão listened carefully to the canon's words, since of late, they had become good friends. 'You are within your rights to raise your banners, but I advise you to remove them. You know it will only incite the crowd and give advantage to the Portuguese in their aims to frustrate our king's expedition.'

After a moment to consider the options, he replied with cautious reluctance, 'Very well. 'I will only do so to ensure our mission proceeds on schedule.' Fernão turned to the crew. 'Remove the banners!'

The flags were stored away, the mob retreated, and the men returned to their work. However, it was not long before the alcaide returned with the port-captain. They climbed up the gangway to find Fernão conversing with Dr. Matienzo. 'Where are the banners of the King of Portugal that you have brazenly displayed?' the port-captain asked emphatically. 'Bring them to me now!'

'I am not responsible to you for my actions,' Fernão replied defiantly, and then turned his back on the two as he returned to his duties.

The port-captain's face turned red, and he barked an order to his escort of armed guards, 'Arrest him!'

Dr. Matienzo bravely stepped in front of the guards. 'If you lay hands upon the king's captain and interfere with the work at hand, you shall answer to the king himself. I advise you to leave now.'

'Arrest him also!'

The guards rushed forward and raised their swords over the canon's neck. Fernão turned his focus from the swords over Dr. Matienzo's neck to the crewmen departing for fear of arrest, and thus leaving the vessel to the impending peril of the rising tide. He stared the port-captain in the eyes. 'You can assist the remaining crew to right the ship before high tide sets in or do nothing and take full responsibility for what happens to the king's property. As for me, I shall depart and leave these matters for you to resolve.' With these words, he defiantly walked down the gangway planking toward the beach.

The port-captain and alcaide stared at one another in shock at such a stubborn affront. A simple nod between them and then to the guards signaled their withdrawal.

Fernão stood on the beach with his arms crossed as he stared down the retreating officials and their armed escort. After the matter was settled, Fernão met Dr. Matienzo as he disembarked. 'Thank you, doctor. Your help was substantial and duly appreciated.'

'That was nearly a catastrophe, but your determined will and quick thinking prevailed.'

Fernão boarded again and found Rodríguez wrapping his bloodied hand. 'Thank you for your assistance in defending the ship. I know you served with the great Admiral Colombo. You are an experienced veteran at sea, and I will need you to pilot the *San Antonio.*

'Thank you, sir, for the honor,' Rodríguez replied. He nodded and left to finish preparing the ship.

For the next two nights, Fernão's sleep was fitful, as he wrestled in his mind how to persuade the king to right the wrongs done to his loyal servant. It was dawn and he tossed and turned in bed. Beatriz awakened next to him. 'You must sort this out so you can sleep,' she said. 'So that we both can sleep.' She smiled. 'Let me prepare some tea and we can talk about it.'

Fernão arose and sat in a chair overlooking the courtyard. Beatriz soon returned with tea and took a seat near him. They watched the sunlight gradually lighting the grove below them. 'You must inform the king about the Portuguese agents,' she said. 'They are causing strife.'

'Of course. And the officials in Seville have acted even more treacherously, for they have delayed the king's work and have treated us as villains.'

She looked into his eyes. 'You are the king's captain. You deserve all due respect, as a royal commander in service to the crown. Set forth your case with all details and demand justice be done.'

'I will pen my letter today. We cannot afford any more delays.'

She kissed him and went back into bed. Fernão knew he was lucky to have her advice, for he knew his own temperament. She was the calm to his storm, and this proved out somedays later, when the court had responded to his queries.

Beatriz met Fernão in the Dance Garden. They sat on a bench and discussed the royal letters. 'King Carlos favors you much for he has dispatched correspondence with all expediency. He lends you support well beyond most of his subjects.'

'He has indeed. Quite the opposite of Dom Manuel.' Fernão stared off to the garden fountain. 'He promises a thorough investigation into the matter. Any attempt to thwart his own fleet captain have been deemed as acts of treason. It appears the king was so incensed and vexed by the betrayal of officials in his own jurisdiction that he ordered those found guilty punished with maximum severity.'

'Did you say there was a second letter?'

'Yes. It was delivered to Dr. Matienzo with a royal commendation for his dutiful actions and requested his service to inform on any progress concerning the punishment of the guilty.'

'Any other news?'

'I was raised from rank of Knight—to Knight Commander in the Order of Santiago.'

'I am so proud of you. Such an esteemed rank earned by achievement and not court bribes is indeed a worthy accomplishment.' She rested her head on his shoulder and stared at the fountain.

'I am beginning to really like this young king,' Fernão said with a grin. 'I shall see this project through to the end.'

Throughout the winter, Fernão Magalhães supervised the outfitting, repairs, and arming of the fleet to completion while the Faleiro brothers updated and modified the navigational charts and instruments. Fernão decided to see how work was progressing at the Casa. The room was full of desks, all cluttered with charts and astronomical tables. Ruy was hunched over a wide flat solid-edged box.

Ruy turned his head. 'So, you finally decided to pay me a visit.'

'I have been busy,' Fernão said. 'The good news is our flagship floats.'

'Yes. Of course. Forgive my presumptions. Look at our new compass units.'

Fernão leaned over the compass box. It had a wide, flat 360-degree graduated face surrounding a pivot needle. An arched needle crossed between the N and S markings. 'My brother helped develop these modified compass boxes,' Ruy said. 'We have four ready and can measure compass variation quite well.' He then retrieved a wooden astrolabe from a shelf. 'I have combined the astrolabe function into a compass box.'

Fernão noticed the sun-style set above the pivot needle, and a revolving pelorus or compass card with two sighting vanes on the ends.

Ruy continued, 'I believe both devices can best be used to locate the pole star position by my double azimuth technique. Take a reading at sunrise and sunset on the same day and then one can ascertain the altitude zero point.'

Fernão scratched his beard. 'This is good.'

'With this device one can take a reading in any given hour to ascertain the meridional line, the poles, and the equinoctial line of the horizon.'

'This is really good,' Fernão said.

'As you know, longitude is our greatest challenge,' Ruy said. 'My brother, Francisco, has assisted me in finalizing a 30-chapter manual for such computations at sea.'

Fernão thumbed through the book taking notice of its diagrams, astronomical tables, and instructive notes.

'We have revised and updated the Zacuto Almanac and the Ephemerides of Regiomantus. By these, one can calculate the lunar distances. By the way, I have fixed our prime meridian to Mount Teide in Tenerife.'

'Very useful tools,' Fernão remarked. 'But will they work in uncharted waters with unfamiliar landmarks and skies?'

Ruy looked at him flatly. 'You know how to sour the mood, don't you?'

'Just trying to prepare.'

'Well, they will be invaluable for taking readings. And always remember to compensate for magnetic compass variation. Of course, you will have to rely upon your dead-reckoning skills.'

Fernão smiled as he considered the challenges. He would have to take careful notations on their course heading and make constant adjustments for directional changes. All the distances covered would have to be measured and recorded, including all the tacking maneuvers. Any storm disrupting their course would have to be accounted for and adjustments made on best guess estimates. It would be challenging, but not impossible. 'Thank you Ruy. These tools will be invaluable,' Fernão said. 'We will speak again soon.'

4

Barcelona, Spain – April, 1519

Fernão and his page, Cristovão Rebêlo, dismounted their steeds just outside the Grand Royal Palace of Barcelona, also known as the *Palau Reial Major*. Fernão's leg buckled under him as his foot hit the ground.

Cristovão hurried to lift him back up. 'Are you alright?'

'I will be fine. Must be the cooler weather and the humidity from the sea.'

'It will be an honor to meet the emperor,' Cristovão said.

'It was for me every time,' Fernão said with a smile.

Fernão struggled as he limped up the outdoor stairway. It was an odd design, for it began with wide steps, but as they climbed, each step became narrower, until converging to a narrow point in the right corner of the royal palace.

After introducing themselves, the guard allowed them to enter. Inside the doorway, Fernão stopped for a moment to admire an exquisite altarpiece dedicated to the Epiphany, which adorned the royal chapel of Saint Agatha. The guard then led them to the adjacent ceremonial hall, a vast chamber with numerous Gothic round arches layered under high Romanesque vaults. Unannounced, they happened to walk in on a conversation between King Don Carlos, Cardinal Adrian of Utrecht, and another unfamiliar ecclesiastical prelate.

'The Curia in Rome has informed me of a situation,' Cardinal Adrian said. 'A professor of theology in Wittenberg, Germany has circulated a document of 95 thesis and a sermon against indulgences. It challenges the authority of the church and the pope. The heresy is spreading across the empire.'

'And what is that of concern to me?' Carlos replied.

'Perhaps it will pass,' he replied. 'But if it persists and you succeed your grandfather as Holy Roman Emperor, it may *become* your problem.'

'What is the professor's name?'

'Martin Luther.'

Carlos took notice of Fernão's presence. 'Excuse me. Ahh, my fine commander. How proceeds your work? And who accompanies you?'

'This is my page, Cristovão Rebêlo. I expect he can be of great service to us on the expedition.'

Carlos nodded.

'Equipment has been readied, repairs complete, and supplies en route as we speak,' Fernão said. 'We only need to acquire the barter goods for the journey.'

'So, we must not delay any further,' Carlos said. 'The fleet will sail by the end of May, correct?'

'Well, there is another issue regarding delays.'

'What is this?'

'The new comptroller, Recalde, has been spreading rumors and allegations among the captains and pilots. He implores them to refuse sailing, claiming I have concealed the planned route, and have sinister motives. Furthermore, he denied the disbursement of enlistment bonuses authorized prior by Dr. Matienzo.'

'Is that everything, concerning delays?'

'Yes.'

'Then I will take care of it,' Carlos replied and turned to the sunlight beaming through the windows. 'Please, let us all enjoy this fine spring day.'

The entourage followed the king into the courtyard. Birds chirped as they perched among the orange trees. They walked on paving stones surrounded by flower beds and green grass. They casually stood apart.

In private, Don Carlos resumed his conversation with Cardinal Utrecht about the Luther affair.

Meanwhile, a finely dressed young man near 30-years of age approached Fernão and Cristovão. He asked, 'Have you heard about the Roman ruins?' Fernão noticed his Italian accent.

'Ruins?' Fernão asked.

'This courtyard has been built over the old Roman city of Barcino with all its factories, wineries, and housing. Even the walls of this complex are intertwined with preexisting Roman structures. Later, the Visigoths built Christian churches among these ruins. A fascinating site.'

'Indeed.'

'It is so amazing to stand here surrounded by such history. Imagine, the great admiral himself stood in this very place, reporting on his first voyage to the Catholic Monarchs. I also wish to experience such great sights and wonders. Have you read the books by Duarte Barbosa and Ludovico di Varthema? Their accounts of the far-off lands to the east?'

Fernão felt as if he was looking at an image of himself before he first set out to the Indies in quest for adventure and glory. A keen mind and attention to detail were especially valued in such missions.

'Actually, I know them both,' Fernão said. 'Duarte is my brother-in-law and will join our fleet. I met Varthema in India.'

The young man stared, speechless and amazed.

A prelate stepped forward, the one in attendance during the discussion concerning Martin Luther.

'Please allow me to introduce my companion, and myself,' he said. 'I am Monsignor Chieregati, the Pope's ambassador to Spain and this is Antonio Pigafetta, my assistant. I value his writing skills in our service to Rome. But perhaps his talents could be of greater use for the interests of our lords in your mission. My young friend has heard of your own exploits at sea and would like to join your fleet. He has quite the combat experience at sea, fighting against the accursed Turks. He served with the Knights of Rhodes under the command of Grand Master, Philippe de Villiers l'Isle Adam. He is even knighted in the Order of St. John of Jerusalem.'

'Ah, a gentleman and Hospitaller,' Fernão commented, quite impressed. 'I am honored. If you can arrange it, his presence would be considered a great asset.'

Later, Cristovão asked Fernão about the contract as they departed for Seville. 'If I may ask, did the king grant your requests?'

'He did indeed,' Fernão replied with a grin. 'I have heard it often said: Ask and you shall receive. So, I asked *and* received.'

'Everything you asked?'

Yes. My wife shall receive all my annual pay while at sea. If I shall die, then she receives it for life. I also pressed for my captains and pilots to receive extra honor by elevating their ranking to knights.'

'You are loyal to your men,' Cristovão remarked.

It was late July and Seville was burdened with a scorching heat. Fernão made his way to the Casa for a briefing with Ruy and found him in his office hunched over a desk scribbling mathematical notations. 'Good morning Ruy.'

'With all these delays can you really believe it is a good morning?'

'At least we now have the funds to complete the outfitting. The purse of Cristóbal Haro has opened wide. He will cover one-fifth the entire cost of the expedition.'

'Yes,' Ruy said, with disdain. 'But at what cost? Can we trust a Jewish banker? He represents the House of Fugger banking consortium in Augsburg.'

'I am not sure if it matters that he is Jewish.'

'Then why has he made a pact with Fonseca to open their own Casa, a separate trading house?'

'I was unaware of this,' Fernão said. He scratched his beard. 'Unfortunately, you may have a point. In Barcelona I witnessed Fonseca accuse and sentence Aranda of illegally using his official position for personal gain at the expense of the crown. He then cut out Aranda's entire share and relieved him of his position as agent at the Casa. Nobody knows who brought forth the charges; Fonseca, Recalde, or Haro. I suspect the former. He had the most to lose in securing lucrative profits for himself. Ironic is it not? Fonseca uses his position for profit yet accuses Aranda of the same.'

'Speaking of Fonseca. Rumors circulate that the new inspector general for the fleet, Juan de Cartagena, may be his son,' Ruy's hands shook with agitation as he spoke about it.

'Quite possible, for his pay exceeds ours,' Fernão said, concerned but not too alarmed at Ruy's state. 'He receives salary as the new inspector general, retains his guaranteed annual pay as a royal guard, and now appointed as captain of the *San Antonio*, he accumulates an additional third salary. Even more disturbing, Fonseca has managed to manipulate the king into granting Cartagena sweeping new powers, nearly equal to fleet commander.'

'But it gets worse,' Ruy added. 'Fonseca has appointed two more Castilians, personal friends, as captains in the fleet. So, now he has control over three of the five vessels. Damn Fonseca!' Ruy threw a book across the room.

'You are right,' Fernão said. 'They distrust us. Orders were given to fill a roster of 234 crew with preference to Spaniards. I tried to recruit in Castile, but few are willing to risk their lives for dubious profits while opportunities for employment on shore remain safe and plentiful. So, I enlisted whatever Portuguese seamen I thought I could trust who seemed willing to venture out. And of course, the Casa vehemently objected to the number of our countrymen and complained to the king. So, as you may have already been informed, last month orders were given to limit the enlisted Portuguese to five.'

Ruy's face reddened as his rage burst forth. 'This is ridiculous! Such absurd nonsense!'

'It is. I shall continue leading recruitment efforts myself, but if no locals enlist, we may have to sail with more of our kin and other foreigners. You know the Portuguese agent, Alvarez. He came to my residence and tried to dissuade me once again from proceeding with the mission. Even though he uttered enticing words, I politely refused to stray from my course. But in our conversation, he warned me about trusting Cartagena and the other Castilian captains. I begin to believe he may be right.'

A rapping sounded on the closed office door.

'Who is it?' Ruy asked with a raised voice.

'Excuse me,' said a man's voice from outside. 'I have a letter from the crown. It concerns you both.

Ruy opened the door, snatched the document, then closed the door on the courier. He carefully read it over. After some moments, his face began to contort and flush red. 'Damn them! Damn them all!'

'What is it?'

'I told you many times, over and over, they cannot be trusted. They claim I am unfit for a command at sea. And they have cut my pay.'

'What?' Fernão asked, startled.

Ruy handed him the letter and continued to rant, 'They are sending a second fleet, after ours. The Haros and Fonseca conspire with their plots to cut us out. They have the audacity to offer me a mere 30,000 maravedis to supervise the second fleet! They have assigned Andrés de San Martin to take my place as the fleet's chief astronomer.'

Fernão shook his head in disbelief as he read over the letter. 'Outrageous!' He read past where Ruy abruptly left off. 'That is not all. They have now given Cartagena position as joint commander. I will only have two advantages over him, administrator of justice and the command of the flagship.'

'Can you do something? Ruy pleaded. 'For both of us? Send word to the king?' His head drooped in despondence.

Fernão knew the reason for dismissal was due to Ruy's deteriorating mental condition. He slept little and often walked about as if in a daze. Lately, his sudden irrational fits of rage were triggered at the slightest offense. But today's news was justifiable grounds for outrage. Fernão tried to diffuse his anger and offered a sympathetic response. 'If I had the power to revoke the cedula, you know I would do so.' He knew the king would never rescind his order, for Ruy was indeed gradually succumbing to insanity. 'I will appeal the decision regarding Cartagena's new powers and suggest your brother take your place.'

Ruy stared blankly in despair.

'I am sorry Ruy,' Fernão said, placing a hand on Ruy's shoulder. He withdrew it, and walked toward the door, then turned. 'When you have completed your manual, I could really use it.'

Ruy continued to stare without any response as Fernão walked out.

In early August the intense dry heat was at its peak. With incessant delays, desertions begun to hamper efforts to complete the rosters. Fernão knew he must personally oversee the demanding task to recruit. He sent officers to the seaports from Cadiz to Malaga, all with funds to pay enlistment bonuses. Meanwhile, Fernão hired a public crier, and walked the streets of the mariner's section of Triana—a district of Seville. They drew near an outdoor tavern with sailors lounging at tables, many drinking red wine paired with sardines on flat bread. The crier bellowed: 'Last chance to join the Armada for the Discovery of the Spicery!'

'What's the pay?' a local sailor asked.

'Depends on enlisted rank,' replied the crier. 'Wages for a servant boy, 600 maravedis. For a sailor, 800. Mariner is 1,000. Senior mariner, 1,500. A master, 1,800, 2,500 for a pilot, and 4,000 for captains.'

'How long is the voyage?' another seaman asked.

'Estimates range up to two years.'

'Two years, at those wages?' balked another.

'Any officer shall receive a bonus of five-months of salary prior to departure.' The crier's extra incentive was answered with silence. He looked over the men and continued, 'In addition, space will be allowed for

75

prizes acquired on the mission and sized according to rank.' Still with a tepid response he added another caveat. 'And advances may be paid from 6 to 12-months of salary.'

'Who is the captain-general?' a brutish mariner asked.

'I am,' Fernão replied in broken Spanish. He stood with his hands on his hips and chest out.

'A Portuguese commander?' The mariner huffed with impertinence. 'Count me out.'

'What route will you take?' another sailor asked.

'West to Brazil, then we sail beyond the New World via a pass to the south.'

'Never been done before,' the sailor responded. 'Why should we risk our lives for such paltry wages?'

The sailors murmured among themselves and shook their heads, unconvinced.

Fernão and the crier looked at one another undecided how to respond any further. Just then, a tall-muscled man with blond hair and a thick beard stood up from among the tables. He walked toward Fernão. But along the way, he turned his head towards the sailors and asked in a Nordic accented Spanish, 'What is the matter, afraid of a little adventure?'

'What is your name? Fernão asked.

'Hans.'

'I assume you wish to enlist as a—'

'Gunner sir. I have many years of experience.'

'Your accent, never heard it before.'

'I am from Bergen, Norway.'

'Ahh, a Norseman—a Viking!' Fernão grinned. 'We can definitely use a Viking gunner.'

From sunrise to past sunset, Fernão was constantly busy with every down-to-the-wire detail crowding the rapidly approaching departure date. He supervised the last-minute deliveries in the millstone docks along the Guadalquivir River. Armaments, sailing equipment, and preserved items such as wine and hardtack, were loaded on the vessels. The wine was stored in casks, sealed with cork and pitch, then stored below deck. The hardtack was a main staple consisting of wheat flour along with its husk. It would eventually be kneaded with hot water and cooked twice to produce biscuits.

Then, on August 9, all the enlisted men were ordered to attend a high mass in the church of Santa Maria de la Vittoria de Triana. The king's delegate—Sancho Martinez de Leiva, had earlier suggested the captain-general enter last, for he wished to orchestrate and heighten the solemnity of the great event. Fernão tried to conceal his limp as he walked the center aisle. Colored linen and silk banners of the five vessels were displayed along the sanctuary walls. The leading captains and officers flanked the center aisle while the crews stood among the pews. Dr. Matienzo smiled as he watched his friend approach and take his position at the front along the wall. All remained standing as the mass was performed. Once concluded, Sancho Martinez beckoned for Magalhães to come forward. Kneeling before a statue of Mary and with head bowed, he swore to obey the king and dutifully accomplish the mission tasked to him—to discover the Spicery. Next, all the captains and leading officers swore allegiance to the king, to obey all the commands of the captain-general and follow all his directed routes. As they exited the church, bells rang to proclaim the occasion.

The following day, the armada discharged a thunderous salvo and weighed anchor. Galleys accompanied the fleet to tow and guide the vessels through the hazardous sandbars of the winding

Guadalquivir as they made their week-long journey to the seaport of San Lúcar de Barrameda. Fernão and the captains remained behind to complete the remaining administrative tasks and secure final enlistments. The king had responded to his request for allowing more Portuguese to sail and had approved up to 24. Over the next five weeks, Fernão ferried back and forth on galleys between Seville and San Lúcar to finalize last-minute provisions and orders.

On Aug 24, Fernão had formalized his will in a lengthy document. Among the declarations were orders to disperse his share of profits of the expedition to various religious orders. He stipulated one share be given to the Monastery of Santa Maria de la Vittoria in Triana, and to where he also requested burial if he should die in Seville. If he should perish on the voyage, he asked to be buried on the grounds of the closest church dedicated to Our Lady. Other shares were to be divided between the Monastery of Santa Maria de Montserrat in Barcelona, the Monastery of San Francisco in Aranda de Duero, and S. Domingo de las Dueñas in Oporto, Portugal.

His wife Beatriz was to receive her entire dowry. His son—Rodrigo and any other legitimate male heirs with his wife, were to receive all the rights and titles the king had granted him in the lands he should discover. His page, Cristovão Rebelô, was to receive 30,000 maravedis. Enrique was to be set free and receive 10,000 maravedis for his support.

He also completed his *Memorandum* detailing the objectives and routes of the voyage. He delineated the locations of the Far East islands in respect to their reference to the antemeridian and claimed the Moluccas lay within Spanish domain.

Fernão was relieved when Ruy delivered to the fleet the 30-chapter astronomical manual, plus the updated nautical almanac and tables. The vessels were nearly readied. The wine and hardtack comprised nearly four-fifths of the consumables. Fernão read over the list of final provisions and quantities of each to ensure the amounts would sustain them. The list included: flour, beans, chickpeas, lentils, rice, cheese, vinegar, dried large fish, anchovies, onions, garlic, lard, capers, almonds in the shell, mustard, dry figs, olive oil, quince jelly, honey, raisins, salt, sugar, and dried pork. Six live cows and three pigs were brought as fresh meat for the early stages after departure.

He had been updating the rosters and had counted a final tally of 265 crew, 165 of which were Spaniards. The remaining were foreigners; Portuguese, Italian, French, Fleming, Greek, German, English, Irish, Norwegian, Malay, and two black slaves. The diversity of languages would prove to be a challenge. He also knew the limitations concerning sheltered space would add to their woes. The forecastle and stern were assigned to the captain, pilot, master, priest, clerk, and supernumeraries. The remaining covered areas of the quarterdeck, and below the main deck, were limited. A typical crewman could only expect a six-foot by two-foot space, just enough for their body size.

Finally, on the evening before departure, Diogo Barbosa had hosted an elaborate farewell dinner for his son-in-law, after which the family accompanied Fernão to the Alcazar gate. 'Keep an eye on Duarte for us,' Diogo said. 'And may the Lord bless your mission.'

'I will do my best.'

Diogo embraced Fernão. 'I will leave you now with Beatriz,' he said upon departing back inside the fortress.

Beatriz held their six-month old son, Rodrigo. He tickled the baby's face and chest, bringing forth a spontaneous giggling. Fernão then rubbed his wife's belly. 'Sorry I will not be able to greet our new addition.'

As she embraced him, a tear rolled down her cheek. 'I will miss you so much. But you must follow your destiny, your dream. We shall wait for your glorious return.'

After a last passionate kiss and embrace, Fernão exited the Alcazar for a waiting galley which would take him down the Guadalquivir River to his flagship.

5

San Lúcar de Barrameda, Spain – Sept 20, 1519

The last week before they were to set sail out of San Lúcar, the officers and crew paid daily visits to the church of Nossa Señora de Barrameda to hear mass and make confession. Fernão was aware of the risks in undertaking such a perilous voyage, so on the evening before departure, he led the men in a final confession and prayer.

Then, on September 20, the five black ships unfurled their sails, caught the winds, and sailed southwest toward the Canary Islands. The *Trinidad*, with its royal standard raised, led the fleet, until it reached Tenerife, and the port of Santa Cruz. The island was a stopover point for Portuguese and Spanish vessels to load final provisions before the open seas. With its signature volcanic peak of Mount Teide rising to over 12,000 feet, and Spain's highest elevation, the island was easily sighted by the lookouts. The lush forest of Evergreen pines and laurels rising on the horizon were sustained by microclimates; clouds descended midday and the mists produced condensation upon the foliage thereby providing an ample supply of water. The armada remained in Port Santa Cruz three days to load extra wood, fresh water, fruits, vegetables, salted fish, and fresh meat. Here they acquired two more able seamen—Alfonso Blas and Master Pedro. In addition, a supernumerary—Hernán López was enlisted to replace Lazaro Torres on the *Trinidad*. From Santa Cruz the fleet sailed to Punta Roja of the same island to procure loads of pitch from the locals, a necessary commodity to maintain vessels on long journeys.

During the two-day layover, a caravel arrived from San Lúcar. A skiff was sent by the vessel and tied up to the *Trinidad*. A courier climbed on board and was escorted to the captain-general's quarters. Pigafetta, enlisted as a supernumerary, was seated around a small wood table assisting his commander in checking over the supply inventory lists. From behind the barred cabin window, they noticed a uniformed man approach.

'Captain-General Magalhães?' the courier asked through the window.

'Yes?' Fernão replied.

'I have two dispatches for you; one is from the Casa de la Contratación, the other was sent by the alcaide in Seville, Diogo Barbosa.'

Fernão creaked open the wood cabin door and retrieved the sealed documents. 'Wait for a short while. I may have to send a reply.'

The courier nodded and stood a distance away, along the deck railing.

Fernão returned to take his seat at the table, read over the document from the Casa, and then passed it over to Pigafetta for a second review. He had come to trust his new assistant; a knight of Rhodes—of the famed order of Hospitallers, an astute diplomat, a skilled writer, and with the keen eye of a naturalist.

'Looks like the Casa wants you to confirm the planned route to your captains,' Pigafetta remarked. 'The remaining, appears to repeat former instructions.'

Fernão unsealed the second document from Barbosa. His eyes narrowed as he read it through, then handed the letter to his supernumerary.

Pigafetta commented as he read, 'Your father-in-law is indeed loyal and gives you a warning. He says, local mariners in Seville have confessed they have overheard the Castilian captains bragging about removing you from command and if required, to kill you.' He paused and looked at his commander. 'Diogo Barbosa warns of mutiny.' Pigafetta scratched the corner of his eye. 'I do not understand why they hate you so vehemently.'

'It is because I am Portuguese and have the command of their flagship. Please dictate my response:

> I will try not to provoke any servants of the king and will continue to further the crown's interests. I have pledged to serve the emperor and to this end—if needed—I offer my life.'

He read over Pigafetta's dictation, signed his name, and then signaled for the courier to return.

Before departure, the captain-general summoned a meeting of all the captains and pilots. He confirmed that the planned route would sail southwest out of the Canaries, until they reached the designated point of crossing to the Atlantic, just west of Cape Verde. Before the meeting concluded, instructions concerning signals and watches were reaffirmed and strict compliance was ordered. The flagship was to lead, and the other vessels were to follow.

So as not to lose sight, the poop deck on the aft of the *Trinidad* would always maintain a light at night; it was often a lantern but at times could be a thick cord of sun-dried rushes lit on fire. Whenever the captain-general signaled, the others were to send a return signal to know if they were all still following. If he wished to change course due to weather conditions, or the wind was contrary, or he wanted to reduce way; two lights would be displayed. If he wanted them to haul in a bonnet—the part of sail attached to the main sail, he displayed three lights. If he wanted to strike sail, four lights would be shown and quickly extinguished. Then one light would be displayed to signal all vessels to hold and remain in position, just as his own. And if he ordered them to sail again, four lights would be shown. If he sighted land or reef, he would use many lights or fire off a mortar.

Three watches were established in the night: The first at the beginning of night, the second at midnight, and the third toward daybreak, commonly called the *diane*—the watch of the morning star. Every night the watch was to be changed; those who had the first moved to the second, the second to third, and third to first. Every subsequent night was advanced in the same forward rotation.

The crews were divided into three companies: The first was the captain's, second was the pilot or boatswain's mate, and third was the master. At dusk, all ships were to come alongside the flagship, salute the captain-general in an exact order, give the reports, and receive sailing orders.

Once provisioned, the fleet weighed anchor at midnight of October 3. They set on a southwesterly course until they reached a latitude of 27 degrees north. The *Trinidad* then signaled an unexpected course change that altered between south and southwest. Fernão had unexpectedly altered the route from that agreed upon prior in Seville and Tenerife— which was to sail direct southwest to 24 degrees north. He gave no explanation for the change during the evening salute at dusk and proceeded through the evening and next afternoon—south by southwest. It was the evening of October 5, when Captain Juan de Cartagena of the *San Antonio*, hauled alongside the flagship and asked what course they were on. The pilot of the *Trinidad*, Estevão Gomes, replied: 'South by west!'

'Let me speak with the captain-general,' Cartagena demanded.

The pilot summoned Fernão Magalhães who returned to appear at the rails on the main deck.

Cartagena asked in a booming voice across the water, 'Why has the course changed from our original?'

'The sailing plan has been amended,' Fernão replied in kind. 'Do your duty and follow me.'

'Changes should not be made arbitrarily, but only after consulting with your captains and pilots,' Cartagena belligerently responded. 'If we pass too close to Cabo Blanco, we may encounter Portuguese vessels. It is too risky!'

Fernão Magalhães barked his final order: 'The fleet only needs to follow my flag by day and light by night. You should not ask questions.'

Cartagena's face turned red with rage as the captain-general turned his back and walked away without any further explanation.

Fernão noticed his pilot and master staring at one another in confusion. They walked off to their duties, unwilling to pry or question their commander's course decision. After the two separated, he followed the master who began to inspect the rigging. 'Join me in my quarters.'

'Yes, yes captain-general,' he stuttered nervously, uncertain if he had angered the commander.

Arriving at the cabin they found Pigafetta still at the table poring over documents. He looked up. 'Shall I leave sir?'

'No. Please remain here. Master Polcevera is also Italian and maybe we could use your assistance in translation if required.' He then gestured for the master to sit. 'I know you and pilot Gomes are curious about the sudden course change.'

Polcevera's eyes widened.

'I am almost 40-years-old, but you are nearly 52. You have served many captains loyally over your career and proved yourself to me in your persistent recruiting efforts in Cadiz.'

Polcevera nodded.

'I can only divulge my intended route to those few I trust.' Fernão looked out the cabin window to see if anyone was within audible range before continuing. 'I am uncertain of Gomes. He is a good pilot-general, yes, but a jealous breed. I expect he still holds a grudge after the Casa approved my mission to the Moluccas over his own proposed expedition. Anyway, we are stuck in the middle, between those who suspect all Portuguese, and all Portuguese worthy of being suspect. I know there are Portuguese spies infiltrating the Casa and they will know where to intercept us based on the pre-planned route confirmed in Seville. I cannot allow the mission to be compromised and have amended the route. I expect if Dom Manuel sends a fleet against us, it will be on the west side of Cape Verde. I intend to sail to the east side, between Cape Verde and the African coast, then continue to a latitude of 6 degrees north, where we should encounter southeast winds to guide us west to Brazil.'

'Excuse me,' Pigafetta said. I understand it is an appropriate plan, but what if we cross one of the Portuguese fleets en route to the Indies? They usually sail along the coast.'

'If so, those vessels will likely be unaware of our mission,' Fernão replied. 'I doubt they would risk offending Spain without any direct orders from Dom Manuel.' He turned to Polcevera. 'So, do you see? We must walk a fine line to have any chance of finding passage west.'

Master Polcevera scratched his beard, concerned. 'I understand your route, and the reason why. But many have entered the doldrums here.'

'Yes, but a better risk than fighting a well-armed Portuguese naval armada, is it not? Besides, crossing off the Guinea coast is the shortest distance. It should prevent us from overshooting too far north on the Brazil coast and force us to sail back against headwinds. But let us keep this among ourselves.'

'Aye sir.' Master Polcevera nodded Magalhães, then Pigafetta, and returned to his duties.

The fleet continued its southerly course for 15 days of fair weather. They passed between Cape Verde and the African coast until reaching Sierra Leone at a latitude of 14 degrees north. Here the weather turned on them. Fernão stood on the quarterdeck watching storm clouds converge and winds picking up in strength. In the face of the sudden squall, he quickly ordered three lanterns lit, signaling the others to haul in the bonnet. The first squall hit as the bonnet was finally reeled in. It quickly became apparent this might not be enough. Powerful squalls increased in magnitude and tossed the fleet like bobbers in a wash bucket.

The crews scurried across the deck to man the rigging. The relentless winds slammed the sails and the masts creaked under the strain. Tidal waves tossed men across the slippery deck, pinning many against the ship rails, one step away from plunging into the deep. They watched in horror as the massive squalls caused the yardarms to dip below the waters. With imminent danger of capsizing, the pilot asked, 'Sir, should we cut the masts? We may go under if this continues.'

'No,' Fernão said emphatically. 'Give the signal to strike sails. We run bare poles. Our only chance.' He knew if they cut the masts the fleet would be permanently immobilized.

The men prayed fervently for mercy until the storm finally abated. It was a short respite, for they endured another 20 days of raging storms and the men feared it would never cease. Veteran mariners who had sailed these seas before proclaimed they had never heard of, nor expected, such phenomena. Based on the experience of such men, the rest had been prepared for easy sailing in these parts.

One dark evening, a mighty tempest of strong winds and thunderstorms suddenly enveloped the fleet with relentless fury. In the chaos, all watches reported for duty. Fernão, Pigafetta and Enrique stood on the deck, all braced for the battering waves that crashed over the flagship. For hours, the storm raged, and the men again feared the entire armada would capsize. He could see it in the men's faces, an impending doom leading to certain death in the murky dark abyss. Lightning discharges lit up the sky as nature's onslaught continued.

Suddenly, a violet-hued torch of light appeared at the top of the mainmast. The luminous body remained steady. 'What is that sir?' Enrique asked in wonder.

'Never seen anything like it in all my years at sea,' Fernão replied.

'It is the holy body of Saint Anselmo,' Pigafetta declared. 'Some believe it is Santo Pedro Gonzalez, or Santa Clara, or Santo Nicholas. Nevertheless, they all intercede for mariners.'

'What does it mean?' Enrique asked, still unclear.

'Pigafetta turned to both. 'Any time the light appears, it means our lives will be spared.'

After remaining stationary for two hours, the violet light began to pulsate, and for a quarter of an hour it had morphed into a blinding white light, causing many to cry out for mercy. Then the light suddenly vanished, the seas calmed, and the men thanked the holy apparition for their salvation from certain death.

As both a man of science and a devout believer in the supernatural, Fernão pondered. Was this some sort of phenomena caused by the lightning discharges, or were these indeed apparitions of divine assistance, or perhaps both.

After the storms had finally abated, they sighted a mountain off the coastline. Fernão met Gomes on the quarterdeck, who was manning the whipstaff and taking compass readings. 'You recognize that mountain?' Fernão asked.

'The mountain of Sierra Leone, a key landmark on the charts, latitude of 8 degrees north.'

Fernão tugged on his beard and frowned. 'Yes. I figured so. But was hoping to be wrong. Not much progress due to the headwinds. I suspect we have only covered three leagues since we first encountered the squalls. The delay will cost us dearly. We need to ration our supplies.'

During the dusk salute, the captain-general issued the order for rationing; only four pints of water daily per man, a smaller measure of wine, and hardtack biscuits reduced to a pound and a half.

The doldrums had set in. It was a duration of windless days and nights, and which could last for weeks. Sailors feared to be caught in these miserable conditions. Relentless downpours in the high tropical zone brought the humidity to nearly 100 percent. The food began to rot and the smell from the bilge turned rank. Sleep was near impossible and crew dissentions began to stir. With rations draining their strength, men boldly hunted ferocious man-eating Tiger sharks, all with menacing jaws full of sharp jagged teeth. They stabbed and grappled them with iron hooks. The large ones were barely palatable, but the small ones were tolerable, and deemed prizes worthy of consumption. Meanwhile, Pigafetta scribbled daily notes in a journal describing the various exotic bird species they encountered. One day they witnessed a massive school of flying fish that were so numerous it appeared as though it were an island.

The slow monotonous doldrums began to demoralize the crews. The Castilian captains were furious that the fleet commander had altered course and brought them into such a miserable state. Once again, it was Cartagena who instigated the rebuttal. It occurred off the coast of Guinea, during the customary rendezvous at dusk, and when the *San Antonio* sailed near the *Trindad*. Cartagena had delegated his reporting duty to his ship master, Juan de Elorriaga, who saluted with the following: 'God save you, captain and master, and good company!'

Captain-General Magalhães and Master Polcevera looked at one another, stunned.

'How come Captain Cartagena does not give the salute?' Polcevera asked. 'And he does not address you as captain-general, but only as captain?'

'Double insolence,' Fernão muttered. He regained his composure and gestured for Polcevera to give a reply. The master leaned over the rail and yelled: 'The salute must be given in the prescribed manner!'

Cartagena stepped forward and interjected loudly for all to hear, 'I have sent my best man to salute him, but if he wishes, on another day, I will send one of our cabin boys!'

Fernão's face reddened. But he once again composed himself and walked away.

For the next three days the *San Antonio* did not render any salute. During this interlude, an incident occurred, and had come to his urgent attention. The master of the *Victoria*—Antonio Salamón had been caught sodomizing a cabin boy—Antonio Varesa. Fernão sent a skiff to each vessel to convene a court-martial hearing. The offense was considered a capital offense under Spanish maritime law and would have to be addressed. As captain-general, he knew this would be a test of his leadership; any lapse in discipline at this juncture could further endanger the expedition, for already insubordination was evident with the high command, and any appearance of weakness or vacillation in his command would likely end in disaster.

On deck of the *Trinidad* all the captains, pilots, and masters were present for the hearing. Considering Master Antonio Salamón was nearly 47 and had been caught by witnesses abusing the young apprentice, the verdict of guilty went unopposed, and punishment was pronounced: Death by strangulation. They clamped the master in irons while the apprentice boy walked away in shame and scorned by all.

After the hearing was adjourned all the captains met in the captain-general's cabin. He addressed them: 'We need to continue our salutes in the proper manner according to what has already been clearly established. I expect this to be obeyed in all future reporting at dusk.'

'Perhaps if you were consistent yourself, we could do so,' Cartagena rudely interrupted. 'You have altered the planned route and taken us into dangerous storms and now we are mired in the equatorial doldrums.' He glanced over to his Castilian co-conspirators—Captains

Quesada and Mendoza. 'Perhaps you have ulterior motives. You feign obedience to Don Carlos but still serve Dom Manuel and plan to destroy the entire fleet. Remember, I was appointed as joint-commander.'

'You are gravely mistaken captain,' Fernão replied. 'I command the flagship and have the power to administer justice. Your duties are as captain of one single vessel and to supervise the fleet accounts. No more!'

Cartagena fumed, 'I will no longer take orders from you! You are unfit for command.'

Fernão turned his head to the iron-barred cabin window and gave a distinct nod to his muscled *alguacil*, the master-of-arms—Gonzalo Gômez de Espinoza, who charged into the cabin with sword raised. Joining were Duarte Barbosa and Cristóvão Rebêlo, both armed and at the ready. At that moment, Fernão leaped out of his chair and seized Cartagena by his shirt collar. 'This is mutiny! You are under arrest!'

Cartagena turned to Quesada and Mendoza. 'Seize Magalhães! Do it!'

The two captains froze, for the captain-general had preempted their conspiracy by his prepared response. Cartagena was brought to the main deck and locked in the stocks—a demeaning punishment usually reserved for common young sailors. Watching their fellow captain humiliated with treatment and unworthy of Castilian nobility, Mendoza and Quesada pleaded for his release. They assured Magalhães they were not conspirators since they did not rise against the captain-general and could thus be considered loyal. Fernão knew he could have pronounced a verdict of guilty and sentenced Cartagena to death. But knowing his backers—namely, Bishop Fonseca and the Holy Roman Emperor Don Carlos—such a judgment could be considered too harsh and a provocation of unwanted strife. He reluctantly agreed to place Cartagena in the custody of Captain Mendoza of the *Victoria.*

Any foul mood in the fleet might have been easily attributed to the internecine squabbling of opposing cultures, but it ran deeper than that.

It had been 60 days of misery since they first encountered the storms, then the monotonous doldrums, and finally the endless heavy rains which drenched their vessels. Finally, in answer to all prayers uttered, the wind began to stir and gradually increased in strength. Fernão plotted a southwesterly course with the eastern winds blowing on their port side. They crossed the equator on November 20 and soon entered the South Equatorial Current which carried them west across the Atlantic. He assigned the skilled master's mate, a Greek from Rhodes—Francisco Albo, to assist the pilot, who then recorded his first log entry on November 29—the day they sighted the Brazilian coast. Albo took the altitude of the sun and placed them at 7 degrees south, and in proximity of Cape Santo Agostinho. They continued to sail past the Cape, south by southwest, until they reached the entrance to Guanabara Bay on December 13 at a latitude of 23 degrees south. Fernão named it Bahía Santa Lucía since they had arrived on the patron's day of honor. They passed around a peninsula with a tall conical-shaped peak and anchored offshore. He remembered how Vespucci once recounted to him the details of his third voyage to the New World. He was assigned as chief navigator for Captain Gonçalo Coelho's exploratory vessel commissioned by Dom Manuel. The explorers, Vespucci and Coelho discovered this bay in January of 1502, and accordingly named it the *River of January*—Rio de Janeiro.

6

Rio De Janeiro – December 13, 1519

A steady rain set in as the fleet anchored offshore. The captain-general issued orders to lower the longboats and have them loaded with objects for barter. He then sent a skiff to the *Concepción* to summon its pilot, João Lopes Carvalho. After some time, the skiff returned and tied up to the *Trinidad*. The pilot climbed on board and stood at attention. Fernão and Pilot-Major Gomes stared him over.

'If it were not for Gomes, you would have grounded the fleet on the approach to Cabo Frio,' Fernão angrily remarked. 'I thought you knew these waters.'

Indeed, Carvalho had sailed the Brazilian coastline before and had lived in Rio de Janeiro from 1511 to 1516 as steward of a Portuguese storage facility.

'Sorry sir. I was not aware of the strong inshore current.'

Fernão knew the coast was only recently navigated and errors could occur. He decided to move on. 'Not long ago, you lived in this bay. I assume you have acquired some of the local dialect.'

'Yes sir.'

'Perhaps you can serve as translator and give us any relevant information about these people.' Fernão gestured for Pigafetta and Enrique to approach. 'You can work with our two linguists on shore.'

'The natives in these parts call themselves Tupinambá,' Caravalho informed. 'Most speak Tupi and some know the Guarani dialect. I speak Tupi.' Soon long oval crafts approached from shore. 'The locals call their boats, *canoes*; they are trees hollowed out in one piece with stone tools and paddled with wood oars.'

Drawing near, the crews curiously stared. The natives were all painted face to toe in patterns of red dye, all extracted from the abundant supply of brazilwood. The men had only parrot feathers covering their loins and backsides. From three holes in their lower lips hung an alabaster stone, green or white, and a finger's length in diameter. All were well-built, with long black hair and olive-skinned. The women were completely naked.

Fernão took careful notice of his men, for they were awestruck and gaping in open lust. After almost three months of misery and near death at sea, he knew they had deserved a good shore leave in this garden paradise but providing a modicum of discipline would not be an easy task to enforce.

Caravalho recognized one of the native leaders approaching. 'Sir, I know this one.'

'Bring him aboard,' Fernão ordered.

The crew gestured for the warrior to climb up a dangling rope from the *Trinidad's* port side. Carvalho immediately questioned him in Tupi and then reported, 'He says you must have come from heaven, for after two months of draught, the rains returned on the day you arrived.

'Ask him if they wish to trade.'

After a brief inquiry Carvalho commented, 'They are eager to trade.' He then noticed the crews mesmerized by the beauty of the young women. 'A word of warning captain-general. The men here are very jealous of their wives. They have no compunction in trading their daughters for a specified time, but never the wives. You do not want to become their enemy, believe me.'

Fernão, Pigafetta and Enrique looked at him puzzled.

'They may kill you and eat your flesh for dinner.'

Fernão's eyebrow raised. '*Canabali*. Vespucci once mentioned of them during his stay in these parts. So, it is true?'

'They eat the flesh of their enemies, but it is more of a custom than for the taste,' Carvalho replied, then continued with the backstory. 'It has been said, the custom began with an old woman's vengeance upon an enemy who had killed her only son. The killer was captured by the woman's friends and brought to her. When she recognized the murderer, she leapt upon him like an angry she-wolf and bit into his shoulder with great ferocity. The culprit narrowly escaped, relayed the incident to his tribe, and showed the deep bite mark. After that, many captured in war were eaten. But the entire flesh is not consumed at once. They will cut up the victim in pieces, salt the flesh, and then hang it in a chimney or beam to dry. Thus, by adding only a piece to their daily meals will allow them to relish the victory over their enemy for a prolonged period.'

'So, you believe they are a danger to us?'

'They are unpredictable. I have lived here four years and have learned of their habits but still do not comprehend all their reasoning. For instance, they worship nothing and live like beasts in nature. There is a king here they call *cacique,* but he is more of a spokesman for the elders. These latter will often stir up the young warriors to wage war. But it is strange how they eagerly commit savage wars for no reasons like ours. They do not recognize private property, do not have any strict tribal borders, and do not crave power or great wealth. They vow only to war for the sake of avenging their ancestors. But know this, those who do not succumb to war may be expected to live a long life, for the land is teeming with life. I have heard some live up to 125-years-of-age, others even 140.'

They were all captivated by Carvalho's report.

'This seems to corroborate Vespucci's accounts,' Fernão replied. 'I will give leave to trade but only in disciplined order. No trading for any local wives and strict adherence to assigned times on shore will be enforced. We will rotate based on the night watch schedule, one day per watch.'

The men were given articles for trade according to rank. Once the orders were disseminated, the first designated crews eagerly clambered into the skiffs and longboats. The natives escorted them to shore as the young maidens fawned over the sailors dressed in their finest attire. The captain-general remained on the *Trinidad* to maintain command on the flagship while his crews rotated shore leaves.

Pigafetta always brought a journal to record his findings. He soon discovered the natives had constructed long communal houses they called *boii* to which more than 100 may live in, and fastened to the great beams were cotton nets called *amache* (hammock) which they slept in. In the evenings, they lit small fires below these nets for warmth. There was an abundance of herbs, fruits, and fish. Shellfish, such as: oysters, crabs, lobsters, and mussels, provided much of their sustenance. They also made a bread of sorts in round loaves, made from manioc root, also known as cassava or yuca. Their primary source of meat was primarily human flesh, but they would also consume wild animals and birds. They do not catch many, because the jungle was so thick, and full of dangerous beasts that they preferred not to hunt in such places unless in great numbers. The crews bartered for fresh provisions such as fowl, sweet potatoes, and pineapples. Much trading ensued. Common exchanges were a knife or fishhook for five or six fowls. A comb could trade for a goose and a small mirror or pair of scissors for enough fish to feed 10 men. A bell or leather lace could garner a basket full of sweet potato called *battate*, which tasted like chestnut.

Pigafetta recorded one of his own trades. A local warrior took an interest in a deck of cards he carried. When the colorful king of diamonds was shown, the native eagerly traded five fowl for the single card and believed he had emerged the winner of the deal.

There were a great number of parrots, and 8 or 10 could be acquired for one mirror. A knife or hatchet could be traded for one or two daughters as sexual escorts. The men were enamored by the beautiful, exotic maidens, and was not long before their passions inflamed and escalated into orgiastic escapades of unbridled debauchery.

One day, an exceptionally beautiful young girl boarded the *Trinidad* in search of trinkets. Fernão and Pigafetta were on deck when they noticed her presence. She found the captain-general's cabin to which she found a nail about a finger's length. Believing it was of great value she hid it in her private area, bent slightly forward, and scurried away. The two looked at one another in disbelief, but soon broke out in laughter at the absurdity.

Meanwhile, before dawn on December 17, the fleet astronomer—San Martin, took a celestial reading to estimate the longitude by shooting the elevations of the Moon and Jupiter passing at the same azimuth. The Ephemerides of Regiomantanus and Zacuto's almanac did not match the reading, for it was almost 18 hours off. He blamed the modifications done by Ruy Faleiro as the cause for the discrepancy. Fernão still believed his friend Ruy Faleiro's navigational manual was useful and requested San Martin to give it further review and application in future readings.

On December 20, the master-of-arms—Espinosa, was tasked with the hanging of Antonio Salamón for the crime of sodomy. Salamón was publicly executed in front of all the natives who looked on in bewilderment.

In contrast to the prior grisly event, Fernão took a day of shore leave to attend mass. As Padre Valderrama performed the service, the natives unexpectantly joined by kneeling and folded their hands with great reverence. Soon after, they constructed an extra longhouse, and it was filled with stacked redwood in eager anticipation the fleet would remain for some time.

While on shore, Carvalho and two natives approached. 'Captain-general, this is my woman and my young seven-year-old son, Joãozito. Would it be possible for them to join our voyage? I can pay for the extra rations from my salary.'

'You know the rules regarding women, none may be allowed to sail,' Fernão replied. However, he wished to accommodate his loyal pilot and pondered the options. 'Perhaps we can allow the boy to serve as a page on your vessel.'

'Thank you, sir.'

Fernão Magalhães' attempt to maintain a moral decorum with the religious service on shore proved short-lived. The liaisons with the tempting young women proved too enticing for the men. Duarte Barbosa had always had a propensity to become ensnared in amorous affairs with the exotic females in far-off lands, and this was no different. He shirked his duty and went missing for three days and nights—he went native. The captain-general fumed at the insubordination by his brother-in-law. Regardless of his relations, Barbosa was soon found on shore and brought back in irons. He would remain in shackles while his comrades continued to continue their dalliances.

Defiance began to spread. The newly appointed captain of the *San Antonio*, Antonio de Coco, had conspired with Captain Mendoza of the *Victoria* to release Cartagena and brought him to shore. Fernão immediately arrested both and threatened to maroon Cartagena upon the fleet's departure. But once again, the other captains requested they take responsibility to watch Cartagena. In another attempt to avoid a mutiny, he agreed to place him in the custody of Quesada on the *Concepción*. Needing a new captain that he could trust to command the *San Antonio*, his cousin was selected, Álvaro de Mesquita. Fernão assigned Pilot-major Gomes to assist Mesquita in navigating. Gomes was furious, seemingly demoted as fleet pilot of the flagship *Trinidad* to a standard pilot of the *San Antonio*, and worse, he now would serve under a captain, who until now, was ranked as a mere supernumerary. The insult was taken to heart and not to be forgotten.

The captain-general was growing impatient. The men had deserved two weeks of relaxation and time to acquire provisions but now it was time to depart. He cleared the fleet of any female stowaways and made final preparation to sail.

On Christmas eve, mass was performed with great solemnity. The following day the fleet departed the paradise of Rio de Janeiro. The crews hung upon the rails with remorse as they watched their new lovers wave them goodbye. The fleet sailed southwest, in search of Cape Santa Maria, the strait which Solis had discovered in 1516, and the possible gateway to the vast ocean beyond.

7

Montevideo, Uruguay – January 10, 1520

On the quarterdeck of the *Trinidad*, the captain-general stood with the newly appointed pilot from Rhodes, Francisco Albo. Fernão sighted a large hill in the distance rising above an immense plain and loudly exclaimed: '*Montevide!*' He handed Albo an astrolabe and ordered, 'Take a reading.'

The pilot sighted the sun at 75 degrees with a declination of 20 degrees. With a careful look at the navigational charts, they both calculated a position of 35 degrees south latitude, and just northeast of Cape Santa Maria.

'Those hills in the distance coincide with the discoveries of Lisboã and Solis,' Fernão remarked. 'Rounding the Cape will bring us past the demarcation line and into the Spanish domain of Rio de la Plata.'

'Do you believe that could be the strait?' Albo asked.

'I am expecting the strait closer to 52 degrees south, but we must check any possibility from this point onward to be certain.'

After passing the Cape they had lost sight of land. Here the fleet encountered a heavy storm and had to turn back north. Fernão decided to anchor in a secluded bay to wait out the storm.

Once the skies cleared, they sailed southwest until gradually turning to a more westerly course. Frequent soundings were performed as they cautiously entered the Rio de la Plata estuary. Due to their shallower drafts, the *Santiago* and the *Victoria* led the way.

The water was brackish at first but as they sailed further up the estuary the water turned fresh. But with the depth at only three fathoms the captains warned they were in imminent danger of grounding. Fernão heeded their words and ordered the fleet to drop anchor. For six days they cleaned the vessels, took on fresh water, and caught a great quantity of fish. Wanting to be certain whether this was the strait, he ordered the lowest draft vessel, the *Santiago*, to venture further northwestward through the estuary, and to investigate the two main tributary rivers, the Paraná and Uruguay. Meanwhile, the remaining vessels explored the southern inlets of the estuary.

A few days into their own reconnaissance mission in the estuaries, Fernão, Albo, and Pigafetta stood on the quarterdeck of the flagship keeping watch of the shoreline. Suddenly, they noticed a contingent of natives boarding canoes and rowing with great power toward the fleet. 'What the—,' Pilot Albo blurted out as he noticed the immense stature of the natives.

'Sir, do you think those are the same *Canabali* that murdered Solis?' Pigafetta asked.

'Afraid so, but worse . . . they are *giant* man-eaters,' Fernão answered somberly. He immediately barked orders to the shipmaster, 'Ready the boats with 100 armed men.'

As they mounted their defense, Pigafetta interjected, 'Requesting permission to join the party sir. I would like to have a closer look.'

Fernão, admiring the young knight's bravery, smiled, and nodded his approval.

With the men armed and ready in the longboats and skiffs, the natives cautiously halted their canoes. In front, a massive giant bellowed out loudly like a bull and raised his arms in defiance, an apparent display to show strength. The natives then turned and rowed back to shore with the Portuguese following in close pursuit. Fernão ordered the men to capture a few to interrogate but this proved futile, for the giant's strides were double in length and power compared to that of the crews, and they soon disappeared into the bush.

Later that evening, a lone native dressed in animal skins boldly paddled a canoe toward the *Trinidad* and signaled he wished to meet. Granted permission, the giant climbed on board in a matter of seconds with great ease. The captain-general and all the men were awestruck. The giant was nearly twice their height, proportionately built, and apparently fearless.

Fernão turned to his shipmaster, 'Bring the largest shirt and coat you can find, and some silver items as well.'

Meanwhile, Pigafetta, and Enrique tried in vain to communicate. The master soon returned with the articles requested. Fernão presented the native with a cotton shirt and a red coat. The giant held it up and found it was too small. He thought a moment and then gestured to himself, then held his hand midlevel.

Pigafetta understood and smiled. 'Seems he has a young son, and it will fit him for a time. He is very pleased with the gift.' Next, a silver plate was presented, along with several hand signals questioning if there were similar metals on land. The giant understood and gestured to affirm there was a great quantity. Pleased with prospects for future trade, Fernão lavished him with a fine meal and more precious objects. The next morning the giant left to shore, but to their disappointment, he never returned.

It had been 15 days since Captain Juan Rodríguez Serrano began his reconnaissance of the tributaries. The *Santiago* had run deep west up the Uruguay and

Paraná, with a total of 300 nautical miles traversed. Serrano reported there was no existing strait, but only meandering rivers, and with this disappointing news they decided to leave the region.

Since entering the estuary, the armada suffered two casualties. On January 25, an Irishman named Guillen Irés of the Concepción, had fallen overboard, and drowned. Then, on February 3, near Montevideo, an able seaman named Sebastián Olarte of the *San Antonio* was buried at sea for mortal wounds sustained in a fight with another sailor. Before they set out to sea, a leak was discovered near the keel of the *San Antonio*. After two days of repairs, the fleet finally weighed anchor, and ventured further south.

On February 12, off Cape Corrientes, the fleet encountered heavy storms with thunder, lightning, and rain. Fernão ordered all anchors lowered to prevent the currents from pulling them toward the sandbanks.

Enrique was with the captain-general just outside the cabin as the storm began to wane. 'Look sir, Santo Anselmo appears again!' The luminous display radiated a violet glow upon the mastheads. Even the ship rails lit up. Enrique felt the top of his head. 'It tingles.'

Fernão chuckled as he noticed the frayed ends of Enrique's bandana glowing a bluish-violet hue. He snatched it from Enrique's head and waved it around. The emanating light followed the cloth in a trail to their amazement. By the following morning, the tempest subsided but they were now among the dangerous shoals. The *Victoria* bumped the seafloor several times, unnerving the men, not knowing if the shoal was rocky or sandy. A jagged ground could easily tear open the hull and destroy the vessel and a sandy bottom could ensnare them in a permanent death grip.

Fortunately, they just skipped off the seafloor. The fleet continued southwest by south exploring the coastline for the elusive strait leading to the great ocean beyond.

On February 24, they found a large bay. The captain-general named it San Matias Bay to honor St. Matthew's feast day. Finding no strait, they departed the same night. As the fleet continued toward the southern latitudes, they encountered the first of the arctic blasts causing many of the crews to dread how much worse it would become as the winter season approached and as they continued further into the southern latitudes. Their fears intensified as a wave of powerful storms battered the armada and separated the vessels for over three days.

On February 27, they were able to regroup off an inlet at 45 degrees latitude south. Fernão ordered six men to row a skiff to locate fresh water and firewood. Fearing another encounter with cannibal giants on the mainland, they opted to land on a nearby island. Upon arrival, the men found an ample supply of meat with an innumerable number of flightless goslings busily hunting fish; all these duck species had fat bellies, black feathers, and long beaks. They also found a greater prize, what appeared to be massive sea wolves resembling a calf with small round ears. Strangely, they had feet attached to their bodies which looked like human hands. The feet had nails and skin between the toes like the goslings. With their large teeth and immense body weight they could have been extremely dangerous, if only they had legs to run. It would be for another generation to rename these species as sea lions and the goslings as penguins. The crew killed an ample supply of both and loaded them into the boat near the rocky island shore.

Just as they were about to return to the fleet a violent storm of mixed snow and rain forced them to remain on the island in subzero temperatures. It was not until dawn that the storm abated. The captain-general ordered 30 men to row a longboat in search of the missing crew. They came across an unmanned skiff and feared the crew had either frozen to death or worse, eaten by a mass of sea creatures they saw lumbering about on shore. They shouted for their comrades which only awakened another herd of these creatures, later known as sea lions. Finding a new source of meat, the sailors hunted 50 of them as the sea lions tried to escape to the sea. After the herd dispersed, the search party stood in amazement, for the missing crew was suddenly revealed from amid the last pile of fleeing sea lions. They had survived the frigid night by huddling among the masses of these strange creatures. After the rescue, and finding the large beasts were good for eating, Fernão sent three longboats in a hunting expedition to acquire more, but upon arrival the expedition only found the strange goslings had remained. Due to the great abundance of them, the place was named *Bahia de los Patus*, or Duck Bay.

Just as the sails were raised on the *Trinidad*, a sudden squall pummeled their vessel. The anchor cables were ripped away, and the flagship was dragged perilously toward the rocky shore. The crew lowered their remaining spare anchor and prayed it would hold. All made confessions and vows of pilgrimage to the monastery of Nuestra Señora de la Victoria. The storm finally subsided in the evening. But with the winds now absent, they were left helpless in the bay and at the mercy of nature. Fernão commandeered spare anchors from the other ships and ordered the fleet to prepare themselves for a possible secondary onslaught. His foresight was correct, for at midnight, a ferocious storm pounded the armada mercilessly. All five ships lost their forecastles in the violent winds and many of the stern-castles sustained heavy damage. Again, the mariners prayed and vowed to undertake pilgrimages if they survived. Finally, after three days of terror, their prayers were answered, and the tempest abated.

The fleet now sailed with an urgency to find a suitable harbor to winter and repair their badly damaged fleet. They soon located an inlet and found it teeming with sea lions and penguins. Fernão immediately sent a shore party to look for fresh water. But just like in Duck Bay, a powerful storm stranded the small crew. The vessels were protected by their position in the bay but the men on shore endured lashing winds and frigid temperatures. For six days, they survived solely on mussels and other assorted shellfish that washed in from the waves. Before they were able to finally depart, they named the inlet, *Bahia de los Trabajos* or the Bay of Toil, for they found no water and endured harsh weather the entire duration. Fernão knew they must quickly find a suitable harbor to make repairs and wait out the brutal winter season, so they sailed further south in the quest.

On March 31, the fleet entered an inlet at approximately 49 degrees south. They named it St. Julian's Bay. Fernão sent a scouting patrol to search inland for fresh water, firewood, and any natural foods they could find. Once the party returned with favorable news of provisions, the battered and broken armada sailed through a narrow waterway surrounded by high cliffs and emerged in a sheltered inner harbor which they called Port St. Julian.

Fernão and representative crews from each vessel went on shore to gather fresh water and firewood. Later, the frozen mariners had kindled fires on shore to warm themselves. Fernão stood in the middle of the groups of worn sailors to make an announcement: 'Men, as you are aware, we still have a long distance to reach our destination and regrettably, I must issue a new order.'

The tension in the crowd became palpable. All they wanted was respite. The men stood in tense anticipation and listened.

'Rationing will begin now, and to be strictly enforced by all commanders during our wintering here.'

The men grumbled and murmured.

'You have endangered us all!' Captain Mendoza blurted out. 'Look at our fleet, all the forecastles smashed to pieces and much of our stern-castles damaged. All because you lead us into these frozen wastelands in search of a strait that does not exist.'

'It exists and I will find it,' Fernão said.

'Then why not give us your route?' Mendoza pressed further.

Before the captain-general could respond, another mariner boldly spoke his mind, only because he knew many other officers and crew were of the same opinion, 'We could winter back in Rio de Janeiro.'

With these enticing words the men rallied in a chorus of agreement.

One of the shipmasters interjected, 'Or we could return to Spain. We have enough provisions and if we leave now, we can escape the winter. Next season, another expedition can be sent and continue directly from where we left off.'

Again, the men erupted in support of this second comforting option.

Fernão composed his thoughts and then addressed his men which he began to sense were skirting on the edge of mutiny.

'I hear your words!' he said. 'It has been difficult. But listen, we have plenty of provision to survive on— water, fish, shellfish, and wild game. There is plenty of wood for cooking and fires to stay warm. Also, to construct housing and make repairs to our ships. In the spring, we continue onward with our reserves of biscuit and wine adequately preserved, and our vessels stocked full of extra supplies from this land.'

He paused to measure the response. Many still appeared wary. He then eyed Hans, the stout Norwegian gunner he had enlisted. Fernão walked over near him and nodded. 'The king has royally commissioned me, *us*, to complete this voyage. If required, we shall sail to the icy Cape and round it.' He then gestured with his arm to Hans. 'What about the Norwegians? Have they not sailed to more extreme latitudes and far off places?'

The Scandinavian mariner grinned at the compliment to his people.

'Do you fear to accomplish what they have already done? I thought the Castilians were fearless, known throughout the world for their bravery and fortitude. Yet you would cower and retreat to Seville with dishonor? I cannot imagine such a thought would ever arise in such nobility. As for me, I would rather die than present myself to the king in shame and everlasting scorn. Please, listen to me. Our goal is the Spice Islands, a tropical paradise with fine women and abundance. You shall achieve great fame and bountiful rewards. Do not squander your opportunity! Only follow me to glory and honor!'

With this lengthy speech, cheers erupted from most of the men. For the moment, they were appeased and comforted. But the Castilian captains and their leading officers murmured among themselves as they dispersed.

8

Port St. Julian, Argentina – April 1, 1520

The captain-general requested all to attend Easter mass on shore. Only those assigned on watch duty would remain with the ships. He also extended a goodwill invite to all the captains to dine with him at his table on board the *Trinidad* after the services were concluded.

Immediately after the Easter celebration of the resurrection event, the men relaxed along the shore.

Master Polcevera approached Fernão who was staring out toward the natural harbor. 'Sir, I hear rumors of a conspiracy. The Castilian captains have circulated disinformation among the men. They claim a strait does not exist and you secretly plan to destroy the fleet for the Portuguese king, Dom Manuel.'

'It seems we have entered a new phase of insubordination,' Fernão said. 'Captains Quesada and Mendoza have refused to attend Easter mass in outward defiance and visible to all the men.'

Fernão waited on board the flagship for his guests to arrive. Only his cousin, Captain Mesquita of the *San Antonio* attended. The two sat to dine with three empty chairs.

'I expect Captain Serrano does not wish to partake in political intrigues and dismissed the invite,' Fernão surmised. 'But understandable considering the situation.'

'So, you expect the others conspire?' Mesquita asked naively.

'Yes. I was hoping to maintain goodwill, but that appears elusive at this moment. Let us at least enjoy our dinner.'

Magalhães was exactly right about the good will.

During the second night watch, and under the cover of darkness, a longboat rowed silently across the harbor. It carried the master of the *Concepción*—Juan Sebastian del Cano, Captain Quesada, the deposed Captain Cartagena, and 30 armed men. The boat pulled up silently next to the *San Antonio*. With most of the crew asleep the invaders climbed on board unnoticed. The two captains rushed directly to the captain's quarters. They broke in and roused Mesquita with the point of their swords. They escorted him to the main deck where all the crews were forcefully gathered.

Captain Quesada stood in front of the *San Antonio* mariners. 'Men, you shall no longer be mistreated. The so-called captain-general has put the fleet at unnecessary risk far too often in his mad quest. It is *he,* that disobeys the king, for he will not reveal his true route to the king's captains. So, the fleet captains, pilots and chief officers will maintain order from now on, and rations will return to normal apportionment. We only ask you to follow our lead in restoring proper order.'

Captain Mesquita struggled against the armed invaders. 'This is mutiny! Do not follow these mad men!'

'Subdue the captain,' Quesada ordered. 'Place him in irons.'

The armed men took the cabin keys from the ship clerk, Gerónimo Guerra, and placed Mesquita under armed guard. Quesada went to flush out any remaining holdouts in the sheltered crew areas. He found Pedro de Valderrama hearing the confession of a sick mariner.

Taking notice of the captain's approach, the chaplain turned his head toward him and quoted from Psalm 18: 'To the pure you show yourself pure, but to the crooked you show yourself shrewd. You save the humble but bring low those whose eyes are haughty.'

'Who said that?' Quesada asked with irritation.

'The prophet David.'

'Father, there is no prophet David today,' Quesada angrily remarked and then returned to the main deck.

Meanwhile, the noisy commotion had roused the shipmaster, Juan de Elorriaga, from his sleep. After a quick survey of the mutinous situation, he confronted Quesada in a face-to-face standoff. 'Release our captain and return to your ship, now.'

Quesada did not flinch and stared with indignation.

Finding the captain uncooperative, Elorriaga turned to the master's mate, Diego Hernández. 'Take some armed men and free our captain.'

'We cannot be foiled in our work by this fool!' Quesada cried out as he leaped upon Master Elorriaga and stabbed him repeatedly until the deck was covered in blood and the victim hanging on for life.

The recently deposed fleet accountant, Antonio de Coca, commandeered the weapons from the few remaining loyal crewmen. Three Portuguese holdouts were placed in irons and the master's mate, Hernández, was shackled and informed he would be held on the *Concepción*. With the shipmaster lying in a pool of blood and barely alive, the *San Antonio* was now short of a senior commander.

Quesada approached the acting pilot, Juan Rodríguez de Mafra. 'We no longer have a master. I need you to take over his command of the men.'

'I cannot mutiny against the captain-general,' Mafra said, and defiantly refused to acquiesce.

'Very well. Now we have no master or pilot. Lock him up with the others.' Quesada turned to his co-conspirator and shipmaster of the *Concepción*, 'Master Cano, it is all yours to command, and ready the guns.' Quesada then found the ship steward. 'Open up the stores and distribute whatever the crew desires.'

'I cannot sir, it will jeopardize the mission.'

'Do it or you will join the others in shackles, or worse—' He pointed to the bleeding shipmaster lying on the deck spitting and gurgling blood. 'You may end up like him.'

The steward reluctantly opened the stores. Biscuit, wine, and other assorted delicacies were given out to entice loyalty among the crew. The *San Antonio* was now captained by Quesada, and Cano assumed the role as both pilot and master. The vessel was now under control of the mutineers. Cartagena returned to command the *Concepción* and Mendoza remained on the *Victoria*. Thus, three ships of the armada were commanded by the mutinous Castilians.

The next morning, April 2, a skiff from the *Trinidad* was sent to the *San Antonio* to acquire some men for assistance in gathering fresh water and firewood on shore. As they approached, a loyal marine warned the men of the mutiny to which they prudently rowed back to warn the flagship. To ascertain the depth of the mutiny, Fernão immediately sent the skiff to the four ships with a single question: 'To whom do you proclaim loyalty?'

Quesada replied: 'For the king, and for me!'

Cartagena and Mendoza gave similar responses of defiance.

Serrano was taken by surprise upon the question, but dutifully responded his loyalty was to the king and Captain-General Magalhães.

Later, a longboat was dispatched from the *San Antonio* to the *Trinidad* with a declaration of grievances. The message was delivered to Pigafetta while he was conversing with Fernão about the rationing of their provisions.

Pigafetta looked at the note. 'It is for you personally sir.'

'Go ahead and read it,' Fernão said.

Pigafetta relayed its contents. 'The Castilians insist upon the captain-general's culpability in the mistreatment of the crews by forced rations and unnecessary risks at sea. Therefore, the captains had taken command of the three vessels to restore order. But they would agree to once again, follow his flag upon the following conditions: the captain-general would have to obey the king by consulting them on all matters including the route to be taken, maintain adequate safety, and restore ample rations for the crew.'

'What are you going to do, sir?' Pigafetta asked.

The captain-general crumpled up the note and tossed it aside. 'These pompous so-called captains have never seen a war. But I have seen many. If they desire a war, I will give them a war they will never forget.'

Fernão carefully planned his stratagem and then began the execution of it. His first move was to send a longboat back with a message that the three captains should meet with him on the *Trinidad* to discuss matters. After the message was delivered, the longboat returned again with their response: 'We do not dare to board your ship. You could choose to treat us unfairly.

But we can all meet on the *San Antonio* where we will do as you command.'

In a subtle maneuver, Fernão detained the longboat crew and offered them an exquisite dinner in his quarters. After sunset, he had their longboat secured out of sight from the view of the mutinous vessels.

Next, he consulted with his powerful master-at-arms, Espinosa. 'Bring your best mariner and a rowing crew in a skiff to deliver this letter to Mendoza. If he does not heed the message, kill him.' Fernão walked to the other side of the ship and found his brother-in-law, Duarte Barbosa, with a squad of crewmen about to climb into the longboat.

'Are ready for this?' Fernão asked.

'Indeed,' Duarte replied. 'I only hope it redeems me for my actions in Brazil.'

'Take back control of the *Victoria* and it will.'

They nodded and the crew of 15 armed men of the *Trinidad* clambered into the boat.

'Remember,' Fernão said, just before they departed. 'On my signal row hard for the *Victoria*. Timing is crucial.'

Duarte nodded.

Fernão and Pigafetta stood on the quarterdeck watching events unfold. 'Why the *Victoria* first?' the young supernumerary asked.

'Many on that ship are foreigners and less loyal to the Castilians. I expect it will be the easiest of the three to take.'

Pigafetta considered the logic and nodded.

Meanwhile, Espinosa's skiff had come alongside the *Victoria*. Espinosa asked for permission to come on board to deliver the letter. But the wary Mendoza refused.

Espinosa then taunted him, 'You, a captain of nobility afraid to entertain an unarmed messenger? I thought Castilians were brave.'

With all his men watching, Mendoza acquiesced and even allowed Espinosa's mariner to accompany him. The captain, fully armored except a helmet, escorted the two messengers to his quarters. Espinosa handed him the letter and waited. At first, Mendoza grinned, but then his reaction turned into a mocking laughter as he crumpled up the paper and threw it away. Fernão had carefully written the note with preposterous terms intended to elucidate a precise response of derision—a clear signal for his agents of wrath. Espinosa grabbed Mendoza's beard, pulled his head with great power, and then plunged a dagger into his neck. Almost simultaneously, the other mariner stabbed a blade into his head. Blood spurted everywhere and the rebel captain dropped dead.

Meanwhile, Fernão had calculated the mission should have already concluded and signaled for Duarte Barbosa to approach the *Victoria*. As they drifted closer, Espinosa came on deck and lit a lantern near the captain's quarters on the stern-castle as a sign to board. They climbed with great speed and quickly subdued the night watch. The crews did not oppose for they had already grown tired of the haughty Castilian captain. Barbosa raised the flag of Magalhães, and later in the evening they weighed anchor to catch the reversing tide to take their position aside the *Trinidad*. Now with the *Santiago* and *Victoria* flanking the *Trinidad* the port exit was effectively blocked.

Fernão convened with his flagship's senior command. He turned to his shipmaster, Polcevera. 'They have raised sail, turned their bow to us, and opened their gun ports. Ready our guns and distribute the small arms to the men. Make plentiful provision of many darts, lances, stones, and other weapons, both on deck and in the tops. And double the watch.'

Master Polcevera nodded in affirmation.

'When do you think, they will try to break our blockade?' Pilot Albo asked.

'At dawn, they will have enough light to aim their broadside guns. I do not want a full-scale sea battle to destroy our vessels.' Fernão pondered his options, then turned again to Polcevera. 'Send one of your best mariners silently on a skiff to the *San Antonio* and cut the anchor cables. The current will drift them into our trap.'

The mariner went undiscovered and was able to cut the lone anchor cable. Apparently, the commanders of the *San Antonio* wished to make a rapid assault and had already weighed the other two anchors in preparation. After midnight, the *San Antonio* helplessly drifted with the current and came alongside the *Trinidad*. Captain-General Magalhães could see the rebel Captain Quesada on the quarterdeck, fully armored and with lance and shield. He roamed back and forth, barking orders which nobody followed.

Fernão grinned, knowing he now had the advantage and gave his own order to his crews, 'Fire a few warning shots.'

The *Trinidad's* guns thundered with heavy iron balls piercing the hull of the *San Antonio*. Below deck, the loyal pilot—Juan Rodríquez de Mafra, had been held in chains by the mutineers when an iron ball shot clean between his legs without injury. The *San Antonio* drifted closer and closer until it was grappled by the *Trinidad* on one side and the *Victoria* on the other. Armed boarding parties stormed the deck and shouted: 'For whom do you stand?'

The crews responded: 'For King Carlos and for Magalhães!'

Quesada and his mutineers were seized and placed in irons. Meanwhile, the crew of the *Concepción* watched the events transpire and when Fernão sent a longboat with 40 armed men, they capitulated without resistance. Cartagena and his conspirators were all arrested and secured.

After the suspenseful evening, Enrique and Pigafetta were on deck discussing the affair. 'It was a decisive victory,' Pigafetta remarked.

'Of course,' Enrique said. 'The captain-general has a lifetime experience in war at sea, and on land. He often spoke about his own commander's stratagems, including those of Viceroys—Almeida and Albuquerque. I witnessed firsthand their cunning tactics in the conquest of Malacca.'

'You are right,' Pigafetta affirmed. 'He never wavered or hesitated, acted swift and utilized his knowledge of the shore currents. Most importantly, he knew most men would choose to follow his flag.'

On board the flagship, Fernão ordered a court martial hearing with his nephew, Captain Álvaro de Mesquita acting as judge. The dead body of Mendoza was secured to a chair during the lengthy proceedings. After a serious inquiry of all witnesses, 40 men were condemned to death. Mendoza's body was taken on shore, decapitated then quartered. The bloody body parts were spitted on poles as a warning to all.

On April 7, Quesada's sentence was to be administered—according to maritime law—for mutiny and the brutal attack on Master Elorriaga. Finding nobody willing to carry out the execution, Fernão promised Quesada's page—Luis Molino, a commutation of his sentence, if he performed the task.

Luis nodded his assent.

Thus, Quesada's head was lopped off by his own page and then his body quartered. They spit the bloody limbs on poles next to Mendoza's rotting flesh, a grisly reminder for any considering future transgressions.

Once again, Fernão could not find the will to carry out the death sentence of Cartagena for fear of future reprisals. Similarly, he could not justify executing the others, for the fleet required their skills. Instead, they were bound in chains to perform the menial work of cleaning the bilge, pumps, and other repulsive chores.

9

With winter approaching, Fernão ordered the crews to completely refurbish the heavily damaged fleet. This involved a laborious process of deep cleaning, followed by extensive repair work. The wide tidal range of the inner harbor allowed the vessels to remain midway to shore, conveniently situated near two small islands. On the first island, a forge was constructed for metal working. On the second, a house was built for the captain-general's quarters, along with an attached warehouse to store and inventory fleet provisions.

Fernão had given the mutineers clemency from their death sentences but not from a grinding daily penance, and these would continue to be carried out for the length of their winter sojourn in Port St. Julian. The mutineers were to remain bound in iron shackles, while they exclusively performed the exhausting and demoralizing task of working the bilge pumps and hauling the fetid ballast from below deck. Everything was carried outside to be cleaned. The captain-general had specified all the mutineers would share equal time, so even high-ranking commanders were not exempt from the most demeaning of duties, including the deposed, Captain Cartagena, and the chaplain from the *San Antonio*, Bernard Calmette.

The two were alternating turns on the wooden bilge pump as they watched their comrades in mutiny in chains lugging out ballast. Several had vomit-stained shirts and one threw up as he walked by. They continued pumping out the waters from below until an especially putrid stench belched forth from the bowels of the ballast tanks. Cartagena gagged and quickly covered his mouth with a scarf, but the priest reacted too slow and vomited uncontrollably.

After some moments of violent heaving, Calmette composed himself, then barked at Cartagena: 'Will you not do something? We have been conscripted as mere slaves!'

'Damn Magalhães! Cartagena fumed. 'He will surely pay for this aggression. But we must be patient. Wait until the men have had enough. Then strike.'

After the ships were cleaned inside, they were tilted in preparation for careening. The caulkers filled the seams and once the rotted wood was replaced, the men added new pitch to the lower hulls. Later, the vessels would be set back upright for the carpenters to repair the forecastles, stern-castles, and other broken sections.

Pigafetta was outside the island warehouse checking inventories from the offloaded provisions and comparing the counts to the invoicing documents. Suddenly, his mouth gaped in alarm. He rushed to find the captain-general who stood near the island edge watching the crews working. 'Sir, we have a problem.'

'We can add it to our list then,' Fernão joked.

'Yes sir, but this is, well, if I am not mistaken, quite dire.' Pigafetta handed over the invoice and inventory lists.

The captain-general's face turned white as he read. 'Are you sure the counts of our *actual* provisions are correct?'

'Yes. I had two of us counting to be certain all accurate. It looks like the invoicing was doubled, perhaps on purpose.'

'So, it appears the Portuguese agents have conspired with the merchants of Seville. The agents hamper our mission on behalf of Dom Manuel and the merchants fill their pockets with double profit. I was rationing based on a fully supplied armada and now this.' Fernão sighed. 'We will have to hunt and fish to make up the difference.'

In the following days hunting proved to be difficult. The small game, such as rabbit, fox, and small rodents were just as elusive as the large game of ostrich and llamas. Likewise, fishing near shore yielded only small catches of mussels.

The morale of the men was turning bleak with the effects of full rationing and an increase of inclement weather. Frigid wind chills brought misery of frostbite, and eventually resulted in three deaths from exposure.

Then, on April 27, the young, sodomized Antonio Varessa, could no longer endure his mental anguish and committed suicide by leaping into the icy harbor waters.

Fernão wondered if it was only the taunts and cold stares of the men that made him take his own life, or was it the deprivations and hardships, adding to his inner torment, that pushed him over the brink? But it seemed certain, that despair had taken hold upon all of them.

Fernão suffered along with his men, for the cold damp air caused his knee to ache worse than ever before, and the frequent images of home flooding his mind added to the misery. Beatriz should have already had their second child by now, but unfortunately, no communication was now possible, for they were now at the edge of the known world. But he had already resolved there would be no turning back without a victorious discovery of the Spice Islands. He therefore decided to bury his personal ruminations and physical pains under a renewed focus upon the successful prosecution of the voyage.

Meanwhile, Cartagena decided this time of peak of despair among the men may be his last opportunity to take back command. Fernão's page, Cristovão Rebêlo, had been frequenting between the ships assisting the carpenters transporting wood planks when he overheard some alarming conversations among the crews.

Cristovão rushed to the captain-general's island cabin. 'Sir, Cartagena and his priest accomplice—Calmette . . .' he slowed to catch his breath and then resumed, 'are stirring dissension and attempting to recruit another band of mutineers.'

'Thank you Cristovão. I have heard similar rumors from others. We have enough witnesses now with yours included.'

Fernão then called to his master-at-arms, Espinosa, 'Bring a significant force of armed men and then accompany me to the ships. It appears we have another mutiny to quell.'

Later, they found Cartagena cursing at some men, and as they drew near, watched silently from behind. 'Damn you—fools! Follow us and your troubles will cease. You shall have full rations once again, and if we depart now, we can still return to Spain. If you follow that crazed lunatic Magalhães, you will all be doomed.'

The men had enough of his empty promises and inept leadership and just stared back without a response.

'If you follow us, I will see to it your ranks are increased.'

Again, no response, but several focused their stares past Cartagena's shoulders and to the captain-general with his armed contingent. He turned and swallowed hard.

'Your days of mutiny are at an end,' Fernão declared. 'No more clemency will be given. You and the priest are hereby condemned to be marooned in this land upon our departure.' He then turned to his master-at-arms, Espinosa. 'Secure these men in quarters. I will have no further incitement.'

The caravel *Santiago* was the first vessel repaired and readied for winter sailing. Fernão ordered Captain Juan Rodríguez Serrano to sail a course of south-southwest along the coast in search of the strait or a harbor more suitable for provisions.

Throughout the month of May, the remaining crews continued to make repairs and scavenge for food. Winter was near and the temperatures dropped further. A land expedition was sent inland for supplies and to plant a cross on the tallest peak. But they returned downtrodden and haggard, and reported finding no water, nor natives, and had to forage among the scrub to supplement their provisions. With lack of supplies, they settled for planting a cross on a closer peak overlooking the shoreline.

It had been nearly two months since the fleet had settled in Port St. Julian and without any signs of inhabitants. But one day, in early June, as the crews were busily working to finalize repairs and reloading provisions on the ships, a monumental spectacle interrupted all.

On the shore, a native man of immense stature appeared, all the while dancing, leaping, and throwing sand on his head. He was naked except for a cape and shoes made of animal skins. His male member was bound tight to his body with a cord, apparently due to the cold. Pigafetta and Fernão were near the island house taking breakfast when they noticed the commotion on shore and stared in disbelief at the odd gargantuan personage, dancing and leaping about.

Fernão turned to one of his able seamen. 'Lead him back here. Make friends by singing and dancing like him. I will await your return.'

The mariner followed the instructions and was able to entice the giant to the island, for it was low tide. Along the island shore, the captain-general stood with an armed squad of men. When the giant approached, he held one finger to the sky.

'It appears that our visitor believes we have come from heaven,' Pigafetta surmised.

'Amazing, he must be nearly 10 feet in height!' Fernão remarked, for even the tallest of the sailors, only reached the waist of the giant.

His face was large, painted round with red, and his eyes were painted round with yellow, and in the middle of his cheeks he had two hearts painted. His head was shaven like a friar with only a few white-painted hairs dangling in the breeze. The animal-skin cape was skillfully stitched together. It was an animal with a head and ears as large as a mule's and a neck and body like those of a camel. Its legs resembled those of a stag and the tail like a horse. Pigafetta pointed to the animal-skin, trying to ascertain the local name of what the crews believed to be some sort of wild llama.

The deep loud voice of the giant bellowed, '*Guanaco.*'

The men then turned their attention to his weaponry. He carried a short thick bow, with a thick bowstring, made from what looked like guanaco intestines. A bundle of feathered cane arrows was fastened with a cord to his head. There was no iron pointed tip, but only sharp black or white stones, resembling the arrows of the Turks.

'Bring him food and water,' Fernão ordered.

After the giant consumed a great quantity of provision, enough to feed several men, the captain-general handed him a steel mirror. When the giant saw his own image, he was so frightened that he leaped backward causing four men to crash violently to the ground. To calm the native, Fernão gave him the mirror back, along with two bells, a comb, and a chaplet of paternosters, then sent him back to shore with four armed men.

Another giant stood on shore watching cautiously and aloof, but when he realized his comrade was safe and full of presents, he led the visitors several miles inland to where their village was concealed in a grove of trees. The tribe of giants received the visitors as before, by a display of dancing and leaping while raising one finger to the sky. They brought forth earthenware pots filled with a white powder made from roots of herbs and indicated this was one of their primary meals. The crew then made signs to indicate they should all return with them to the ships, and they would assist in carrying the provisions for trade. The male giants carried only their bow and arrows, apparently in caution for any treachery, while the women loaded themselves full of provisions, including four young guanacos led on leashes.

Fernão and Pigafetta had returned to their flagship in anticipation of the native guests. At low tide, 18 village adult giants led by the 4 mariners slowly approached the flagship in a procession.

Pigafetta carefully estimated their stature and recorded his findings in his journal. 'It appears most of the males, range between 8 and 12 feet in height. The women perhaps 7 to 7 ½ feet,' he wrote. He paused in awe upon their other features. 'Their breasts must be at least 10 inches long. The women were painted as the men and wore animal skin clothing, but unlike the men, they covered their private parts with these skins.

Fernão turned to Pigafetta. 'I wonder how they capture those elusive creatures?'

Pigafetta then pointed to one of the leashed guanacos and indicated by signs they wanted to catch some of them.

One of the giants gestured a reply. Pigafetta replied to his commander, 'I suppose they will show us.'

So, the 18 giants split into 2 groups to hunt on opposite sides of the port, accompanied by the fleet crews to learn the technique. The giants tied the young guanacos to wooden stakes firmly imbedded into the ground and then hid themselves in the rocky ledges above. When the older guanacos came to play with the young ones, the giants would slay them with a volley of arrows. Once the hunt was finished, the natives traded the animals and other provisions for trinkets, and then retreated inland.

Six days later, during a shore patrol excursion to cut and gather firewood, another painted giant appeared. He approached the crew, all the while touching his head and body, then pointed to the sky. When Fernão was informed, he immediately sent orders for the native to be brought to his island abode. This giant was exceptionally friendly and loved to dance and leap with great enthusiasm. He leaped so high that when he landed his feet left imprints to a palm's depth. Fernão was so impressed by their size that he decided to name the natives *Patagones*.

Pigafetta spent several days with the giant and jotted down words in his journal to build a working vocabulary, beginning with simple equivalent translations of anatomy to more complex associations. The giant was intelligent and able to pronounce with a perfect Spanish accent the name of Jesus, the Lord's prayer, Ave Maria, and his own name of Juan—given to him at his baptism. Fernão gave Juan a shirt, a cloth jersey, a cap, a mirror, a comb, bells, and other trinkets before sending him away and taking satisfaction that he left in a joyous mood.

The next day, Juan returned with some large guanacos in gratitude for the gifts. Fernão then loaded him down with more precious objects in hopes for further trade, but he never returned, and some among the crew, including Fernão, feared he had been killed by his clan for the visitations.

It was about this time when two emaciated and frostbitten men appeared on shore, both in tattered and blood-stained clothes. At first, nobody recognized them in their condition until they gave their name and rank, both assigned to the *Santiago*. Their wounds were tended, and food was given them, before they were sent to give a report. It had been six weeks since the *Santiago* was dispatched on its exploratory mission. Fernão was eager to hear their story, for he had feared something was amiss since they never returned. The two seamen recounted the events for him. Captain Serrano had sailed south against headwinds until, on May 3, they discovered a long deep estuary, located at 50 degrees S and 60 nautical miles from Port St. Julian. The captain named it Santa Cruz and gave orders to anchor inside the harbor. With a plentiful supply of seals and penguins, the captain decided to remain for six days to hunt fresh game to replenish their supplies.

Once they set sail on May 22, they set upon a southwest course to further survey the coast, but only three leagues in, an ominous storm enveloped the vessel. A sudden violent wind ripped apart the sails, and the rudder was damaged by the pounding seas. Fortunately, there was enough sail left to steer the bow straight into the rocky beachhead, which enabled the crew to leap off the jibboom safely. All had survived, except for Captain Serrano's black slave, Juan, who had earlier been swept overboard by a monstrous wave and was lost at sea.

It was only a matter of minutes before the *Santiago* was dashed to pieces in the rocks. The captain knew if they were to return to Port St. Julian, they would have to cross the wide estuary of Santa Cruz and therefore ordered the crew to forage for wooden planks from the shipwreck to construct a raft. They remained on the beachhead eight days until enough wood was salvaged. Starved and frozen, the men carried the planks over the rocky shores, but in their weakened state most of the wood was discarded along the way. Arriving four days later, only enough materials were left to build a two-man raft. The crew were relieved to find an ample supply of fish enabling them to restore their health.

Once they recovered their strength, the captain decided to send their two strongest seamen on the journey to Port St. Julian and report to the captain-general their dire predicament. After hiking the barren snow-covered route inland, they found little sustenance and thus turned east to the coastline where they were able to find an adequate supply of shellfish. Heading along the water's edge was a short-lived idea, for the marshes prevented them from traversing to the north. It was a grueling terrain and the only sustenance to acquire were roots and leaves. After an 11-day journey in the frigid wasteland, they arrived at Port St. Julian.

The captain-general looked with compassion upon the two brave survivors. 'I have never abandoned my men and never will,' he solemnly remarked and then looking out the window at the dark cloudy sky continued. 'Weather is foul, we cannot risk another ship. But we can send a rescue party by land and provisioned with biscuit and wine.'

'Thank you, sir,' one responded. 'Shall we guide them?'

'No. We have their co-ordinates from your report to the other commanders. You have endured your share.'

A priest with a silver cross dangling across his black robe approached the captain-general's timbered house. Holding a bible with gold embossed lettering in Latin, he rapped on the door. The door creaked open. 'Ah, my trusted chaplain, Pedro Valderrama,' Fernão remarked with a smile. 'You are now our last official priest.'

'It is unfortunate about Father Calmette, but he deserves the fruits of his insurrection.'

'Yes, unfortunate,' Fernão said. 'I know you will not abandon us. We need your services in these trying times more than ever.'

'Yes, captain-general. Always in your service.'

'So, what can I do for you this day?'

'The mighty men of renown. Have you heard of these?'

Fernão scratched his beard in thought. 'It sounds familiar. I recall vaguely some passage in the book of Genesis during my studies as a youth in the royal court of Lisbon. Please enlighten me.'

'Let me translate from the Latin a passage from Genesis chapter 6. It refers to a time just before the great flood in Noah's time.'

'I have studied Latin, but it has been a while, please go ahead and translate, so I do not miss anything.'

'Very well. It reads: The Nephilim were on the earth in those days—and also afterward—when the sons of God went to the daughters of men and had children by them. They were the heroes of old, *the men of renown.*'

'The Nephilim?' Fernão asked.

'The Nephilim are giants, and the sons of God are the angels of God. A rebel group of the angelic host lusted after the human women and left their heavenly domain to couple with them. Their progeny were the giants . . . the Titans . . . the *mighty men of renown.*'

'So, you believe the giants in this land are their ancestors?'

'These were descended from the second nefarious incursion. Notice the phrase, *in those days* refers to the first incursion before the great deluge, but then the verse continues, *and also afterward.*' There was a race of giants bred after the flood, encountered by Joshua during their early years of settling in the Holy Land. The nine-foot-tall Philistine, Goliath of Gath, was one of these. Apparently, these races spread throughout the world, as we see for ourselves today.'

'It is indeed an amazing discovery, but what do you propose?'

'Bring some back to show the emperor and the world. Your fame will be firmly established in the annals of history.'

'I am intrigued, but Don Carlos ordered no slaves to be taken.'

'Yes, but is there not an exception that if we lose men, it is therefore acceptable to enlist them as crew to substitute our losses and continue our mission? And is it not customary to bring back a small sample from the cultures we encounter?'

'Yes. Your logic is always impeccable. But they consume three times the amount per man, a drain on our limited resources, especially considering I have already ordered strict rationing.' Fernão pondered his options. 'But it is a fantastic discovery and worth the risk. If we encounter more, we shall enlist them. Priest, you shall have your Goliath.'

The chaplain grinned in satisfaction that his persuasion was effective, nodded, and then walked away.

It was another two weeks before another native appeared. But this day, four unarmed male giants stood along the shore. Fernão sent the pilot of the *Concepción* and eight armed men to lure the natives to the island with promises of marvelous gifts. Arriving on shore, the crew inquired by signs why they were unarmed, to which they confessed their weapons were concealed in the bushes. Upon their return, the giants eagerly waited for the items of trade.

Pigafetta stood near the captain-general and observed. 'It appears that 2 of the 4 appear to be under 18 years of age and are painted different to signify their status as youths.'

'Perfect,' Fernão said. 'We shall select these two young ones. They will consume less provisions than the adults. Load them with gifts.'

The men overloaded the two young male's arms full of knives, scissors, mirrors, bells, and various glass objects. With calculated subterfuge, the captain-general ordered the men to bring two sets of leg irons and dangled them in front of the young giants. Their eyes opened wide in anticipation of receiving these intriguing metal objects but were upset they could not carry them away, for their arms were already full of gifts. The older giants offered to help but Fernão refused them. He then made signs indicating the youths could wear them on their ankles and then return home. The youths looked at one another then nodded in agreement. But once the irons were fastened, and a bolt between them was securely locked by hammered rivets, they suddenly became frightened. Fernão signaled they should not be troubled. But once they dropped their gifts and tried in futility to loosen the clamps, they blew and foamed at the mouth, calling *Setebos* to save them, apparently one of their deities.

Alarmed at the trickery, the older giants rushed to free their young ones, but Carvalho and his eight men intercepted them. The first giant snatched two of the crew and slammed them against the wood house. The other giant grabbed two more by the neck and forcefully threw them into the ground. After several minutes of bloody back and forth pummeling, Fernão signaled for the men to attack their legs. He then distracted the giants by banging on bells while the men thrust their shoulders behind their knees sending both to the ground. With the giants face down in the dirt, the men bound their arms from behind with heavy rope. One of the young giants began to weep and cried out in his native tongue.

Fernão turned to Pigafetta. 'What is he saying?'

'I recognize the word *iohoi*. It means to copulate with one's mate. I think he wants his wife.'

Fernão grinned. 'Well then, we shall find her. The emperor shall now have a complete menagerie of giants in his court.' He turned to Carvalho and the older bound giants. 'Have these two adult prisoners lead you to their village and bring back his wife.'

'Yes sir.'

They escorted them to shore, but it was not long before one of them broke his bonds and ran with great speed into the bushes. Likewise, the other giant tried to break his bonds but was struck with great force upon the head by one of Carvalho's burly men. The giant held his bloodied head and roared angrily, but after some time calmed, and reluctantly led them seven

138

miles inland where they entered some pathless woods. Nestled among the trees was a low makeshift animal skin hut. The men cut the giant's bonds to appear benign. They discovered that 13 women and children were living with 5 adult males. A divider within the hut separated the men from the women and children. Finding one of their own among the strangers, the natives felt at ease. To entertain their guests, a feast was prepared. A great fire was stoked and an animal, like a wild ass, was half-cooked then presented to the men, but without any other accompanying food or drink. Two of the male giants performed an odd feat. They each inserted a two-foot-long arrow all the way down their throats, then extracted them without harm, and they were well pleased with their own skill. But one of them began to shudder, then vomited a green and bloody bile. The men were stunned by the display, unsure if the man was sick or injured. Carvalho gestured with signs to ascertain from the others what was happening. They answered by passing him a bowl of green weeds and invited him to partake. He picked up one of the itchy rough weeds and tossed it back in the bowl.

Carvalho rolled his eyes and turned to one of his men. 'Thistles . . . really?'

His comrade chuckled and passed the bowl onward.

By hand signs, Carvalho repeatedly questioned the giant that had led them to the village to ascertain which woman was the wife they were in search of. The giant only shook his head in response. Carvalho was unsure if he was refusing to cooperate, or the woman was not present in this group. Dusk had precluded them from returning safely so they accepted the invite to spend the night in the hut. He set a watch as did the male giants.

It was a miserable night, sleeping under animal-skins and heavy snoring giants.

When they awoke, the hut was empty and most of the native's possessions had been left in their hasty escape. Apparently, the watch had dozed off just long enough for their captured giant to warn the others to flee. Carvalho led his men out of the wooded area to see if there were signs of any other native clans. Finding none, they marched toward the east. Soon they heard a rustling behind them. From the wood line, armed giants emerged; two of them approached closer and drew back their thick bows. One of the arrows struck Diogo Sanchez Barrasa in the thigh and he quickly bled out and died. Carvalho's men fired back with crossbows and matchlocks but could not hit any of the giants, due to their agile prancing about. The natives soon retreated, and the men buried their comrade. Without knowing which female giant was the correct one to retrieve, he ordered a return to the armada to avoid any further confrontation.

In mid-July, the vessels were nearly seaworthy. The young giant that grieved his missing wife was consoled and brought on board the *San Antonio*. Meanwhile, the other giant youth was assigned to Pigafetta on the *Trinidad*. Enrique and Pigafetta worked as a team to build a working vocabulary of the giants by constant communication with their captive.

At this time, the captain-general had been notified by the priest on the grave condition of Master Elorriaga who had been suffering from the deep wounds inflicted upon him by the mutinous Captain Mendoza. Fernão accompanied Chaplain Valderrama to see their dying comrade who was now under the care of Surgeon Juan Morales on board the *Trinidad*. They entered the doctor's quarters and found Elorriaga pale, his breathing sporadic. The surgeon gave a subtle wave of his hand near his waist to signal it was the end. The priest administered last rights.

The shipmaster seemed only half conscious when looked at Fernão. 'Sorry sir. It is best anyway. I will only be an extra burden to bear on this arduous journey.'

'You are a loyal shipmaster. I will never forget and always honor your name.'

Elorriaga smiled and exhaled his last breath. Fernão put a hand on his shipmaster's head and stood for a moment. His emotions surged suddenly, and he was overcome with grief, forcing him to depart in haste, for he was unwilling to show any weakness in front of his men.

On July 21, the fleet astronomer, San Martin, was tasked with taking a longitudinal reading. Of all the pilots, he was the only one able to decipher Ruy Faleiro's mathematical calculations delineated in his navigational manual. Using Faleiro's modified instruments he took a reading based on the conjunctions of the moon and planets to arrive at a position of 61 degrees west of Seville.

It was late July when Captain Serrano's men returned to Port St. Julian. He reported to the captain-general and thanked him for the timely rescue. When they were found, it had been 35 days since they had eaten any biscuit or wine and had lived off the fish in the bay. Fernão marveled at their stamina and courage, for they had survived a shipwreck, and then lived on meager provisions for nearly three months. He was ecstatic to have his loyal captain return safely. The surviving crewmen were distributed among the four remaining vessels and Serrano was assigned to captain the *Concepción*.

Pigafetta continued to build a working vocabulary of the natives by frequently working with the young giants on board the *Trinidad* and the *San Antonio*. They would say *oli* when they wished to drink water and could drain half a bucket in one sitting. If they wished to eat, they would say *mecchiere*. It was not uncommon for them to eat an entire bucket of biscuits and due to their custom in partaking of raw flesh, they were quite pleased to consume unskinned rats. Even the hardened crew were appalled by the disgusting cuisine.

On August 11, Fernão carried out the sentence upon Cartagena and the priest, Calmette. They were left in his abandoned island house with ample provisions of biscuit and wine. In addition, they retained their personal weapons along with gear to hunt and fish. With that, all crews returned to the ships and made ready to get under way.

Before departure, on August 24, a final latitude reading was taken. The captain-general convened with all his pilots, and they reviewed their charts, logs and all measurements taken. They concluded by recording their final consensus in agreement with San Martin's readings of: Latitude, 49 18' degrees south, with the final notation of 18' a unit of seconds out of 60' for greater precision, and a longitude, 61 degrees west of Seville. Once the logs were updated, general confessions made and mass attended, the fleet weighed anchor. From the island, the marooned captain and priest watched forlornly as the ships raised their sails and left the harbor.

On August 26, a mere two days out, the fleet encountered rough seas and winds as they crossed the bar into the secluded estuary of Santa Cruz. Captain Serrano's report of abundant fish and game assured Fernão they could remain here to accumulate more provisions while waiting for winter to pass. He placed a carpenter named Martín de Garate in charge of salvaging the wreck of the *Santiago*. Unfortunately, during the crossing of the river to complete his survey, he drowned. Another seaman also died during their seven-week layover in Santa Cruz.

Finally, on October 18, with their ships provisioned with fresh fish and game, salvaged materials retrieved from the wreck, and winter concluded, Fernão ordered the fleet to weigh anchor and sail southwesterly in quest of the elusive strait which would lead them to the western sea.

10

Cape of the Eleven Thousand Virgins, Argentina – October 21, 1520

Francisco Albo, the Greek pilot of the *Trinidad* took a reading of their position and entered it in his daily log:

> On the 21st of the said month, I took the sun exactly 52 degrees, at five leagues from the land, and there we saw an opening like a bay, and it has at the entrance, on the right hand a very long spit of sand, and the cape which we discovered before this spit, is called the Cape of the Virgins, and the spit of sand is 52 degrees latitude, and 52 1/2 degrees longitude, and from the spit of sand to the other part, there may be a matter of 5 leagues.

The captain-general had consulted with the fleet chaplain, Pedro Valderrama, concerning which name to attribute to the newly discovered cape. It happened to coincide with the feast day of St. Ursula, a Romano-British princess martyred in the late fourth century. Fernão remembered that Admiral Colombo had named the Virgin Islands in the Caribbean in her honor. The legend of the virgin saints had spread throughout Europe in various telling. Chaplain Valderrama relayed one version. Princess Ursula had vowed to make a pilgrimage to the Holy Land before she was to wed a pagan king through an arranged marriage. She departed with an entourage of 11,000 virgin handmaidens. On the way, they encountered an army of Hun fighters from Central Asia who were besieging Cologne, Germany. In retaliation for refusing to surrender their bodies to the invaders, the leader of the Huns struck Urusla dead by an arrow shot. Afterward, the Huns beheaded all her 11,000 virgin escorts.

The fleet rounded the Cape of the Virgins and continued past the spit of sand before dropping anchor on the north end of what would later be named Possession Bay, for Captain Cook had claimed it as a new territory of Britain.

Fernão summoned Pilot Carvalho of the *Concepción* to assemble a crew and climb the peak of a small hill to ascertain if the waters led further inland. It was not long before Carvalho returned with his report to the captain-general who was eagerly awaiting on the flagship. As the skiff paddled closer to the *Trinidad*, Fernão leaned over the deck rail and yelled: 'Is there a strait beyond?'

Carvalho looked up and replied, 'I cannot see any waterway leading to the south nor the west. It appears closed off.'

Fernão's hands clenched hard on the rails and ordered, 'Wait there a moment.' He then hobbled off to find the pilot on the quarterdeck. 'Albo. Are you certain your latitude reading of 52 degrees south, is correct?'

'Yes sir, positive.'

'Very well,' Fernão responded and made haste to his quarters. He glanced around for any prying eyes. With nobody in the vicinity, he unlocked his storage chest to retrieve the old chart Martin Behaim had given him as a young man in the India House. Fernão unfurled it on the wood table and traced his finger over a strait leading west, across the dragon's tail of the southern continent, and then muttered to himself: *'It has to be here. Vespucci thought they saw an opening*

146

at 52 degrees south, before the storm forced his retreat. Behaim's chart also shows the strait to be here.' He rolled up the chart, secured it in the chest, and returned to the main deck.

Fernão returned to the rail to address Carvalho, 'It has to be here. Take the *Concepción* and the *San Antonio* to explore for any outlets. Return within five days. We will remain here waiting for your report.'

'Yes sir.'

The two exploratory vessels had already sailed off before a mighty storm arose in the evening. With their anchors dragging, the captain-general gave orders for the two remaining vessels to put out to sea and ride out the inland storm. Once the winds abated, they returned to Possession Bay and once again dropped anchor. After two days had elapsed, there was still no sign of the *Concepción* or the *San Antonio*. In the distance, smoke billowed, and all wondered if it was a signal warning of shipwreck. By the fourth day, with uncertainty concerning the fate of the missing vessels, a fearful dread began to take root in the minds of the men. Fernão stood on the high position upon the quarterdeck anxiously watching for any sign. Later, on the same day, two vessels emerged from a channel in the western end of the bay and approached with flags raised and artillery booming. The crews cheered and gave thanks to God for their safe return.

The two captains of the exploratory vessels gave their reports of what transpired. During the first night's storm they had already entered far into the bay. They would have had to fight against powerful headwinds if they wished to retreat out to the sea. The winds drove the *San Antonio* southwest toward Cape Orange, past Anegada Point, and into a channel about two miles wide. With the powerful winds at their back, they cruised through the First Narrows and entered St.

Philip's Bay, where they found a calm from the tempest. The *San Antonio* pushed west through the Second Narrows and emerged into a wide gulf. Captain Mesquita and Pilot Gomes noticed the waters were salty, deep, and the current flowed strong. With these clues, they were convinced the strait continued to a great sea beyond, and thus turned back to report the good news. Along the way, they encountered the *Concepción* in St. Philip's Bay, and the two vessels sailed back to the rendezvous point in Possession Bay.

With this stellar report, Fernão was invigorated with a renewed zeal and ordered the fleet to sail back through the First Narrows. As they approached, a lookout spotted a large structure inland which indicated the existence of indigenous tribes. The captain-general ordered a crew of 10 men to explore, but after trekking inland for one mile, they only discovered the edifice was filled with 200 graves. Upon return to shore, they found a gigantic rotting whale carcass and many large white bones. With no other signs of inhabitants, the fleet continued onward and anchored in a sheltered area between Isabel Island and a peninsula off the mainland.

Fernão knew the lack of inhabitants to trade with, and further lack of food supplies, could become a problem. Furthermore, if he was thinking it, he could be sure the crew was already talking about it.

On October 27, the captain-general summoned all his captains and pilots to his flagship. Outside his cabin, Fernão addressed his leading officers in the fleet, 'We have reached a crossroads of sorts. I have always considered it my duty to consult with my captains and pilots regarding crucial decisions. My query to you is this: Shall we continue to press onward through the strait and then to the Spice Islands?'

Finding the other captains reticent to confront their fleet commander, Pilot Gomes boldly interjected, 'I believe this is indeed the strait and will exit into the western ocean beyond, for it has salty waters, and the currents are strong. But we are not yet even halfway to our destination. If we encounter anymore delays such as storms or doldrums, we shall run out of provisions, and surely die. I recommend we return to Spain and then outfit another expedition based upon our discoveries.'

Fernão looked over the officers, and perceiving no others wished to second the reasoning of Gomes, he limped forward and retorted, 'Even if we are forced to eat the leather hides on the yards we must go forward and discover what has been promised to the emperor. God will help us and bring us good fortune.'

The officers nodded in approval, except for Gomes, who gave an icy stare of contempt, for his jealous hatred was deeply rooted. Fernão knew Gomes had been passed over for the Moluccas project, and if they returned to Spain in defeat, he would make accusations of incompetence against the captain-general and soon have a second chance to lead his own expedition.

On Nov 1, the armada continued south into another waterway they named All Saints Channel, and later to be named, Broad Reach. To the east, they saw numerous campfires and named the lands accordingly, *Tierra del Fuego*. The days here were often overcast with light mists engulfing the ships as they meandered through the extensive labyrinth of channels. It was almost summer in the southern hemisphere and the daylight hours were nearly 16 hours long. Additionally, the remaining hours continued to provide an ambient hazy light. Even with frequent cloud cover, the sun periodically shined forth, and reflected brilliantly off the snow-capped mountains over the horizon. One majestic peak to the south towered nearly 7,000 feet. They continued south through the wide channel until they arrived at a split near Cape Valentín, located on the northern point of an islet, and to which subsequent expeditions would name Dawson Island. Uncertain which of these two passages led to the ocean, Fernão decided to split his fleet. He ordered his cousin, Captain Mesquita of the *San Antonio*, to explore the eastern side of Cape Valentín and after three days to rendezvous on the western side of the island at Cape San Antonio—located just below several snow-capped peaks.

Fernão sailed with the three remaining vessels southward until they reached Cape Froward. Here, the channel turned west-northwest and appeared to be a wide direct pathway leading them to the ocean beyond. With renewed confidence, Fernão ordered Captain Serrano of the *Concepción* to the rendezvous point, off Cape San Antonio, and to escort the *San Antonio* back to Froward Reach where the other two vessels would be anchored.

But, prior, the *San Antonio* had already explored the eastern channels off Dawson Island and returned to the rendezvous point before the *Concepción's* arrival. Thus far, every attempt by the *San* Antonio crew to find an exit waterway had ended in dead-ends and imposing snow-capped mountains and glaciers. Finding the crews disheartened and frustrated by their apparent futile mission, Gomes seized the moment. He convinced the new fleet accountant, Gerónimo Guerra that the only prudent course of action was to return to Spain while their provisions lasted and only a fool would lead them further around the world to a certain miserable death. Utilizing his prestige as a renowned pilot, it was not difficult to persuade the others. Only a few, such as Captain Mesquita, held loyal and refused to partake in the mutineer's schemes.

On November 8, Gomes and Guerra pushed their case again upon Mesquita to join them but a staunch rebuttal led to a heated exchange and a shoving match ensued, to which Mesquita stabbed Gomes in the leg and in return was knifed in the hand. The mutineers bound their captain in chains and tortured him until he capitulated. He was forced to sign a document accusing his cousin, Captain-General Magalhães, of murdering the Castilian captains in Port St. Julian. With command of the *San Antonio* secured, Gomes promoted Guerra to captain, and forthright sailed for the Guinea Coast, en route to Spain.

Soon afterward, the *Concepción* arrived at the rendezvous point, at Cape San Antonio, but found no vessel, it had simply vanished. Knowing the missing ship had the greatest apportionment of the fleet's provisions, Captain Serrano desperately searched the nearby channels but all in vain.

Meanwhile, the captain-general led the *Trinidad* and the *Victoria* in a quest for a suitable harbor. They passed Cape Froward and entered the channel of English Reach, a scenic wonderland with high 1,000-foot cliffs above and thick forests below. After a short reconnaissance along the peninsula, Fernão discovered a suitable anchorage in Fortescue Bay. Since the fleet had sailed westward, the strait had increased in depth dramatically and no bottom could be found, thus they anchored to the granite cliffs by 40-foot cables and makeshift attached spikes.

The scenic bay was surrounded by fields of yellow and white orchids blooming across fields of green tundra. Further inland were dense forests of cedars with lush ferns and moss growing below. The men shuttled back and forth to shore on the skiffs and longboats. They gathered herb berries called *appio* which were of two types, one sweet and the other bitter, all which grew near the springs from the waterfalls cascading over the cliffs. The variety of fauna produced a pleasant fragrance that carried with the breeze. The harbor was teeming with small fish they called *missiglioni,* and thus Fernão accordingly named the place, the Bay of Sardines. As the men gathered firewood, they encountered scavenging artic foxes and giant black and white condors circling above.

Pigafetta had returned from shore duty and met Fernão near the ship rail where they admired the beautiful landscape. A snow-covered mountain peak contrasted against the colored foliage surrounding the bay.

Fernão interrupted the moment with a query, 'How is our giant?'

Pigafetta cleared his throat. 'Well, uh . . . fine, but . . .'

'But what?'

'Well, you see, the priest and I have been trying to instruct him in the faith . . . at least the basics for salvation. *But,* when I made the sign of the cross and kissed it, then showed it to him, he cried out loudly— *Setebos.* He made signs to me, indicating if I did so again, it would enter his stomach and cause him to burst.'

'*Setebos?*'

'It is their chief deity, but in reality—a demon of high rank. We have been able to communicate enough to understand some things. Apparently, when one of them dies, 10 or 12 demons appear, and dance around the dead man. They appear as if they were painted, and it is why the natives paint themselves in similar colors. One of these demons is taller and makes more noise with greater rejoicing than all the others. They call this demon, *Setebos,* and the others, *Cheleule.* The giant also indicated by signs that they had seen these demons with two horns on their head, long hair down to their feet, and through their mouth and backside belched fire.'

'It appears you will have to continue praying and teaching our guest until the demons are exorcised. Keep steadfast faith and you will have success.'

'Yes sir.'

While awaiting the return of the *San Antonio* and *Concepción,* Fernão dispatched a reconnaissance party to confirm how far the strait continued. Three crewmen were selected: Roldan de Argot, a Flemish gunner; Hernando de Bustamente, a barber; and Bocacio Alonso, an able seaman. The explorers sailed a skiff past Carlos III Island, entered Crooked Reach, and halted at Santa Inez Island on the western end of the Ullos Peninsula.

There, Roldan de Argot climbed a helmet-shaped hill and stared down Long Reach Channel. It was a cloudless day, and he clearly saw the strait ahead appeared to open into a great sea beyond.

The next morning, the reconnaissance party retraced their route 11 nautical miles to Fortescue Bay to report their findings. Alerted to the approaching skiff, Fernão was waiting at the deck rail to receive the news.

As the skiff approached the *Trinidad,* Roldan yelled out, 'We cannot be certain, but it looks like the strait exits into a great sea!'

Even without absolute confirmation, the crews cheered loudly and embraced one another. Fernão was standing with his companions and kin: Pigafetta, Enrique, Father Valderrama, Pilot Albo, Master

Polcevera, Cristovão, and others. Tears ran down his cheek as he rejoiced by hugging and clasping hands with all those near him.

But. it was now November 12, and neither the *San Antonio* nor the *Concepción* had returned. Fernão, justifiably concerned, decided to weigh anchor, and sailed his two ships toward the rendezvous point, back at Cape San Antonio, near Dawson Island. En route, they met the *Concepción*.

Captain Serrano reported the *San Antonio* had vanished, that there was no sign of her at all. Fernão immediately ordered the smallest of the vessels, the *Victoria*, to search the channels leading toward the entrance of the straits. The *Trinidad* and *Concepción* would search the channels near Dawson Island.

Captain Duarte Barbosa brought the *Victoria* all the way to the entrance near Virgin Point but found no vessel. They left two markers on shore in Possession Bay and another on a small island. The markers were tall crosses with inscriptions giving the dates erected. A small jug was buried nearby with orders to proceed westward and rejoin the fleet. Fernão also left a cross on San Juan Island, readily visible to any approaching ships.

On November 18, nearly a week since the sighting of the western sea, all three vessels gathered off Cape San Antonio. The negative report from the *Victoria* brought Fernão to a point of desperation. He requested their fleet astronomer to cast a horoscope to perhaps divine what happened to the missing vessel. San Martin already knew the mind of Gomes and his tenacity, thus he feigned the divination and simply reported that Mesquita was taken prisoner and the *San Antonio* had sailed back for Spain.

Fernão was upset upon their loss of provisions and crewmen, but as always, he endeavored to push onward. Retracing their route, they sailed past Fortescue Bay or what Fernão preferred to call the Bay of Sardines. Pushing onward through the various channels to the south, they discovered a magnificent arctic paradise. Beautiful glacier walls sloped down from the cliffs as they entered a harbor full of humpback whales. They watched penguins and seals going about their business diving into the channel for their daily intake of fish. Eventually, they anchored off Rio del Isleo on the eastern shoreline of Carlos III Island for a last chance to gather much needed provisions of firewood, fish, and fresh mountain water.

Pigafetta was working the nets when he noticed the gunner from the *Concepción* approach. 'Are you here to fish, Hans?'

'Yah, we shall need as much as possible. A long journey ahead.'

Pigafetta looked southward to the snow-capped mountain peaks and imposing glaciers covering the cliffs. A massive chunk of ice crashed into the waters with a thunderous echo. A whale leaped high with a mid-air twist. 'Look! Have you ever seen such a sight?' Pigafetta asked. 'I think there is no more beautiful country or better place than here.'

Yah, it is marvelous, but it cannot match the wonders of my homeland.'

'Really?'

'Out fjords have cliffs much higher and majestic. I prefer our fish as well.'

'What fish?'

'We call them *laks*, or salmon to others. We also have salted cod in the far north.'

'*Bacalao?*' Pigafetta asked.

'We export much to your lands. We dry it four months in the open air and preserve it with salt. It is easy to export, for it is cured and will not spoil.'

'And it tastes exquisite,' Pigafetta remarked with a smile.

Han grinned and the two continued fishing until their nets were full.

On November 21, Fernão ordered all his leading officers in the fleet to express their opinions in writing about going ahead with the mission, for they had not yet confirmed with absolute certainty the strait ahead led to the ocean beyond. Fernão penned the following letter to Duarte Barbosa and all the leading officers of the fleet:

> I Fernando Magallanes, Knight of the Order of Santiago, and Captain-General of this Armada which His Majesty sent to the discovery of the Spiceries, hereby inform you, Duarte Barbosa, captain of *Victoria*, and its pilots, masters, and mates, that I am aware of your deeming it a grave matter that I shall be determined to continue onwards, because you think that the time is short to accomplish our journey. As I am a man who never scorned the advice and opinion of others, on the contrary, all of my decisions are taken jointly with everyone and notified to one and all, without offending anyone; and because of what happened in San Julian with the deaths of Luis de Mendoza and Gaspar de Quesada and the marooning of Juan de Cartagena and the priest, Pero Sanches de Reina [Bernard Calmette], you need not be afraid, for all that happened was done in the service of His Majesty and for the security of his fleet; and if you do not give me your advice

156

and counsel, you will be in default of your obligation to the king-emperor, our sovereign, and to the oath of loyalty you swore to me; therefore, I command you, in his name and mine, and I pray and charge that whatever you may feel with respect to our voyage, whether to go forward or to return, each of you will give me your opinion, with your reasons, in writing, letting nothing prevent you from being entirely truthful. When I have your opinions and reasons, I will give you mine, and my decision as to what we must do.

On the following day, San Martin entered his reply on the bottom of the captain-general's order:

Most magnificent lord . . . while I doubt that neither this, All Saints Channel, nor the other two that trend east and east northeast, may be the route for sailing to Maluco . . . since we still do not know how far they may reach, we should take advantage of the weather which favors us during the height of summer. I believe that Your Grace should go forward while we have the flower of summer in hand, to continue our explorations until the middle of January . . . at which time Your Grace will judge whether it will be appropriate to return to Spain, for from then on, the days will grow shorter and the weather more severe than it is now. And should Your Grace leave these straits in January, having in the meantime taken on water and firewood, we will be well enough supplied to sail straight for Cadiz or San Lucar from where we left. And, as for advancing farther toward the South Pole than we are now, as Your Grace stated to the captains at Rio Santa Cruz, it does not seem to me that it would be feasible because of the terrible, stormy weather. If we are now confronted by such labor and risk, what will it be like farther [south] at 70 or 75 degrees to which Your Grace said he would go in search of Maluco? . . . I have said as I feel and understand, to serve both God and your lordship with what I believe is best for the Armada and your lordship.

Fernão was relieved upon the reception of San Martin's letter and the support of the officers. He then made an oath by the cross of Santiago that he wore, promising to lead them through the strait and onward to the Spice Islands.

On November 24, official sailing orders were distributed, and the provisions were loaded. The following day, the crew made last-minute preparations for sailing.

Two days later, the fleet detached their anchors from the shore and with great fanfare; flags were displayed, cannons boomed, and the men cheered. As they sailed west through the channel, iridescent icebergs glistened in the sunlight and floated near the ship's hulls. Entering Crooked Reach beautiful snow-capped peaks and cascading waterfalls appeared off their port side. From Crooked Reach they sailed through Long Reach where exotic caves and rocky cliffs appeared on both sides of the channel. From Long Reach they entered Ocean Reach and from Desolation Island on their port side the crews reported hearing thunderous waves.

On November 28, the *Victoria* sighted a cape on to their starboard side which they named, Cape Desire. It was recorded to be located at a latitude of 52 42' degrees south, almost the same as their entrance point at Cape Virgin with a latitude of 52 20' degrees south. After 38 days of navigating the 338-mile strait, they entered the great ocean, which Fernão named *Mar Pacifico*, or Peaceful Sea.

11

The Pacific Ocean, Chile Coast – November 28, 1520

Fernão Magalhães led the three-ship armada up the Pacific Coast of the unexplored continent. For two days and three nights, they followed the coastline on a course northwest to north, and then north-northeast. On December 1, approximately 50 miles off the coast, they sighted a range of tall conical mountain peaks running north to south. At this point, the captain-general signaled the fleet to assemble for their daily reporting and ordered all pilots to convene upon the flagship with all their charts in hand. Pigafetta's position as fleet chronicler required his attendance in the commander's quarters. Fernão placed his hands on his hips and addressed his three pilots, 'What course have you laid out?'

'As you ordered,' they remarked almost simultaneously.

'Show me.'

The pilots unfurled their charts upon the wood table. Fernão carefully scanned over their marked course plots and then turned to them with a scowl. 'You have all laid it out wrong.'

They stared back in bewilderment.

'You need to adjust the compass needle to compensate for the variation. In these parts, the lodestone does not pull from the side to the Antarctic Pole as it does in the northern hemisphere. So, let us continue to verify our course, for it is of crucial importance in this unknown sea. We should be in better winds by now.' He confirmed their position of

48 degrees south, issued new course directions, and then dismissed them.

In the evening, Fernão was on the quarterdeck observing the night sky. Pigafetta climbed the stairs to join him and remarked, 'We have picked up speed.'

'The north-westerlies.'

'How did you know we would encounter such favorable tailwinds?'

'I suspected this based upon similar patterns in the Atlantic,' Fernão responded with a smile. 'Logic, my friend—and a little faith.'

At that moment, a unique stellar phenomenon appeared along the dark horizon; clusters of stars appeared as two clouds of mist. Pigafetta pointed to the grouping. 'Look, in the middle of those two mists are two large stars, and they are moving!'

'I have never seen such a thing,' Fernão said, as he stared at the night sky. 'This is marvelous indeed!'

It would be for the world, many generations later, to credit the captain-general with the sighting of the two dwarf galaxies, and thus classify them with a suitable appellation—the Magellanic Clouds.

On December 2, the armada passed Cape Tres Montes on the tip of the Taitao Peninsula. Now in warmer climates, the marine species had changed. Pigafetta took note of the varieties of mahi-mahi and tuna fish, and entered his observations into his fleet journal:

> In that Ocean Sea there is seen a very amusing hunt of fishes, which are of three sorts, a cubit or more in length, named "Dorades," "Albocores," and "Boniti." They follow and hunt another kind of fish which flies and is called "Colondriny," a foot or more in length and very

good to eat. And when these three kinds of fish find in the water some of these flying fish, forthwith they make them leave the water and fly more than a crossbow's flight so long as their wings are wet. And while these fish fly, the other three go after them in the water seeing and following the shadow of those that fly. And no sooner have they fallen than they are seized and eaten by those which hunt them. Which is a marvelous and merry thing to see. And this chase we saw several times.

Since their stay in Port St. Julian and the time spent through the strait, Pigafetta had continued to compile a working vocabulary of the giant's language, until 90 words were officially recorded in his journal. Initially, the sight of the cross had caused the native intense anguish and fear, but after some time, Pigafetta and Chaplain Valderrama convinced him it was a sacred object and a sign of the eternal and all-powerful God. The giant had been suffering from an illness during their journey through the strait, and when he was particularly afflicted, he would often ask for the cross, and then he would repeatedly embrace and kiss it with great reverence. Now, near death, he agreed to follow the Christian path as a new believer and was subsequently baptized as Paul. Unfortunately, the giant eventually succumbed to his malady and was given a proper funeral at sea. His massive body was wrapped in an old piece of tattered sail and strapped to a large wood plank with ballast and cannon balls attached near the feet. After Valderrama commended his spirit to heaven, the plank was slid off the deck railing and into the sea. Pigafetta stared out to sea with a tear trickling down his cheek. Fernão knew how close they had become and placed his hand on his shoulder with a nod of empathy before departing to the quarterdeck.

On December 16, and with the fleet positioned at 36 1/2 degrees south, they altered course to a more northwesterly direction and gradually veered away from the coast. Near Christmas, an able seaman and a cabin boy died from sickness and were commended to the deep. It was an ominous portent of things to come.

Between Jan 1 and 18, three more crewmen perished. The cause of death was listed as infirmity. The crews all knew their survival now depended upon acquiring fresh provisions.

On January 24, they sighted a coral atoll covered with trees in the Tuamotu Archipelago. The crew's hopes of finding provisions soared. Pilot Albo took a reading of 16 1/4 degrees south, and named the atoll, San Pablo's Island. They took soundings but could find no bottom and therefore, no anchorage. They were forced to continue onward in bitter disappointment. Soon after departure, they committed another infirm sailor to the sea.

On February 4, another coral atoll was sighted, but the dangerous surrounding reefs made anchorage impossible. In desperation, longboats were dispatched to explore. They found no fresh water or fruit, but only trees and birds. No sustenance was obtained, except an abundance of shark meat fished in the lagoon, and so they named the atoll—*Isla de los Tiburones* or Shark Island. Before departure, Albo entered a log entry of their location of 10 2/3 degrees south, and the disheartened men chose to collectively name these taunting atolls—the Isles of Misfortunes (presently, atolls of the Southern Line Islands). The fleet carried onward with two more deaths on February 6 and 9, both of sickness.

On February 13, the fleet crossed the equator at 164 degrees longitude. They were now in the northern latitudes.

Three days later, Fernão altered course from northwest to west-northwest. For 10 days the fleet sailed on this course, sighting no respite from the wide-open-sea. On February 26, the captain-general changed the heading due west.

By this time, starvation, scurvy, and other maladies had inflicted pain and death on the weakened crew. Many of the officers had unwittingly been able to resist the scurvy by taking daily apportionments from their personal quince preserves and other vitamin-rich sundries. Fernão had packed his own supply before departing Seville and had often given portions to his companions. But not all officers were immune from the dreaded scourge that plagued the men. During this period, Pilot Vasco Gomes Galego of the *Victoria*, had died of sickness. Since the fleet astronomer-pilot—San Martin, was already on board, he assumed the official role of pilot. Pigafetta described the desperate and miserable plight of the crews in his fleet journal:

> And we ate only biscuit turned to powder, all full of worms and stinking of the urine which the rats had made on it, having eaten the good. And we drank water impure and yellow. We also ate ox hides which were very hard because of the sun, rain, and wind. And we left them four or five days in the sea, then laid them for a short time on embers, and so we ate them. And of the rats, which were sold for half an écu apiece, some of us

could not get enough. Besides the aforesaid troubles, this malady was the worst, namely that the gums of most part of our men swelled above and below so that they could not eat. And in this way, they died . . . But besides those who died, 25 or 30 fell sick of diverse maladies, whether of the arms or of the legs and other parts of the body, so that there remained very few healthy men. Yet by the grace of our Lord, I had no illness.

Suffering under the stifling heat of the equatorial zone and with starvation due to scurvy and depleted provisions, the emaciated crews appeared as skeletons as they struggled to attend their duties. With rations in the quantity of mere ounces, some of the men had even resorted to eating sawdust. The pains of scurvy continued to ravage the men. Festering bloody sores in their gums eventually caused their teeth to drop out and along with the swelling made it nearly impossible to eat what little they had left. Hope grew dim throughout the fleet.

A week later, March 6, Fernão was standing on the quarterdeck with Enrique when a lookout in the *Victoria's* crow's nest shouted: 'Land! Land!'

Needing to verify this for himself, Fernão climbed up the ropes of the mizzenmast to look. He squinted his eyes and made out a small island. 'By God, I will give that astute young man 100 ducats as reward,' he excitedly yelled to Enrique below.

The crews could see and hear him, and they reacted to the word from their commander. Men wept and cried with joy as they raised their arms to the heavens in expectation and hope of salvation from their pitiful state. Fernão made his way carefully back down to the quarterdeck.

'Maybe soon we will find your friend—Francisco Serrão?' Enrique eagerly asked.

'We can only hope.' Fernão replied. He considered how far they had come. Since exiting the strait, they had been at sea for over three months and had not found any new provisions. He remembered a recent saying from one of his crewmen: *This sea is so vast that the human mind can hardly comprehend it.*

The sighted land turned out to be an island with a tall mountain peak. As they approached, a second island of greater dimensions appeared beyond. Fernão knew their best chances to locate provisions would likely come from the latter, and accordingly ordered Pilot Albo to pursue it. Coming between the two islands, the fleet veered to southwest and left the smaller island to the northwest. In the distance, a flotilla of small outrigger sailboats from the island closed in on the fleet with remarkable speed. Pigafetta joined Fernão on the quarterdeck for a better view. The proas were colored black and white, or red.

'Look!' Pigafetta exclaimed. 'They glide across the waters like great fish skipping from wave to wave. Have you ever witnessed such agile and fast-moving craft?'

'Must be moving nearly 20 knots,' Fernão observed with keen interest. 'Reminds me of the proas in India and Malacca, but these seem modified for even greater speed.'

As they encircled the armada, the unique watercraft features were now more evident. Each vessel had a triangular lateen sail made of palm leaves sewn together which was positioned to the right of the tiller. The bow and stern were identical thus enabling the craft to sail in either direction without having to come about and giving it the ability to cut through head winds with ease. In addition, the hull was asymmetrical with the leeward side flat, and the windward side rounded to achieve superior aerodynamics when sailing on a tack. The oars were shaped like blades of a shovel.

'What do you think Pigafetta?' Fernão asked. 'Shall we name this place—the Islands of the Lateen Sails?'

'Seems fitting,' he replied with a grin.

The two islands would later receive the names of Rota and Guam, the latter of greater size and to which they neared. As they sailed toward the coastline in search of suitable anchorage, proas arrived in greater numbers. Tall, muscular, brown-skinned men with shaved heads scaled the fleet's vessels with great agility and swarmed the decks. They snatched any object that fancied their curiosity, at least anything not bolted or strapped down securely, and bared their reddish-black betel-stained teeth whenever they found metal objects. Most of the crewmen were so emaciated and sapped of energy they could only watch helplessly as the powerfully built natives stole whatever they desired. The men pleaded for the captain-general to force them off the ship.

Fernão had enough of the brazen insolence of the thieving natives and ordered his crews to repel the invaders. Those who could muster the strength began to shove the intruders toward the rails. The boatswain confronted one of the more unruly ones and slapped him across the face. The native responded angrily with a counter slap to which the officer escalated by grazing his back with a machete. Stunned by the effect of sharp steel and with blood dripping from their comrade's wound, the natives leapt overboard and clambered back into their proas. They soon retaliated by throwing spears and rocks up at the sailors. One of the crew was grazed in the arm by a sharp fish bone attached to a spear head. The men responded with crossbow shots to scare them off. Undaunted, they continued to fight and harass the crews. Fernão was riled with indignation and turned to bark an order at his master gunner: Master Andrew! Ready the guns!' Fernão looked down at the deck below and found his loyal officer who originated from Bristol, England, was perched against the ship rail, gravely ill and in no condition to assume his duties. Instead, he turned to one of his other gunners, 'Fire a warning salvo.'

'Yes sir,'

Soon a booming discharge reverberated across the bay to which spooked the locals and scattered their flotilla in all directions. But, only moments later, another contingent of proas with their customized lateen sails, were seen approaching from shore with great speed. Coming into view the natives displayed fresh provisions of bananas, coconuts, and other varieties of fruit. Pigafetta turned to Fernão. 'Perhaps they had intended to trade all along.'

Fernão nodded and signaled for the goods to be received by rope and basket. The starving crewmen eagerly consumed the victuals and drank fresh coconut water. Once all had their fill—at least as much as possible in their state—the natives unexpectedly resumed their hostilities and spears were again launched at the men above. In return, crossbowmen sent volleys of warning shots. As more proas encircled the ships, the likelihood for a protracted engagement was real and a serious threat, for the men were so weakened that an effective and victorious counterattack appeared dubitable and both sides would endure losses.

Thus, Fernão gestured for the archers to lower their crossbows. Once the natives perceived the foreigners signaled for peace, trading once again resumed. Food was again sent up, and in return glass beads and other trinkets were lowered down in exchange. Once trading concluded, the proas accompanied the fleet as they sought for suitable anchorage. Near dusk and during the process of striking the fleet's sails, the natives quietly cut the rope that was used to secure the captain-general's skiff to the stern of the flagship and towed it away with two outriggers toward shore. Pigafetta rushed to the captain-general's quarters.

'Sir, the natives stole the skiff,' he said through the barred window.

'What!' Fernão exclaimed. 'We need to take it back. It is crucial to our mission.'

Indeed, it was considered the captain's craft, a valuable commodity—often used to communicate messages between the ships and for landing parties on shore.

Fernao rushed out his cabin past Pigafetta and yelled to Pilot Albo, 'Weigh anchor and head out to sea for the night. We cannot suffer anymore losses.'

Albo acknowledged, and had the crew cast off.

Fernão turned to Pigafetta and sternly remarked, 'I retract the name of this place as the Islands of the Lateen Sails. Henceforth, it shall be called, the Islands of the Thieves.'

At dawn, the fleet again approached the island. Fernão ordered an armed shore party of 40 able men to accompany him to shore to recover the skiff and demonstrate the consequences for theft of the king's property. Just before departing, some of the sick and famished men pleaded to him as he stood near the ship rail.

'Please sir,' one sailor feebly said. 'If you kill any of them, bring us their entrails so that we may recover.'

'We beg you sir,' another desperately cried out.

The captain-general turned toward them. 'We will not become like the heathens, men. Hold fast to your faith and the Lord will provide for us.'

Fernão turned and proceeded to disembark the vessel. He sympathized with their desperate pleas, for he led them into this vast formidable sea. He himself was starving. But he would never entertain any sacrilegious acts of cannibalism.

The armed squad stormed the beach and soon encountered a barrage of spears and stones hailing down from a ridge overlooking their position. Fernão was in the lead, spotted the warriors above, and ordered the arquebusiers to fire. Hearing the booming echo and watching the trees splintering nearby, the tribesmen fled. Pushing the offensive, the captain-general commanded the village to be set ablaze. As his men set the houses to the flames, a band of warriors came to defend them, but were shot with crossbow bolts. Whenever one was struck, they withdrew it in astonished shock and fell dead, for they had never experienced such lethal weaponry.

Fernão and the men regretted the unfortunate confrontation, and a feeling of compassion soon welled up in them over the apparently innocent nature of the natives. After the skirmish had ended, the men were able to retrieve the stolen skiff. The damage inflicted during the raid resulted in nearly 50 village homes and several proas burnt. Seven natives were killed. But despite any compassion Fernão may have felt, the mission drove everything. He decided to divide his forces in half, one to return with the skiff to the ships and the other to remain and gather provisions.

Pigafetta approached the captain-general with wobbly legs and a face very pale. 'What's the matter, a little regret?' Fernão asked.

'Not so much, for they are thieves. I just need some time to adjust to the stability of land.'

Fernão laughed heartily. 'You are not alone. I also felt a little dizzy for some moments as we landed, which is a rarity. We have not set foot on land now for—what—98 days? And nearly 11,000 miles.'

'That must be the reason. Maybe I can remain with the provision crew and record my observations of their culture?'

'My friend, as our loyal fleet historian your shore leave is granted as always.' Fernão smiled and as he walked off to join the men back to the ship, he quipped in light-hearted jest, 'And maybe you will get your sea legs back upon your return.'

Since any reading of the astrolabe was preferred to be taken on land due to the stability, Fernão and pilot Albo recorded their observations before returning to the flagship. The large island of Guam was recorded at 12 degrees north. and entered in the log as such. The remaining crews spent two days gathering fresh supplies of food and water. Pigafetta noted his observations:

> Those people live in freedom and as they will, for they have no lord or superior, and they go quite naked and some of them wear a beard. They have long hair down to their waist, and wear small hats after the manner of Albonians, and these hats are made of palm. Those people are tall as we, and well built. They worship nothing. And when they are born, they are white, then they become tawny, and they have black and red teeth. The women also go naked, but that they cover their nature with a bark as thin and supple as paper, which grows between the wood and the bark of the palm tree. They are handsome and delicate, and

whiter than the men, and they have disheveled hair, very black and hanging down to the ground. They do not go to work in the fields, but do not leave their house, where they make cloth and boxes from palm leaves. Their food is certain fruit called "Cochi" (coconut) and "Battate" (sweet potatoes). They have birds, figs a palm in length (bananas), sugarcanes, and flying fish. Those women anoint their body and their hair with coconut and benseed oil. And their houses are made of wood covered with planks or boards with fig (banana) leaves, which leaves are very large, and the houses are six fathoms wide and have only one story. Their rooms and beds are furnished with mats made of palms and very beautiful, and they lie on palm straw, which is very soft and fine. Those people have no weapons, but they use sticks with a fishbone at the tip. They are poor but ingenious, and great thieves. And on this account, we called those three islands the Islands of the Thieves. The pastime of the men and women of that country, and their sport, is to go in their boats to catch those flying fish with hooks made of fishbones . . . Those thieves thought (by the signs which they made) that there were no other men in the world but themselves.

The typical village house was constructed on wooden posts about 3-foot-high, but the more affluent families built their homes on top of 12-foot-high stone pillars, called latte stones. Their society was divided into four classes: *chamorri*-chiefs, *matua*-upper class; *achaot*-middle class, and *mana'chang*-lower class. The name Chamorro was given to them based on the name for their chiefs. They had also discovered their society was matrilineal with the women performing the central role of the family and they remained monogamous.

On March 9, with provisions somewhat replenished, the captain-general ordered a course alteration of west by 1/4 southwest, from their departing position of 12 degrees north latitude, and the armada sailed out of the harbor. Their departure had not gone unnoticed, for over 100 proas approached from shore. As the boats drew near, they displayed fish and gestured that they wished to give it as gifts. But as they encircled the fleet, they began to hurl stones in great quantity, and then fled. Many passed so near the stern of the flagship and with such agility that all the crews were amazed. Pigafetta noticed some women weeping and tearing at their hair in great sorrow in a show of grief for those killed in the village.

Soon after departure, master Andrew succumbed to the dreaded scurvy and was given final repose into the deep sea. Indeed, this was indeed the deepest point on earth, at nearly 36,000 feet below sea level.

Fernão highly respected his master gunner and would dearly miss his skills and loyalty. Knowing the flagship required the best officers, he wondered who could take his place. His mind flashed back to his encounter with the Norwegian. He recalled his loyal service in recruitment and his brave assistance in calming the men back in Port St. Julian. Accordingly, Hans—the master gunner of the *Concepción*—was summoned to join the *Trinidad*. Fernão watched along the deck rail as the tall broad-shouldered Scandinavian climbed up the rope with ease. 'Welcome aboard,' he said with a smile. 'I am relieved to see you are resilient to the scurvy and rationing.'

'Yah, my homeland is a rugged land and my years at sea have taught me how to endure the hard times. Sorry about Master Andrew. He was a good officer.'

'Indeed. But I am now more certain you are just the man to replace him on the guns.' Fernão smiled.

12

Homonhon Island, Philippines – March 16, 1521

After another week of sailing and another 1,100 miles traversed, the lookout sighted a southern promontory off an immense mountainous island, which they would soon discover was named, Samar. The armada sailed northwest towards it. The land trended north. Coasting along the shore they could not find safe anchorage due to the many shoals, and so turned southward and anchored off Suluan Island. Fernão was on the quarterdeck waiting for Albo to complete his readings.

'We are at 9 2/3 degrees north latitude and—' Albo paused with a look of befuddlement.

'And?' Fernão asked.

'My reading shows we are at 189 degrees longitude from the meridian,' he replied. 'If this is true, we are in—'

'The Portuguese domain,' Fernão replied, well-aware of their situation. 'It appears the ocean is vast, more than we could ever imagine.' He pondered the ramifications for a moment, but there was only ever one conclusion. 'Nevertheless, whatever alliances or bases we establish, it shall be for Spain, and we shall take part of the proceeds.'

Just then, canoes appeared, coming off Suluan Island. The captain-general ordered to weigh anchor and pursue. But once the armada started in their direction, the natives fled back to the island. Unwilling to endanger his men who were suffering from scurvy and other ailments, he signaled for the fleet to follow him westward into the Leyte Gulf in search of safer anchorage. Sailing nine miles west they found an uninhabited island surrounded by white coral. Later, they would learn it was called Homonhon Island. It had a nice sandy beach and the fleet anchored off the coast for the evening.

The next morning, the sick men were brought on the beach and two large tents were erected to give them shade and to enjoy fresh ocean breezes during their recovery. Fernão joined Father Valderrama on the shore and remarked, 'What shall we call this place?'

'Well, since we discovered these islands yesterday, we should accordingly name it the Archipelago of St. Lazarus.'

Fernão contemplated the significance. 'Lazarus, resurrected from the dead after three days. It is a propitious name indeed. We shall ask the Lord to resurrect our dying men and thank him in faith.' He reflected upon their epic journey. It had been an arduous sea crossing of 109 days and they had lost 21 men; of the 177 on board since leaving the strait, only 156 remained. The fleet chaplain, Pedro Valderrama held a mass on the beach, the first of such in the archipelago, and only 22 years later was to be renamed, the Philippines, after the King of Spain.

After the service concluded, Fernão dispatched able-bodied men to search for fresh water, fruits, and to hunt anything that moved. Since few men had strength, he also participated in search of provisions.

Fernão called to Enrique who had been stationed near the longboats, 'Bring weapons. We are going on a hunt.'

Enrique retrieved two pikes from one of the boats and brought them to Fernão, who was already well-armed with a black sword strapped to his side and a half concealed kris dagger under his vest. He took one of the pikes and expertly twirled it around to sense its weight and maneuverability. The crews entered the densely forested island interior and split in groups of two or three.

After trekking inland about a mile, Enrique pointed to a large wild pig grazing in a distant meadow. Fernão whispered to Enrique, 'Flush it out from the rear and I will have a clear shot.'

Enrique nodded and eased through the timbered wood line with silent agility. While the pig was engrossed in taking its daily rations, he proceeded to outflank it. Enrique then yelled, waved his arms, and charged toward it. Startled, the pig whirled around and fled in the opposite direction, all the while weaving back and forth.

Fernão held his pike at the ready, but the pig sensed his presence and veered off to the left. If he did not act quickly, the pig would disappear into the woods. Fernão thrust with all his strength to a point just below its shoulder blades. It struck the heart with precision, a perfect kill shot.

Enrique witnessed the skilled pike thrust from his commander and gleefully rushed to their bounty. 'The men will be pleased sir.'

'You did all the work. I just killed it.'

Fernao reached around his back to retrieve a rolled-up piece of sail and wrapped the pig in it. Once tied up, they lugged it out of the woods by its limbs. Nearing the beach, the crews saw the protruding pig limbs and cried out in celebration, and great joy. Immediately, the fresh meat was secured to a spit, roasted over a fire, and later fed to the starving men.

On March 18, of the following day, another party returned with casks full of fresh water and excitedly reported a fantastic discovery. Apparently, they saw what looked like gold flickering in the streams. Fernão reflected upon his time stationed in Malacca and the stories he had often heard from the merchants concerning the vast gold mines of the east and wondered. *'Could this be it? Are there any other such places nearby?'*

After dinner, a canoe with nine natives approached from Suluan Island and landed on the beach. Fernão was acutely aware that many of his men were still recovering from their infirmities and few of the others had any vital energy, and so he did not wish to provoke any more hostile actions. Fernão ordered the men to stand ready, but not to act unless commanded to do so.

The most ornately decorated of the islanders approached the captain-general and signaled that he was pleased of their arrival. Fernão looked him in the eyes and perceived these to be reasonable people and decided to invite them on board the flagship. Five of the best attired natives assisted the men to load the longboats with the casks of water. Meanwhile, the other islanders went to fetch some of their comrades who were fishing in the distance and brought them back so they could join in the encounter.

Once on board the *Trinidad,* Fernão gave them some food and drink from what they had left to give. He then gave them red caps, mirrors, combs, bells, pieces of ivory, and other sundries. Greatly pleased with the marvelous goods, they returned the favor with gifts of fish, a jar of palm wine, bananas of varying sizes—even up to a foot long, and two coconuts. Realizing they had nothing else to give for a fair trade, one of them made signs they would return in four days with rice, coconuts, and other foods.

The islanders were congenial and imparted to the officers a basic understanding of their language and informed them of the names they had given the islands. Finding the natives quite friendly, Fernão deemed them worthy to see the valuable commodities in the ship store, in hopes they knew where to find such items as: cloves, cinnamon, pepper, walnut, nutmeg, mace, ginger, gold, and other valuables. They pointed southward indicating the items could be found there. Fernão and the officers looked at one another with a grin, for their course was already plotted in that very direction—to the Moluccas.

In a festive mood, the captain-general ordered Hans to fire off a salvo. Unaccustomed with such booming power, the frightened natives tried to leap into the sea and would have done so if not for the quick reassurance from the officers. Once calmed, they departed on good terms.

True to their word, and exactly on schedule, on March 22, at noon, the natives of Suluan returned with two canoes loaded with coconuts, sweet oranges, a jar of palm wine, and a chicken to indicate they had fowls in their lands. The men purchased everything they had in exchange for more trinkets. The islanders remained to instruct the men in making use of the coconuts to the full extent, including how to make palm wine. Pigafetta described their process of coconut distillation in a log entry:

> To declare the kind of fruits named above, know that they call "Cochi" the fruit borne by the palm trees. And just as we have bread, wine, oil, and vinegar in their several kinds, these people have the aforesaid things which come only from the palm trees. And know that wine is obtained from the said palm trees in the following manner. They make an aperture into the heart of the tree at its top which is called "palmito," from which is

distilled along the tree a liquor like white musk, which is sweet with a touch of greenness. Then they take canes as thick as a man's leg, by which they draw off this liquor, fastening them to the tree from the evening until next morning, and from the morning to the evening, so that the said liquor comes little by little.

Pigafetta then recorded the coconuts other properties and usage:

This palm tree bears a fruit named "cocho" (coconut), which is as large as the head or thereabouts, and its first husk is green and two fingers thick, in which are found certain fibers of which those people make the ropes by which they bind their boats. Under this husk is another, very hard and thicker than that of a nut. This second husk they burn and make of it a powder that is useful to them. And under the said husk there is a white marrow of a finger's thickness. This they eat fresh with meat and fish, as we do bread, and it has the flavor of an almond, and if it were dried it would make bread. From the center of this marrow there flows a water which is clear and sweet and very refreshing, and when it stands and settles it congeals and becomes like an apple. And when they wish to make oil, they take this fruit called "cocho" and put it in the sun and let the said marrow putrefy and ferment in the water, then they boil it, and it becomes oil like butter. When they wish to make vinegar, they let the water of the said cocho ferment and put it in the sun, which turns it into vinegar like white wine. From the said fruit milk can also be made, as we proved by experience. For we scraped that marrow, then mixed it with its own water, and being passed through a cloth it became like goat's milk. This kind of palm tree is like the palm that bears dates, but not so knotty. And two of these said trees will sustain a family of ten persons. But they do not draw the aforesaid wine always from one tree, but take it for a week from one, and so with the other, for otherwise the trees would dry up. And in this way, they last one hundred years.

During the eight days on Homonhon Island, the captain-general made daily visits in his skiff to shore so he could personally attend his sick comrades. He served coconut water and other fruits with his own hands to nurse them back to health. Along with Father Valderrama, he often prayed among the men, invoking the Lord above for their quick recovery. During one of these visits, Fernão found his trusted pilot, Juan Rodríguez de Mafra, laying upon some stacked palm leaves. He was pale and gaunt, and smelled of sickness. He poured some coconut water into a small cup and handed it to him.

'Please take some of this Juan,' Fernão said.

'Thank you, captain.'

'The least I can do for my loyal veteran pilot.'

Fernão deeply respected his experience. He had been born in 1470, ten years his senior. Juan Rodríguez de Mafra had sailed with Admiral Colombo on his second voyage to Hispaniola, and third voyage to the Paria Peninsula (Venezuela). In 1499, he sailed with Diego de Lepe to the northeastern coast of Brazil and thus one of the earliest to discover those lands. In 1500-1502, he had also explored the coast of Darien (Panama).

'You need to recover my friend. Your services and loyalty are sorely needed. I will never forget your bold actions in Seville against the Portuguese agents and against the mutineers in Port San Julian.'

'I am sorry captain, the hard years at sea and my age—'

'It is called *experience*, my friend, and I admire yours.'

'It has been an honor serving under your command.'

'I will expect your recovery, then. Do your best.' Fernão gave him a pat on the shoulder, and then stopped as he walked away, 'I will see you every day until we sail.'

'Aye captain-general.'

Meanwhile, Pigafetta and an armed escort followed the natives to Suluan and then on to another neighboring island. He described his encounters as follows:

> The lord of those people was old, and had his face painted, and he wore hanging from his ears golden rings which they call "Schione," and the others wore many gold bracelets and armlets, with a linen kerchief on their head . . . Near the said island, there is another where there are people who have holes in their ears so large that they can pass their arm through. These people, called "Caphri," (Kaffirs), are heathen and go naked, except that round their nature they wear a cloth made of the bark of trees. Howbeit some of the better clad wear cotton cloth, fringed with embroidery of silk done with a needle. Those people are brown, fat, and painted, and they anoint themselves with coconut oil and with benseed oil to protect themselves from the severity of the sun and the wind. They have very black hair

hanging to the waist, and they wear small daggers and knives, and lances adorned with gold, and several other things. And their boats are like ours.

On March 25, as the fleet was preparing to set sail, Pigafetta decided to fish before departure. With the recent rains the bulwarks were drenched and when he stepped out on a slippery yard located over the storeroom, he lost his footing, and plunged into the sea. Fortunately, with his left hand, he had snatched the foot of the mainsail dragging in the water, but unable to swim, he frantically called out for help while struggling to keep afloat. Finally, a crewman heard his pleas and dragged him on board. Fernão was unaware of what had transpired and raised an eyebrow as his drenched officer walked past, but from Pigafetta's embarrassed expression, he chose not to query the reason.

The fleet weighed anchor on what all the pilots and even the captain-general assumed to be March 25 but later they would understand to be March 26, for they had already long ago, crossed the international date line. They continued westward until they encountered the eastern coastline of Seilani—later known as Leyte. Eventually turning south along the coast, they entered through the Surigao Strait.

The next evening, March 27, they sighted lights flickering from an island near the southern end of the Leyte Peninsula. Fernão ordered the fleet pilots to anchor offshore. They would investigate at daybreak.

13

Limasawa Island, Philippines –
March 28, 1521

In the early morning, a scouting party of eight natives rowed a canoe toward the flagship. Enrique spoke to them in a Malay dialect and offered them to come on board to trade. Fernão was amazed they understood his servant. But, wary of the foreigners and their imposing black ships, the natives waited a safe distance away. Fernão understood their mistrust and ordered his men to display some fine items, including a red cap, and then fastened them to a floating plank of wood. With caution, the islanders snatched the goods and with great joy retreated to the shore. Two hours later, two long barge-like craft approached and were full of men. Fernão estimated the larger of the two boats was 80 feet in length. It carried an elaborately dressed man who was seated under a palm-thatched awning.

'Enrique, they seem to be cautious,' Fernão said. 'Go out and greet the one seated under the awning. He appears to be the king.'

He climbed down the ship, then swam out to meet with the visitors. Enrique had a long conversation with the ruler, then returned with some of the natives to the flagship.

'What have you learned Enrique?' Fernão said, waiting at the gunwale to help him back aboard. 'It appears he understood you.'

'Yes sir. The rulers here are fluent in Malayan. They say it is important for trade.'

'So, he is the king?'

'Yes. The king introduced himself to me as Rajah Calambu. He claims to rule over Butuan and Caraga, which is a district in the eastern part of Minanao Island. His jurisdiction even reaches to the distant island of Suluan, whence we have since sailed. He refused to come on board but allowed some of these men to do so.'

The captain-general looked at his crewmen and spotted his clerk. 'Ezpeleta, open up the storeroom and bring an assortment of items.'

Ezpeleta and some crewmen returned with their arms full of cloths and trinkets. Fernão then personally distributed them to the natives as gifts and sent them back to their boats. Enrique accompanied them.

Once Calambu found out the generosity of the foreigners, he presented Enrique with a massive bar of gold and a basket of ginger to bring back with him. The crews stared in awe at the large shiny bar of precious metal.

'So, the stories of gold and spices must be true,' Fernão said to Enrique.

'The rajah informed me both are prevalent in his lands. He claims his mines often produce gold nuggets the size of walnuts and eggs.'

Fernão gazed upon Rajah Calambu's boat. It too was greatly decorated in gold trim. 'Return the gifts and thank the rajah for his kind offer.'

'Sir?'

'We do not want to show our keen interest in the commodities. It will only drive up the price and we only have so many articles for trade.'

'I see,' Enrique said, then departed.

With first contact now concluded, Calambu returned with his men to the island.

But good fortune was tempered with bad news. The captain-general was very much grieved to hear the news from the *Concepción* that his loyal pilot, Juan Rodríguez de Mafra, had succumbed to his illness and they had solemnly buried him. Fernão was grateful to have spent several days at his side. During the few moments when his comrade had breath to speak, the two explorers had reminisced on their past adventures.

On March 29, Good Friday, Enrique was sent to shore to procure supplies and to reassure the islanders of their good intentions as friends. The young interpreter's mission was successful enough that, the rajah soon returned with a retinue of eight men to the flagship.

Once on board, Calambu's glory was now visibly evident to all. He was tawny, full of tattoos, and a silk headcloth covering his shiny black hair draped over his shoulders. The rajah also wore an elaborately embroidered silk cloth that wrapped around his waist and down to his knees. Strapped to his side was a beautifully engraved wooden sheath which held a kris dagger with a long gold handle. His body was perfumed in storax and benzoin which brought a pleasant fragrance into the air. Two large gold earrings dangled from his ears. When the rajah smiled to embrace the captain-general, it revealed all his teeth— each one covered with three spots of gold that glistened in the sunlight. Calambu presented gifts of three porcelain jugs covered with leaves and full of raw rice and two large mahi-mahi. Fernão responded by giving him a robe of yellow and red after the Turkish design, and a fine red cap. Knives and mirrors were given to the others.

A small meal was then served with Enrique acting as interpreter. The captain-general had learned of an honored Malay custom from his time in Malacca, namely—the ritual to bond as blood brothers and become one and the same thing. Thus, speaking via Enrique, he asked the rajah to perform the rite of "casi casi," if it pleased him to do so. Rajah Calambu enthusiastically agreed, and they each took their personal kris daggers and slit their chests open until the blood flowed. It was all collected in a glass and mixed with wine. They looked at one another and then each drank one half. A new pact of brotherhood was sealed in blood.

The captain-general was enthused at their new bond of friendship and decided to give the rajah a complete tour. First, he opened the stores to display the varieties of colored cloths, linen, corals, and other fine items. Next, he showed off their artillery and ordered Hans to fire the bombards to which Calambu was thoroughly impressed. Fernão then ordered one of his men to dress in full plate armor and to stand in the middle of three crew mates—all armed with swords and daggers. They struck at the armor with hard blows over and over, with rasps and clanking of steel upon steel, but every attack proved futile. No harm was inflicted and thus it appeared the suit had rendered the defender invincible.

Fernão spoke to the rajah with the assistance of Enrique, 'You see this one man clad in full armor? I believe he is worth more than 100 of your men. Is this not so?'

'I see with my eyes, it is indeed true,' the rajah answered with amazement.

'You must also know that in each of our ships we have 200 of such men,' Fernão remarked with a little exaggeration to impress. He then led his new blood brother to the quarterdeck where he displayed the marine charts, compass, astrolabe, and other nautical devices. Through Enrique, he explained how they had discovered the strait, the vast size of the great oceans, and how many moons it had taken him to reach his land. The rajah stared back in awe upon such incredible achievements.

Before departing, Fernão asked if he could send two of his men to shore so that they may learn of their domain. Calambu readily agreed. Pigafetta and another officer were sent to accompany them. The young supernumerary subsequently recorded the events:

> When I had set foot on shore, this king (rajah) raised his hands to heaven, then he turned toward us, and we did likewise. After this he took me by the hand, and one of his more notable men took my companion, and he led us under a place covered with reeds, where there was a "ballanghai," a boat like a foist (a light oared galley or barge). And there we seated ourselves with the said king on the poop of that boat, always speaking with him by signs. And his men stood round us with their swords, spears, and bucklers. The king sent for a dish of pork's flesh, and wine. And the manner of their drinking is this: At every mouthful we drank a cup of wine. They raise their hands to heaven first, then take the drinking vessel in their right hand, and extend the fist of their left hand toward the company. Which the king did, offering me his fist, with which I thought he would strike me. But I did likewise toward him. Thus, with the ceremony and other signs of friendship we banqueted, and then supped with him. I ate flesh on Good Friday, being unable to do otherwise. And before the hour of supper, I gave the king some things which I had brought. There I wrote down several things as they call them in their

language. And when the king and the others saw me writing, and I told them in their way of speaking, all were astonished. Meanwhile, the hour of supper being come, two large porcelain dishes were brought, one full of rice, and the other of pork's flesh with its broth and gravy. We supped with the same signs and ceremonies. Then we went to the king's palace constructed and built as it were thatch, and it was covered with leaves of fig (banana) and palm. It was built up from the ground on thick high posts, and we had to climb up to it by steps and ladders. The king made us sit on a reed mat, with our legs folded like tailors. And after half an hour, a dish of fish, roasted in pieces, was brought, and ginger freshly gathered, and wine. The eldest son of the king (who was the prince) came where we were. And the king told him to seat himself beside us, which he did. Then two dishes were brought, one of fish in its sauce and the other of rice. And this was in order that we might eat with said prince. And my companion made so good cheer in drinking and eating that he became intoxicated. For candles or torches they use a gum of a tree called "anime," wrapped in leaves of palm or of fig (banana). The king signed to us that he wished to go to bed, and he left the prince with us, with whom we lay down on a mat of reeds, and cushions and pillows of leaves. Next morning the king came and took me by the hand, and we went thus to the place where we had supped in order to breakfast, but the boat came to fetch us. And before departing the king very happily kissed our hands, and we kissed his. And a brother of his, king of another island, came with us, accompanied by three men. And the captain-general kept him to dine with him, and we gave him several things.

On March 31, Easter Sunday, the captain-general ordered Chaplain Valderrama to select and consecrate a suitable location on shore to conduct mass. Enrique accompanied him to inform the rajah they would not be coming to dine but to celebrate their holy day of Easter. Upon hearing of this, the king sent two dead pigs so all would have a fine meal after the service.

When the appointed time for mass had arrived, Fernão led a troop of 50 men to shore, not in armor, but only with swords and dressed in their finest attire. Before landing the boats, the fleet artillery fired six blasts as a sign of peace. The two brother kings, Rajah Calambu and Rajah Siaiu, waited on the beach to greet their guests. They placed the captain-general between them and proceeded to the consecrated grounds located not far from shore. To initiate the event, Fernão retrieved a clear flask and then sprinkled the two lords with rose muscat water. At the offering of the mass the rajahs kissed the cross as they all did. When the host was raised, all knelt with clasped hands in worship, and at that precise moment, the ships fired all their artillery in a resounding salute to the eternal Lord.

Once the mass had concluded, each crewman received communion. Fernão was growing fond of his island hosts and his new blood brother, King Calambu, thus he ordered an entertaining tournament of arms. The men choreographed an elaborate sequence of interactive maneuvers of swordsmanship albeit with dangerous repercussions, since the slightest error in timing could maim or kill. Unaware of the excellent martial skills of the captain-general's militia, the kings were thoroughly delighted and awestruck at the stunning display.

Once the exhibition concluded, a large cross adorned with nails and a crown were brought forth to which the rajahs bowed down in reverence.

Fernão explained to them, via Enrique, 'This is the sign of our spiritual Lord in heaven. But it is also the sign of the emperor, my earthly master and lord, and of whom has charged me to display in all the principal lands we should visit. Thus, it is my desire for the cross to be erected on the highest summit so that if any vessels of Spain arrive, they would know to do you no harm, and if they had taken any of your men, they would return them unharmed. Moreover, the cross will be your protection from thunder, lightning, and storms if you always honor its meaning in reverence.'

The two rajahs answered by the interpreter that they wished to wholeheartedly honor his request.

Fernão wanted to ascertain their former beliefs and asked, 'Are you Moors or heathens?'

'We worship no other but this—' They clasped their hands, looked up to the heavens and said, 'Oh *Abba*, hear our prayers.'

He was stunned, and comforted, for Fernão knew from his biblical studies that *Abba* was the Aramaic appellative used by both Jews and Christians to address their heavenly *Father*.

When Raja Calambu saw the captain-general was pleased at his words, he raised his arms to heaven and said, 'If it is possible, I wish to manifest the love I bear you in granting your requests.'

'I thank you for your kindness, but is there anything I can do for you? Do you have any enemies who wish to make war on you? If so, they are my enemies, and we will destroy them with our fleet and bring them into your submission.'

Rajah Calambu smiled. 'There are two islands who make war with us, but the fighting season has not arrived yet to attack.'

'Well, if the Lord allows my return, I shall honor my word and with many men bring your enemies under your rule . . . so, I shall now take a respite on our ship and return later with the cross to set it on the summit.'

The two rajahs embraced him, and they departed.

Later in the afternoon, the crews dressed in their fine doublets and returned to shore. The brother kings escorted the captain-general, along with Enrique, and his entourage, up a winding path toward the highest peak. As they climbed, Fernão's limp became more painful and visibly evident. Calambu whispered some words to one of his escorts, who scurried off into the lush jungle. He quickly returned with a bamboo stick, which the rajah immediately gave to Fernão.

He smiled in thanks and remarked, 'I suppose you wish to know why I am in this state?'

Calambu simply gestured with a slight nod.

'I have fought in many battles, injured severely in four separate engagements. This last wound has not yet healed as you can see, but it is only a nuisance in the cold or when hiking a long distance. I will survive.'

'You have earned the scars of a warrior. I am proud to be the blood brother of such a brave man.'

They exchanged a look of acknowledgment and carried on.

Upon reaching the summit, the men planted the cross. Meanwhile, the kings, the captain-general, and Enrique reclined upon a long flat rock overlooking the islands in the distance.

After some small talk, Fernão focused on more important matters and asked, 'What is the best place for trade? We need provisions.'

'There are three we may recommend,' Raja Calambu replied. 'Seilani (Leyte), Calghan (the Caraga district of Mindanao)—which I rule, and Zubu (Cebu). But Zubu is the best for trade. We can send our pilots to guide you to any of these.'

Now rested, all the men including the rajahs recited a Pater Noster, an Ave Maria, and bowed to the cross. Once concluded, they made their descent and passed through cultivated fields until they reached Calambu's ballanghai for a picnic of coconut water and assorted fruits. Anxious to leave in the morning, Fernão requested for the two kings to loan him a pilot in exchange for a crewman as a temporary hostage.

On the following morning, Calambu sent a messenger to offer his services as a pilot and he would guide them to the ports in person. However, if they could wait two more days and assist in harvesting the rice crops it would be greatly appreciated. Fernão agreed and sent some men. With the good reply, the rajahs feasted late into the night. When the men arrived to help gather the rice, the brothers sent word they were too ill to work to which all understood was due to severe hangovers. Pigafetta now had extra time on shore and was thus able to record further notes in his journal:

> Those people are heathens, and go naked, and are painted, and wear a piece of cloth from a tree like linen round their private parts, and they are great drinkers. The women are clad in tree cloth from the waist down. And they have black hair hanging down to the ground, and they wear certain gold rings in their ears. Those people chew most of the time a fruit which they call "Areca," (Betel) which is something like a pear, and they cut it into four quarters, then wrap it in leaves of its

tree, called "Betre," (Betel pepper) and they are like mulberry leaves. And mixing it with a little lime after they have chewed it for a long time, they spit and throw it out. And from this they afterward have a very red mouth. And many people use the said fruit because it greatly refreshes them, for the country is so hot that they could not live without it. In that island there is a great quantity of dogs, cats, pigs, poultry, and goats, of rice ginger, coconuts, figs (bananas), oranges, lemons, millet, wax, and gold mines . . . And that island is called Mazzaua (Limasawa).

The gold mines existed in great abundance in these lands. Fernão had already surmised it to be so, all based upon his knowledge gleaned from time spent in the Malacca trading emporiums, for the visiting merchants had often sold their gold acquired from these eastern islands. One day a crewman went to fill a water cask and was approached by an islander eagerly wishing to trade a large, pointed crown of gold, for six large pieces of glass. If the transaction had taken place, it would have been like a robbery, for the gold could garner an astronomical price in Europe. But the captain-general did not wish to reveal how much they desired such a commodity, and prior had refused his men to make such trades, at least for the moment, until they could secure a massive haul at one time.

After three days, the rice was harvested and Calambu appeared with his boat and men, thus honoring his word to serve as guide. He led the fleet northward through the Canigao Channel and kept near the western coastline of Leyte to avoid the dangerous shoals off Bohol Island. They sighted tall hills ahead in a place called Baibai (Baybay) and one of the king's guides on the flagship informed the captain-general it had much gold, provisions, and a vast expanse of land.

The fleet briefly stopped near a group of three islets and specifically—at one island called Gatighan (Apit or Jimuquitan Island). Here, Albo took a reading of 10 degrees north latitude. The crews spotted giant flying foxes (fruit bats) as large as eagles swooping across the skies. They were able to shoot one dead, and after roasting it for a meal, they all concurred it tasted like chicken.

From Gatighan, they veered west into the Camotes Sea. With the winds picking up, the fleet raised full sails and soon outpaced Calambu's boat. Eventually, they had to halt off a pair of islets of the Camotes group to await him. Upon arrival, the rajah complemented their exceptional navigational skills. Fernão then proposed that he should board his flagship with some of his leading men to witness firsthand their nautical expertise. They agreed to the captain-general's invitation, and it was agreed the fleet would spend the night here to dine and rest.

In the morning, they continued onward and Albo recorded in his log the remaining journey:

> And on the next day we went southwest and 1/4 south, a matter of 12 leagues, as far as 10 1/3 degrees, and there we entered a channel between two islands, one called Matan (Mactan), and the other Subo (Cebu).

As they sailed through the narrow channel, villages soon came into view. The houses were built upon tree posts, much like in Limasawa.

14

Cebu Island, Philippines – April 7, 1521

The three black ships of the armada approached the wealthy trading hub of Cebu with banners raised and sails lowered as if ready for war. The captain-general signaled for the gunners to fire all the broadsides in a salute. Unaccustomed to such powerful and thunderous artillery, the islanders were mostly afraid, and many scattered into the jungle. When the ships dropped anchors, Fernão summoned Cristovão Rebêlo and Enrique to report on deck midship.

'You are family to me,' he said. 'I have placed both of you in my will. Cristovão, you are my page, but now my adopted son. Therefore, you will initiate first contact as an important delegate of peace to this kingdom. Enrique, you are also like a son to me. Please interpret for him, as a good brother.'

The two young lads looked at one another, nodded, then walked off to embark the skiff. Soon after entering the town, they discovered the king was surrounded by many people, many who appeared terrified by the previous salvo of guns. The potentate was short, fat, and naked except for a loin cloth. Over his head was an embroidered silk cloth loosely draped over his head. He wore a heavy gold neck chain, and two gold rings with precious stones dangled from his ears. Most conspicuous was his face, completely covered in fire tattoos.

Enrique translated Cristovão's intended words. 'We assure you, O lord, that we come in peace. It is our custom to give an artillery salute upon arrival to new ports as a sign of peace and friendship.

Furthermore, it is considered an even greater honor to the king in that we fired *all* the guns.'

The king, his advisors, and the local chieftains appeared relieved at these words.

One of the leading men of the court spoke. 'Rajah Humabon wishes to know what you seek?'

Enrique stepped forward and responded in the common trading language of Malay, 'My master is a captain of the greatest king in the world—or what you call rajah—and that by his command he was going to discover the islands of Molucca. Yet, en route, he was informed of your honor and fame by a certain rajah, named Calambu, and thus decided to visit you. He also desires to trade our merchandise for provisions.'

'You are welcome in my land,' Rajah Humabon said. 'But we have a custom here that all visiting ships must pay tribute. In fact, just four days ago, a vessel from Siam, loaded with slaves and gold, had paid us tribute.' The rajah gestured for a man in Moorish garb to come forward. 'Here is a merchant from this ship, and he may attest to the veracity of my statements.'

Cristovão whispered in Enrique's ear to translate the following: 'Our captain serves under such a powerful king that he would never pay tribute to any other king in the world. If peace is desired then peace it shall be, but if war is desired then war it shall be.'

The Moor trader from Siam spoke to the king in Malay, 'Take good care, my lord, what you do, for these men are of those who have conquered Calicut, Malacca, and all Greater India. If you give them good reception and treat them well, it will be well for you, but if you treat them ill, so much the worse it will be for you, as they have done at Calicut and Malacca.'

With full understanding of the Malay trade language, Enrique interjected, 'My master's king is even more powerful in ships and land than the King of

Portugal, for he is the King of Spain and of all Christians. Thus, if you do not wish to be his friend and treat his subjects well, he will come with many ships and men to destroy you.'

The king's face turned pale as he pondered the implications and then wisely responded, 'I will consult my advisors and give you an answer in the morning. But please stay for a meal before returning.'

A variety of meats were served in porcelain dishes along with an ample supply of palm wine. Once concluded, the two diplomats returned to the flagship and conveyed the dialogues which had transpired. In the afternoon, Rajah Calambu offered his services as an ambassador to attest to the honorable character and good will of Captain-General Magalhães.

On the following day of April 8, Enrique was dispatched to shore with the fleet clerk, Léon de Ezpeleta, and some crewmen. They found the rajah in the town square surrounded with advisors and chieftains.

Humabon spoke to Enrique, 'Please, have your men sit near me.'

The men obliged and took seats as requested.

'Is there more than one captain for your ships?' he asked. 'Do you wish I pay tribute to your chief rajah—I mean your emperor?'

Enrique translated for the clerk, 'We have one captain per ship. But we have one commander of the entire fleet, Captain-General Fernão de Magalhães. He wishes no tribute, but only wishes to trade our merchandise with your people exclusively.'

The rajah smiled. 'If your captain wishes to be my friend, let us seal the pact as blood brothers. I will send my blood from my right arm, and he may do the same in return.'

The crewmen agreed it would be so.

He then made another request, 'It is custom for all the captains visiting our country to offer a present, and that I do so in return to them. Please ask your captain-general if he will honor our ways.'

'We shall do so,' Enrique replied. 'But to follow your custom well, please offer first, and afterwards, the captain-general will render what is due.'

On Tuesday morning of April 9, Rajah Calambu of Limasawa brought the Moor merchant of Siam to the flagship with a message that Rajah Humabon was currently preparing supplies to be sent to the ship as a gift, then after dinner he would send his nephew (an heir apparent prince), along with his leading men—to forge a peace alliance. The captain-general perceived the Moor trader to be of high intelligence and decided to demonstrate a show of force to which he knew would inevitably be related to the rajah. Fernão ordered a crewman to suit up in full armor and to which he fended off repeated heavy blows from an assorted cadre of weapons. With the metal suit appearing impenetrable, the Moor was impressed greatly.

After the Rajah Humabon finished dinner on shore, he sent the promised delegation to the flagship. The captain-general was dressed in his Order of Santiago vestments and seated in a red velvet chair. The prince and eight leading men were seated near him in leather chairs. The other guests took seats on mats upon the deck.

Enrique interpreted the captain-general's words to their guests, 'Is it your custom to speak in private or public? And does the prince have authority to make peace?'

The leading men of the delegation nodded in the affirmative to both inquiries.

The captain-general then spoke a long discourse on peace and then concluded with an emotional prayer that God in heaven would confirm it.

The delegation replied they had never heard such words and wished to hear more.

Fernão was enamored by such an eager audience and gladly obliged their request with an inspirational elucidation of the Christian faith's basic tenets and meaning. Afterward, he inquired, 'Who will succeed the rajah when he dies?'

One of the rajah's statesmen replied, 'The rajah has no son, but many daughters. The rajah's eldest daughter has married the prince that sits before you, and it is because of his love for her that he is called prince. You should be aware that when the father and mother are old, their authority is no more, and the children rule over them.'

Fernão narrowed his eyebrows. 'And you should know this: God had created the heaven, the earth, and the sea, and everything in the world, and has commanded everyone to honor and obey one's father and mother. Anyone who does not, risks condemnation. You should also know that we are descendants from our first parents, Adam and Eve, and that we all have immortal souls.' With seemingly supernatural inspiration, he continued to instruct them on the principles of God's kingdom—the God they professed—and introduced them to the gospel message, which impressed them greatly, as many understood its beneficence.

'Please lend us two men . . . or at least one, who can teach us the Christian faith,' they begged. 'We promise to do them great honor and company.'

'We cannot afford to leave any men at this time, but if you wish to become Christians, I will have my priest baptize any who desire. Later, we will bring teachers of the faith.'

'We shall speak first with our rajah and then become Christians.'

'If you indeed choose to become Christians, do not for fear of us, or to do us favor, but do it with a good heart and for a genuine love of God. If you choose not to become Christians, we will not show you disrespect. But those who choose the path of righteousness shall be treated better than others.'

With one mind, they all pledged to become Christians of their own free will.

The captain-general then promised he would leave them weapons in honor of their new alliance. He also implored them to have their wives baptized, for a Christian cannot have sexual relations with a heathen.

Following this discourse, they offered their allegiance as his own servants. Fernão openly wept with joy and embraced all of them. He took the prince's hand and that of the rajah Calambu, then promised by his faith in the Lord, and to his master the emperor, and to the Order of Santiago, that he would confirm an endless peace between them and the king of Spain. The prince and others promised the same in return.

Once the peace was concluded, a meal was served. The prince then offered gifts from the rajah as promised: boxes of rice, along with pigs, goats, and chickens. They asked forgiveness since the gifts were not adequate for his command. In return, the captain-general presented to the prince a red cap, a fine cloth, a sizeable amount of glass, and a gilded glass cup. It was a fine gift, for glass was highly prized in these lands. To the other delegates various items were given. Then he prepared an assortment of gifts to bring to the rajah.

Later, Pigafetta and another officer arrived at the royal palace with their gifts in hand. They found Rajah Humabon seated upon a palm-thatched mat and surrounded by many people. In front of him was another palm mat with two porcelain dishes full of turtle eggs and four jars of palm wine. As Pigafetta entered, the king was engrossed with eating the eggs and drinking from a reed straw. The two emissaries bowed and laid the presents before the rajah and explained it was given not in return for the gift given prior, but out of real love for which the captain-general wished to bestow upon him. Forthwith, they dressed him in a robe of yellow and violet silk in the manner of the Turkish lords and a fine red cap. Pigafetta then kissed a gilded glass and silver dish which contained delicately crafted glass pieces, then offered them as gifts. The royal advisors confirmed the vows of peace exchanged on board the flagship and the rajah responded by inviting them to remain for dinner. Pigafetta politely made excuse not to stay, for prior, the prince had already offered more enticing plans. Arriving at the heir apparent's abode, they were pleasantly surprised to find four young women playing an enticing melody on various odd instruments.

After they had returned to the ship, Pigafetta entered a log into his journal describing the evening but with prudent brevity:

> One played on a taborin after our fashion, but it stood on the ground. Another was striking, with a thick stick wrapped at the head with a palm leaf on the bottom of two instruments shaped like a long taborin. Another was striking a larger instrument in the same manner. And the last, with two other similar instruments, one in one hand

and the other in the other. And they struck in harmony, making a very sweet sound. These girls were very beautiful, and almost white and as tall as ours. They were naked, except that from the waist to the knees they wore a garment made from the said palm cloth, covering their nature. And some were quite naked, having long black hair and a small veil round their head, and they go always unshod. The prince made us dance with three of them who were quite naked. And we had refreshment there, and then we returned to the ship. Those taborins are of metal, and they are made in the country of the Sinus Magnus, which is China. There they use them as we do bells, and they are called "Aghon"

On Wednesday morning, April 10, Pigafetta and Enrique were sent back to the rajah with a special request. They explained how during the previous night, one of their men had died and they needed a proper burial ground. The rajah responded graciously and provided a site in the town square. Later, a large cross was setup and Martin de Barrena, a supernumerary on the *Victoria*, was buried. An elaborate funeral ensued, not only to honor their fallen comrade, but to display their regard for the afterlife. The rajah followed suit, kneeling before the cross and kissing it with reverence. Soon afterward, Juan de Aroche, also of the *Victoria*, died and was buried later that evening.

During the following days of April 11-12, great quantities of merchandise were transferred from the ships and stored in a warehouse offered by the rajah to be used as a trading factory. Four crewmen were selected to run the operations. The locals already had accurate scales for making precise measurements of weight. It consisted of a spear-shaft suspended in the middle by a cord. One arm extension had a basin which hung by three strings and the other arm had a lead weight to provide the equilibrium.

Official trading began on April 12, and the people marveled at the merchandise. Pigafetta noted the trades in his logbook:

> For metal, iron, and other large wares, they gave us gold, and for the other smaller and meaner goods rice, pigs, goods, and other provisions. And they gave us ten weights of gold for 14 pounds of iron. Each weight is a ducat and a half. The captain did not wish us to take a great quantity of gold, lest the sailors should sell what they had too cheaply for greed of gold, and he should therefore be constrained to do likewise with his merchandise. For he wished to sell it at a better rate.

Pigafetta climbed the stairs to the quarterdeck to meet Fernão. 'How fares your studies on shore?' Fernão asked.

'I am compiling a vocabulary list. I discovered one word of special interest. It describes a certain sea animal. The locals call it *Laghan*.' Pigafetta then held out his hand and displayed a white shell.

'It is beautiful,' Fernão said.

'Yes, and deadly. It's known in these islands as a whale killer.'

'What? How? It is so tiny.'

Pigafetta cracked open the shell and revealed a squirming, black-fleshed creature with teeth. 'Apparently, the whales swallow these shells, but eventually the creatures come out of their shells and eat the heart of the whale.' Pigafetta then took a bite of the slimy black flesh. 'But it is very tasty for us.'

'I suppose so, after what we have had to eat on this voyage.'

The two men chuckled at this.

Pigafetta had a satchel around his shoulder to which he retrieved a small idol. It was hollow and without any backside. The arms were open, feet turned up, legs open, and had a large face with four large teeth like wild boars, and all painted over.

Fernão frowned. 'I will address this issue of idols at the rajah's baptism on Sunday. I am ordering a large platform built in the town square with palm branches and tapestries. It will be a fine day.'

15

On Sunday morning of April 14, a salute of artillery salvos from all the ships thundered as a party of 40 armed crewmen landed on the shores of Cebu Island. In front, two men in full shining body armor carried the royal banner of the Catholic kings as the procession walked along the beach to meet the rajah who had eagerly awaited their arrival. The captain-general and the rajah smiled genuinely and embraced one another.

Enrique interpreted for them both as they proceeded towards the town square.

'You should know my brother that I bear you great love,' Fernão said. 'It is customary to only carry our royal standard if we have 50 fully armed men as only the two you see here, plus another 50 men armed with matchlocks. But I have made an exception, and have brought it as such, to honor you.'

'I am very much honored my brother,' Humabon replied.

Once they had climbed up the stairs to the decorated platform, the captain-general sat upon a red velvet chair and the rajah upon a violet one. The advisors and local chieftains sat upon cushions and the others on palm mats.

Fernão confided to the rajah, 'I am clad in this white robe to share with you in this momentous occasion, all in complete solidarity and love. I also thank God for inspiring you to become a Christian and thus I have a greater desire to conquer your enemies. Your enemies shall be my enemies.'

'I wish to become a Christian,' Humabon replied. 'But you should know there are some other chieftains and rajahs who refuse to obey me and will not become Christian.'

The captain-general's smile of joy quickly became a scowl of consternation. He knew from his experiences in Africa, India, and Malacca, that a trading hub in a fractured kingdom would never last long. The surrounding principalities must be unified under one leader in the trade port of Cebu, namely, Rajah Humabon.

'I wish to speak with these men now,' Fernão demanded. 'Please bring them forth to answer before us.'

The rajah's messengers and several of the crewmen dispersed to locate the recalcitrant chieftains from the nearby villages.

Later, when they assembled, Fernão addressed them, 'We cannot have a divided kingdom. Rajah Humabon will be the sole power and you must submit to him. Anyone refusing will be put to death and then all your goods will be given to the rajah.'

With dread, they all affirmed their allegiance.

The captain-general then turned to the rajah. 'If I return to Spain, I will then return here with a great fleet and make you the greatest potentate in these lands because you were the first to become Christian.

The rajah raised his arms to heaven. 'I thank you my brother. Please leave us two men to instruct us further in the faith.'

Fernão was previously reluctant to spare two good men, since their rosters were already depleted in numbers. But such a receptive audience was difficult to deny. 'Very well, I will leave two men, but please give us two of your young leading men so they may learn our language. Upon returning from Spain, they may relate all knowledge acquired during their sojourn.'

Next, a great cross was placed in the center of the square and all stood in front of it.

The captain-general then explained, 'If anyone wishes to be a loyal Christian, they must burn every idol in this land, and in place of every idol setup a cross. Every day, one must kneel and bow before it, always with clasped hands held up to heaven.' He then demonstrated how to perform the sign of the cross.

All the people promised to obey his commands.

The captain-general, with his long black beard contrasting against the white robe, took Humabon by the hand and led him back up to the platform. Chaplain Valderrama awaited on top. Fernão gave a brief history of the honorable Christian names he wished to bestow upon them at baptism. Rajah Humabon would be named Don Carlos (the emperor), the prince—as Don Fernando (the emperor's brother), Rajah Calambu—as Don Juan, and the Siamese Moor trader—as Cristóbal. All others received any Christian name they preferred. In total, 500 were baptized and then the mass was performed. The captain-general offered the rajah and his leading men to dine on the flagship, but he politely declined. However, Humabon accompanied them to the shore where they were welcomed by a salvo from the ship's artillery. The rajah embraced the captain-general, then departed.

After dinner, Pigafetta, the priest, and a few crewmen, went on shore to baptize the queen. She was young, and beautiful, with very red lips and nails. The queen wore a white and black dress, a large hat of palm leaves, and a crown on top fashioned of the same material, after the likeness of the pope. She was accompanied by a train of 40 ladies, and they were all led to the platform where she took a seat upon a cushion with her women around her.

While the priest was preparing for the event, the queen was shown a well-crafted piece of wood carving, depicting the virgin with child and a cross. The queen was very enamored by the piece and confessed it induced her greatly to become a Christian. The priest baptized her as Juana (the emperor's mother). Subsequently, the queen's daughter, who was also the prince's wife, they baptized as Catarina, and Rajah Calambu's wife as Isabella. In all, 800 men, women, and children, were baptized on that day. Once the ceremony had concluded, the queen pleaded to have the wood carving of the Madonna and child. She promised to set it up in place of the idols. The men agreed and she departed.

During the next week, villagers poured in from the surrounding lands and were baptized, over 2,200 in total. Every day, the captain-general visited the rajah to instruct him in the faith and attend mass. On one of those days, the queen came with her maidens to hear mass. Three young women went before her, and each carried a hat in her hand. The queen was clad again in black and white, and she wore a gold embroidered cloth over her head that reached her shoulders. Her royal hat was worn over the cloth. In addition to the three maidens, another entourage accompanied behind, all naked except their privates were covered by palm cloth, and they wore a linen cloth on their head. The queen bowed in front of the altar and then took a seat upon an embroidered silk cushion. The captain-general was also there and decided to participate in the mass. He sprinkled muscat water over the queen and her maidens, to which they thoroughly enjoyed.

Fernão had heard that the queen highly revered the wood sculpture and presented it to her in this moment. 'I wish you to have this and not your idols. It is a reminder of our Lord and worthy of your care.'

The queen accepted it with many thanks, and then departed.

On the following day, the captain-general summoned the local chieftains to swear allegiance to Rajah Humabon and King Carlos of Spain.

They all swore to obey.

Then he drew his sword before an image of the Virgin Mary and declared, 'When one swears as such, one must sooner die than to break such an oath.'

The rajah borrowed the sword and made the oath in the same manner, pledging loyalty to the emperor.

Once fealty was affirmed, the captain-general presented the rajah with a red velvet chair and instructed him how it was to be carried for diplomatic missions and royal events. The rajah responded in kind by describing how he was preparing a special gift of jewelry: It included two large gold earrings, two gold bands for the arms, and two to wear on the ankles, as well as a variety of precious stones.

A few days after this, the captain-general visited the rajah. Enrique interpreted his words, 'My brother, why are the idols not burned? And why do the people still offer food sacrifices to them?'

'I am sorry my brother. But the people are asking the idols to heal the prince's older brother, who is considered the most wise and valiant man in the island. He has been bedridden and unable to speak for four days now.'

With the success of the mass baptisms, Fernão was full of faith and boldly declared, 'You should burn all the idols and believe on Jesus Christ. If the sick man is baptized, he shall be healed. And if this is not true, you can cut off my head.'

213

This was a moment of testing. He knew if the man was not healed the people would think the Christian faith would be considered a powerless and futile enterprise. They would not only retain their idol worship, but they may indeed cut off all their heads.

'We shall do as you ask,' Humabon replied. 'I truly, believe in Jesus Christ.'

A great procession was then made from the square to the sick man's abode where they found him in bed and unable to speak. The priest immediately baptized him, his wives, and 10 young girls. After some minutes, the captain-general asked him how he felt. The man was now able to speak and with joy declared, 'By God's grace this is indeed a miracle!'

They had already prepared some almond milk and gave it to him to recover his strength. Fernão arranged for a mattress with all the sheets and pillows to be given him.

Over the next five days, provisions were sent to the prince's older brother, including: almond milk, rosewater, oil of roses, and sweet preserves. On the fifth day, he was able to walk. The man brought forth an idol that some old women had hidden in his house and presented it to the rajah to burn. The prince's brother was well respected, and the people followed his crusade to purge the land. They burned the temples on shore and any idols they could find, all the while crying out, 'Castile! Castile!'

As the captain-general baptized the natives, and the chaplain instructed new converts, the crewmen were undermining the effort by consorting with the women of the island. Fernão knew he had to maintain some leniency with the men. If he denied this new paradise to them after suffering the perils and misery at sea for so long, he would surely have another mutiny.

Pigafetta had observed how the locals enhanced their sexual exploits and pleasure to new levels, such as a custom they referred to as Palang. He noted a detailed account in his journal:

Those people go naked, wearing only a piece of cloth of palm around their shameful parts. They have as many wives as they wish, but there is always a chief one. The males, both large and small, have the head of their member pierced from one side to the other, with a pin of gold or tin as thick as a goose feather; and at each end of this pin some have a star-shaped decoration like a button, and others, one like the head of a cart nail. Often, I wished to see that of some young men and old men, because I could not believe it. In the middle of this pin or tube is a hole through which they urinate, and the pin and the stars always remain firm, holding the member stiff. They told us that this was the wish of their women, and that if they did otherwise, they would not have intercourse with them. And when they wish to cohabit with their wives, the latter themselves take the member without its being prepared or rigid, and so they put it little by little into their nature, beginning with the stars. Then when it is inside it stiffens, and remains there until it becomes soft, for otherwise they would not be able to withdraw it. And those people do this because they are of a weak nature and constitution. Whenever any of our men went ashore and landed, be it by day or night, everyone invited him to eat and drink. Their viands are half cooked and very salty. They drink often and much, and their meal lasts five or six hours. The women loved us very much more than the men of the country. And all the women when

215

they are above the age of ten years, have their nature covered little by little, because of the men's member made in the aforesaid fashion.

The captain-general had given liberty to his crews but now he realized it must be held in check. Once again, his brother-in-law, Duarte Barbosa, left his station to pursue amorous pursuits on shore. However, this time he had not left his duties as a regular officer, but as captain of the *Victoria*. Fernão was so furious and removed him from command, replacing him with Cristovão Rebêlo, whom at least he knew he could trust.

Meanwhile Pigafetta continued his linguistic studies and had now compiled a 143-word vocabulary list of the Bisayan dialect of Cebu. During his interviews he had often inquired why a black bird appeared every midnight hour and screeched so loud all night that it caused the dogs to bark incessantly. Nobody knew why, but some of the crewmen had begun to sense an ominous doom behind the veil of paradise.

16

Cebu & Mactan, Philippines – April 26 May 1, 1521

Fernão Magalhães' blood oath with Humabon was tested almost immediately. The chieftain of a small village refused to render a tribute to the Rajah of Cebu. The captain-general ordered the village torched, and a cross was erected on the ashes. A week later, the captain-general had just finished mass when he was met by the son of another village chieftain named Zula, from Mactan, who presented a tribute of two goats and offered an apology on behalf of his father.

Enrique functioned as interpreter and translated the words of the young prince: 'Zula apologizes that he is not able to receive baptism, nor pledge fealty to the King of Spain, for the most-powerful Rajah of Mactan, Lapu-Lapu, will not allow it. But if the captain-general would be willing to provide one boat and some men, Zula is sure he could defeat Lapu-Lapu, and bring him into submission.'

'Zula's message is welcomed, and his tribute accepted,' Fernão said. 'Tell him I will take this matter up with my captains and the Rajah of Cebu immediately.'

The captain-general dismissed the messenger, had the goats taken to the ship, and proceeded into the village with Enrique. They had not gone far when they ran into Humabon, who had come looking for his blood brother. Enrique again translated.

'I understand Zula's son has come to meet you and brought you a message. Is it good news? Anything of import?'

'Lapu-Lapu refuses to submit,' Fernão replied.

'Yes, I expected,' Humabon said. 'He thinks himself my rival. When he first came to Mactan from Brunei, we were friends. I appreciated his efforts at organizing the people. But then he began doing things that were not permitted—raiding trading vessels visiting our ports—things such as this. He has since openly defied me and set himself up as ruler of Mactan. He even dares to rule over part of Cebu!'

'He is a pirate?' Fernão asked. 'You know, we have effective means of dealing with them. Know this, my brother, Our Lord in heaven has taught us that a kingdom divided against itself cannot stand. Are these islands not a kingdom?'

'Yes,' Humabon replied. 'But we are bound only under alliances, not by one ruler.'

'Then you are divided,' Fernão said.

'Perhaps,' Humabon replied. 'But you do not understand, Lapu-Lapu has organized a large army of many men. They are fierce warriors, very skilled in combat. No one has stood against them. Perhaps we can—'

'Force him to submit,' Fernão interrupted.

Humabon took a deep breath and exhaled. 'I see you are determined. In this case, I must insist on accompanying you along with my own warriors.'

'I will only need 3 ships and 60 men to crush this renegade army,' Fernão said, wondering if such doubts ran among his own men. He knew his plan would encounter resistance in his own fleet. He returned to the ship with Enrique, prepared to face down criticism. As soon as he boarded the *Trinidad*, he sent for Captain Juan Serrano of the *Concepción* and Hans, the master-gunner of the flagship.

A short time later, Captain Serrano boarded the Trinidad and reported to the captain-general's quarters. Hans followed close behind. When the door opened, Fernão slammed a book shut and stood up from the table where he was sitting with Pigafetta.

'Ah, my most loyal captain and my trusted gunner,' Fernão said. 'I wanted to hear your thoughts about this renegade chief on Mactan, this pirate they call Lapu-Lapu.'

Serrano frowned and thought for a moment. 'I understand your zeal to convert the heathens to the faith, and to forge solid alliances for Spain, but I cannot help to think this is a reckless and needless enterprise. Would it not be prudent to continue to the Spice Islands, as mandated by the king? Nearly all the men believe this way.'

Pigafetta, still seated at the table with pen in hand, nodded. 'This is true,' he said.

Hans cleared his throat. 'The men of the *Trinidad* wish to continue the mission for the spices.'

Serrano continued. 'Our ships need repair and we have lost too many men. We cannot afford to lose many more, and you know we will if we pursue this course. Not to mention, if we split the force, we risk attack on the undermanned fleet. Would you leave it defenseless?'

'I hear your concerns,' Fernão said. 'I have considered these things myself. But surely you can see the need to solidify our presence here before departing?'

'Under normal circumstances, yes,' Serrano replied. 'But this is no small village chief, and he has a formidable army.'

Fernão smiled. 'I have fought in many battles against overwhelming numbers, sometimes by countless thousands. We have always prevailed. We have the superior weapons and tactics. The courage of our men is without equal. Do not underestimate these advantages.'

'I think it is possible you underestimate this enemy, and overestimate our own condition,' Serrano said.

'And perhaps not,' Fernão shot back.

'Will the captain-general consider remaining with the fleet?' Serrano asked. 'You do not need to personally engage this enemy. We can choose another to lead the men.'

'I can volunteer my services to lead the attack, sir,' Hans said.

Pigafetta nodded in agreement.

'I will lead my flock,' Fernão said resolutely, ending all discussion. 'Make ready the men. Hans, you will command the gun boats. We shall leave tonight.'

At midnight, a fleet squadron of 60 men with swords, lances, arquebuses, and crossbows, climbed over the gunwales and down on to the three skiffs waiting below. Each skiff was armed with a swivel gun. The men wore only their helmets and breastplates, having left their leg grieves behind, for the rajah had informed them that the approach was long and shallow, and they would have to wade in from a distance.

As they readied the skiffs, Rajah Humabon and 1,000 of his warriors rowed up beside them in longboats and canoes. The flotilla navigated the nine miles northeast through the channel separating Cebu and Mactan. Rounding the northern point of Mactan, they entered a small bay and sailed up to the reef. The water was shallow beyond this, but it was still a long way to the shore. Crossbows and swivel guns would be useless at this distance.

Fernão had Enrique call to Humabon, who was alongside in his canoe. 'My brother, send your trusted merchant from Siam to Lapu-Lapu with this message: If he agrees to obey the King of Spain, and pay tribute, we shall all be friends. But if he acts contrary, he shall learn by experience how our lances pierce.'

The messenger returned sometime later with Lapu-Lapu's response: 'We have bamboo lances and stakes hardened by fire and we can attack you any time we wish. But we ask that you wait until morning, so that we have more men.'

'This is Lapu-Lapu's tactics,' Humabon said. 'He hopes you will attack in darkness, for they have dug pits with poison stakes at the bottom so that you will fall into them and die.'

I, too, am sure this is a ruse,' Fernão said. "We will wait for the dawn. But I must request that you remain here and witness how our men can fight.'

'But he has many warriors. Surely you cannot overcome these numbers alone.'

"This is even better. The fear of Spain will spread across the islands and reinforce your rule here.'

Humabon looked at him sincerely. 'This is truly what you wish?'

'It is indeed,' Fernão replied.

'Very well. I will hold my men.'

In the light of dawn, the men could see the approach to the shore, full of stones and rocks waiting to gouge the hulls of their boats. The low tide meant the three skiffs with the swivel guns were stuck beyond the shore, unable to provide any covering fire. Leaving a token force to guard the skiffs, Fernão and 48 men slipped into the waist-deep water and began wading toward the shore nearly half a mile away. Without the heavy leg grieves they were able to maintain a steady pace, but the natives began appearing on the beach, and with every step they took, more islanders joined their ranks. Soon there were thousands of native warriors assembled, waiting for them. As Fernão's men approached, Lapu-Lapu had his men divide into three divisions. He was preparing to surround the Spanish force.

Fernão called out to his men. 'Align on me, V formation! Arquebusses and crossbows, fire at will!' His men fell into two ranks fanning out behind him. Crossbow bolts flew away from the formation toward the natives, and the arquebuses boomed shot at them. But the distance was still great enough that the fusillade lost its momentum and bounced helplessly off any intended or unintended target. The natives on shore ducked and weaved. Shots rifled through the leaves, or hit their thin shields, at best only causing them to crack. It soon became apparent to Fernão that his men were wasting ammunition.

'Hold your fire!' he yelled. 'Hold your fire! Let's close our range! Pikes at the ready! Advance!'

The men, thigh deep in water, pointed their pikes forward and began sloshing toward the shore.

The futility of the initial attack emboldened the natives. They unleashed a torrent of arrows and bamboo lances. They threw fire hardened stakes and pummeled the attacking force with stones. The Spaniards protected themselves as best they could. Fernão had the crossbows and arquebuses return fire as soon as they were in range.

He and his men pushed forward, rising out of the water as they approached the shallows. Noticing their legs were unprotected, the natives began targeting them. But the warriors who did approach were often quickly cut down by Spanish lances. Despite this, Lapu-Lapu's army kept coming at them. Fernão and his men fought through them and gained the edge of a mangrove at the shoreline, which offered some protection from Lapu-Lapu's army, which had begun to respect their lances. Clearly at a disadvantage, Fernão was desperate and looking for inspiration. The native village was visible through the mangroves, and he once more invoked Albuquerque's tactics.

'Pigafetta!' he called. 'We need to draw them off. Take your men over there and burn their huts. We will hold the beach until you return.'

With a steady wind blowing off the ocean, the village huts went up quickly. But the effect was exactly opposite of the intention. The islanders became enraged and threw themselves at the Spanish invaders. Pigafetta's squad was quickly cut off and attacked. Two of Pigafetta's men were killed on the spot. Fighting hand to hand with weapons, Pigafetta and his men battled their way through the mangroves and back onto the beach before they were finally able to rejoin the main force.

At that moment Lapu-Lapu's army launched a storm of projectiles from the cover of the mangroves. Arrows, lances, and stones rained down on Fernão and his men. A poison-tipped arrow lodged into the captain-general's leg. His knee buckled. As he snapped the arrow off, a horde of islanders swarmed from the groves and onto the beach.

'To the boats!' Fernão yelled. 'Hasty, orderly, retreat to the boats!'

Fernao had been accustomed to fighting in the ranks of veteran soldiers. Only a few of these men were experienced in disciplined tactics. Faced with the sheer number of islanders storming onto beach, the men panicked, broke formation, and ran for the boats in complete disorder.

'I said orderly!' Fernão bellowed, helplessly. He was left with 8 men, including Pigafetta, and his son and page, Cristovão Rebêlo. They were in knee deep water, their backs to the sea, and still too far from the skiffs to expect any assistance from the swivel guns. The islanders attacked immediately, launching arrows and spears aimed at the exposed legs of the Spaniards as they swarmed in.

'Protect yourselves,' Fernão said. 'Lances to the fore. Don't let them get close.'

The captain-general was dragging his injured leg as the last of his forces moved back slowly and carefully. An islander screamed and ran at him with a hardened bamboo stake. Fernão buried his lance into the attacker's neck above the collar bone and withdrew it quickly, the man stopping, stumbling, and falling, face first into the water. Another ran at him with a spear, but Pigafetta lunged forward, his lance piercing the man's chest between the ribs. Fernão turned to acknowledge him, but something slammed into the side of his head, sending his helmet tumbling. Dazed, he bent over to retrieve it, but when he placed it on his head, another islander slammed into him and knocked it off again. Fernao steadied himself as another of his soldiers swung his sword and nearly cut the man in two. Other natives were pointing at the captain-general and yelling.

'They know you are the leader!' Pigafetta yelled, just as a poisoned dart cut across his forehead. Pigafetta staggered backward, blood streaming down his face.

The island warriors focused their attack on Fernão, aiming their weapons at him directly. An arrow glanced off his breastplate, another banged off his helmet. He jabbed his pike at his attackers, who backed off quickly. A spear flew toward him, glanced off his breastplate and lodged deep into his arm. Fernão cried out and stumbled backward, nearly dropping his own lance. He grabbed the spear with his left hand and pulled it out, tossing it aside. His son,

Cristovão, stepped between Pigafetta and Fernão, furiously stabbing his lance into one attacker, then another, and was quickly killed in a barrage of spears. Pigafetta and another soldier charged past them both, pushing back the attacking villagers. Still holding his lance, Fernão tried to hold up the lifeless body of his son, but it was a futile effort. The poison from the arrow had begun to affect him, and was overcome with grief, which quickly turned to rage. Adrenaline pumped through him. He held up his pike and stepped past Pigafetta, stabbing, withdrawing, aiming, stabbing again. He saw only targets of brown, and tried to lance them all, until his rage subsided enough to realize he had gone too far beyond Pigafetta and his men, and the villagers were closing in behind him. He was cut off and alone. A warrior lunged at him with a spear. It gouged into his face beside his lips and ripped his cheek away, so that it hung down beside his neck, exposing his teeth like a skeleton. Fernão shoved his lance through the attacker's belly so deep that the man fell away with it embedded in him. The captain-general looked back at his men.

'Get to the boats!' he yelled. 'I will keep them engaged!'

Fernão turned back to the islanders, reaching for the hilt of his sword, grasping it, and nearly pulling it free before the pain from the spear wound fired through his arm. The sword dropped back into the sheath. He tried again, but the pain of the damaged muscle was so great he could not pull it free. The islanders saw this and closed on him. Fernão looked back once more at his men. They were nearly to the boats. Pigafetta was standing some distance away, unsure which way to go. Fernão turned his gaze toward the sky and raised his arms to heaven. The islanders pounded his body with their sharpened stakes. He disappeared beneath them, and the water churned red with his blood.

Pigafetta watched for as long as he could, wiping the blood from his own face with his hand. The poison burned and he squinted and blinked. He turned toward the boats to see a canoe coming toward him. Humabon ordered his Cebu warriors to assist the Spanish retreat. The men in the canoe helped him climb aboard.

In the meantime, Rajah Humabon had sat in his canoe, surrounded by his own warriors, and watched. When it became apparent Fernão's contingent had been overwhelmed, Humabon dispatched some of his Cebu warriors to draw off Lapu-Lapu's army. They were engaged immediately but could offer little assistance. Watching the horror unfold from a helpless distance, he was stunned to silence. His blood-brother was dead. The battle was lost. His dreams were crushed. The grief cut deep. He directed his men to help bring the survivors to their boats, then sat in his canoe and wept openly. As the wounded were being loaded onto the skiffs, the swivel gunners fired on any of Lapu-Lapu's men who pursued them. Lapu-Lapu lost fifteen men to the ship's guns, and untold number on the beach. Unfortunately, four of Humabon's warriors were killed in the crossfire. The fleet had lost eight men in addition to the captain general.

The somber war party made its way to Cebu uncelebrated.

Pigafetta returned to the Trinidad well-bloodied, with half of his face swollen and burning from the poison. After having his wounds dressed by the ship's surgeon, he retired to the captain general's quarters. Pigafetta looked about the room. Neither Fernão nor

Cristovão would be returning. Enrique's hand was sliced open early in the battle but would have to wait for more serious cases to be treated before he could be attended to. For the moment, Pigafetta had the place to himself. He recorded his eulogy in an address to his former commander, Phillipe Villiers de l'Isle-Adam, Grandmaster of the Knights Hospitaller of Rhodes:

> I hope that by your most illustrious lordship, the renown of such a valiant and noble captain will not be extinguished or fall into oblivion in our time. For among his other virtues, he was more constant in a very high hazard and great affair than ever was any other. He endured hunger better than all the others. He was a navigator and made sea charts. And that this is true was seen openly, for no other had so much natural wit, boldness, or knowledge to sail once around the world, as he had undertaken. This battle was fought on a Saturday, April 27, 1521. And the captain wished to make it on a Saturday, because that was his day of devotion.

The very next day, the crew had Enrique ask Rajah Humabon to send a message that they would like to retrieve their dead. In exchange, they offered any merchandise desired from the warehouse. The messenger soon returned with Lapu-Lapu's response. He refused to give up the body of such a man and would keep him as an eternal memorial of their victory.

But Humabon never relayed the entire message to the crew. Lapu-Lapu had concluded by threatening the Rajah of Cebu with the same treatment if he did not drive away the foreigners or exterminate them altogether.

Lapu-Lapu's refusal to return the remains angered the men of the fleet. Most had long desired to get on with the mission, and this latest humiliation only hardened that resolve. The following day, the officers and men convened to address the immediate needs of the fleet, first and foremost who would be in command. Fernao Magalhães, respected and admired by everyone in his command, was the one person who was able to keep such a discordant crew united. Without him, the crew fell into disagreement and mistrust. Duarte Barbosa was Portuguese among all his faults, and the Spaniards would not follow him. In the end, the workable solution was to appoint Duarte Barbosa and Juan Serrano as joint commanders of the armada. Serrano continued to command the *Concepción*. Barbosa would take command of the *Trinidad*. Luis Affonso de Goes, who had been on the *Trinidad*, became the captain of the *Victoria*.

The joint commanders were eager to push on to the Spice Islands and did not wish to delay any further. They immediately ordered the four crewmen managing the warehouse to return with all the merchandise. As this was initiated, an officer approached the rajah's interpreter to request two pilots to guide them to the Moluccas.

Humabon was stunned by their sudden abandonment, which had in-effect broken their promise of trading with him exclusively, for now all merchandise would be gone. He also remembered Lapu-Lapu's threat. Humabon stalled and said he would consult his advisors.

The officer returned to the flagship, where Serrano and Barbosa were discussing preparations for sailing. The officer dutifully reported the rajah's response concerning the request for pilots and his apparent hesitation to comply.

'There must be some misunderstanding,' Serrano remarked. 'Perhaps the rajah's interpreter is not adequate.'

'Where is *our* interpreter?' said Barbosa, agitated. 'Where is Enrique?'

'Nursing his hand,' Serrano replied. 'He got his hand sliced open. Really it is a minor wound. Pigafetta thinks he is maybe depressed about losing the captain-general in the battle.'

'Damn him!' Barbosa fumed. 'He needs to go on shore. I will see to it.'

Pigafetta was in a bunk opposite Enrique's in the captain-general's cabin when he heard a loud rap on the door, then it banged open. Barbosa nodded to Pigafetta whose face was swollen from the poison arrow wound. He then turned to Enrique who was wrapped in a blanket curled up in a fetal position.

Barbosa shook him hard. 'Get up. We need you on shore.'

'I cannot,' Enrique responded with his head still buried in the blanket. 'My wound prevents me.'

'Nonsense. Look at Pigafetta. *He* has a wound. You are barely scratched.'

'I will not. My master is dead and now I am a free man according to his written will.'

'You will obey me, by God,' Barbosa yelled. 'If you do not, then your freedom will be void. Even though the captain is dead, you will not be freed nor released. When we return to Spain, you will still be the slave of my sister—Beatriz—the captain-general's wife. I will see to it. Now get up or I will have you flogged!'

Enrique clenched his jaw and slowly rose from his bunk. 'I shall do as you command,' he said, and then proceeded to shore. But Enrique did not love the sea.

He did not love Barbosa, nor the fleet, nor the idea of continuing the voyage. Fernão Magalhaes had been his savior, his benefactor, in fact, a father to him. His God did not protect him, and he was dead. He had brought Enrique to the far side of the world and abandoned him.

Within a few minutes of meeting with Rajah Humabon, Enrique realized the rajah was going through the same experience. Perhaps there was an answer to both of their dilemmas.

'As I am sure you are aware, the fleet is preparing to depart,' Enrique said. 'But they will surely return one day with a great armada and subdue your kingdom, for they are full of greed and lust for power.'

The rajah frowned. 'You sure they will do so?'

'Do you remember when we first met? Where is the Malay trader—the Moor from Siam? Did he not say this very same thing to you then?'

Humabon looked upward briefly, thinking, then looked at Enrique and clenched his jaw.

'Besides, you already know the answer. Look at your women that they have defiled without any remorse, all the while proclaiming they follow the true faith of Christianity.'

Humabon nodded. He knew the island men were jealous of their wives, sisters, and daughters. They had to watch as they were enticed and lured away by the foreign interlopers, and they had expressed their displeasure openly, sometimes without restraint.

Enrique could tell by the rajah's expression that he had hit a nerve and continued, 'I am sure many of your chieftains will turn on you for making such an alliance with these devils. But, if you were to commandeer their ships, weapons, and merchandise, you would be sole ruler in these lands, even over Lapu-Lapu, if you should choose to do so.'

231

A smile crept across the rajah's face. It was as if fate was playing into his hand. He considered the logistics for a moment, then looked at Enrique. 'Very well. You shall return to your men as if nothing has occurred and tomorrow accompany them back on shore for a banquet before the departure. Everything can be taken care of at that time. But fear not, I will place you under my care.'

On the following morning, May 1, the rajah sent a messenger with an invitation. He had prepared all the jewels and gold as promised for the emperor. But he desired it to be presented in proper custom, accompanied with a great feast and dancing girls for entertainment. The news of a farewell extravaganza spread among the men and the boat crews began to ready the skiffs in eager anticipation. Juan Serrano, who seemed suddenly troubled by something, approached his joint fleet commander, Duarte Barbosa, on the quarterdeck.

'Are you all right?' Barbosa asked.

'I think we should not leave our ships,' Serrano cautioned.

"What has gotten into you?'

'This is an uncertain time. We should not trust everyone.'

'A feast to collect our due,' Barbosa said. 'Then we set sail for the Moluccas. All according to plan. What reason for concern is there?'

'Just a feeling I have,' Serrano replied. 'Besides, how does this honor our captain-general? We should refuse to participate in a feast after such a loss.'

'Is that not like calling oneself sick on Friday, to avoid fasting?' Barbosa scowled. 'My sir Serrano, have you been overcome by fear? Are you suddenly afraid?'

Serrano took this as a slap in the face. 'To prove you the contrary, my sir Duarte Barbosa, I shall be the first.'

The dare was answered as Serrano was the first to disembark. But some men had overheard him, and they chose to remain on the ships along with those who were either too sick or wounded to attend. This included Pigafetta, who could still only see clearly through one eye.

In all, 26 crewmen rowed ashore, mostly officers and skilled men. All three captains, two pilots, two clerks, the master-at-arms, the chaplain, and the interpreter Enrique were among them. When the party landed, Rajah Humabon greeted them as their personal escort to the feast site. However, the master-at-arms, Gómez de Espinosa, was at the rear of the procession with the pilot, Carvalho, when he noticed something odd. The prince's older brother, who had been miraculously healed, had taken Chaplain Valderrama aside, and was escorting him to his house.

'You see that?' Espinosa whispered to Carvalho.

'Yes. Something is not right,' Carvalho replied. 'We should return to the ship and caution the others.'

The two quietly boarded their skiff and rowed back to the flagship. The deck crew helped them aboard.

'What did you forget?' the watch officer joked.

'Something is not right,' Carvalho said. 'All hands on deck. Warn the other ships.' But before the order could go out, loud shouts, and screams emanated from the banquet site.

Carvalho yelled: 'Weigh anchor!'

The crews hustled. The gunners readied the artillery and Carvalho nodded.

'Fire!' the gun commander ordered. The ship's guns pounded the village with their broadsides. By now the other two ships had been alerted and messages passed. They, too, opened-up on the village. In a moment, a group of men were seen moving in the village. Carvalho called a cease fire. The islanders brought Captain Serrano to the beach. He was tied up and bleeding.

Serrano yelled, 'Cease your artillery for you will kill me as well!'

Carvalho shouted back, 'Are the others dead?'

'Yes. All except the priest and the interpreter. They ambushed us and butchered us like animals. Please give them what they want.'

'What do they request?'

'One cannon.'

Carvalho nodded. 'Very well. We will send a boat.'

A skiff was loaded with an iron cannon and sent to the shoreline. But once it arrived, the natives insisted that they send another. Again, the skiff was sent. The villagers insisted on more. It became quickly evident that this was a ruse. The fleet was now in danger from an attack from their own guns. Carvalho refused to comply with any further demands.

Serrano pleaded, 'Do not leave me to these barbarians! Please my friend, send a squad of armed men to my rescue.'

Carvalho and Serrano had been friends, but Carvalho realized any former loyalties were subservient to the safety of the fleet. He waited until the skiff was secure, then yelled, 'Raise the sails!'

'Please! Send a boat!' Serrano began to weep as he pleaded for help. 'Once you leave, they will slaughter me as the others. Have pity!'

Carvalho knew it was the right decision, and there was too much at stake. The fleet had already suffered all the loss it could sustain. Knowing his fate was sealed, Serrano cursed his old friend, 'Damn you Carvalho! On Judgment Day, may God require an accounting of your soul.'

The islanders dragged him away. As the ships left the harbor, the men watched the natives tearing down the mountain-top cross and smashing it into pieces.

The diminished fleet sailed out of the harbor, past Mactan and into the Cebu Strait. Carvalho soon realized he had barely enough men to work the sails. The other ships were slow in maneuvering also. Off the coast of Bohol Island, in the relative safety of an open bay, Carvalho dropped anchor, and called a meeting of the remaining officers in order to assess what was left of the crew, and how they might proceed.

As if the death of Fernao Magalhães was not enough, the fleet had lost most of its senior officers in the massacre. All three captains had been killed, namely, Duarte Barbosa, Juan Serrano, and Affonso de Goes. With the death of fleet astronomer and pilot Andrés de San Martin, only two pilots remained, Francisco Albo and João de Carvalho. Of the shipmasters, only Giovanni Battista di Polcevera and Juan Cano remained. The entire crew was now reduced to 115 of the original 265 who had left Spain.

As the only commissioned pilot, Carvalho was next in line of seniority. He was appointed captain of the *Trinidad,* and designated fleet commander.

To captain the V*ictoria,* the crew elected Gomez de Espinosa, the former master-at-arms of the *Trinidad,* over the more senior Basque ship builder Juan del Cano whom they still resented for his part in the Port San Julian mutiny. Del Cano might have helmed the *Concepción,* but with the severe shortage of manpower, they decided to sail on with the best two ships. They divided up men and supplies, and then the *Concepción* was burned at anchor, off Bohol Island.

17

On May 6, 1521, as the charred hull of the *Concepción* rested at the bottom of the Cebu Straight, halfway around the world a weathered vessel entered the port of Seville. The San Antonio had not been expected to return for many more months. The ship of mutineers had returned with a count of 55 surviving crew. During their return voyage from the South Atlantic to Spain, the giant on board had died, perhaps related to exposure to the tropical heat in contrast to the cool regions of Patagonia. The main conspirators—Pilot Estevão Gomes and treasurer Gerónimo Guerra as acting commander—had overtaken Captain Álvaro de Mesquita in the straits and he remained their prisoner.

The Casa de la Contratación immediately confined the crews until they submitted all their depositions regarding their voyage, for they were all suspects of malfeasance due to their early return. The leading officers had already formulated a coordinated and unified response among the crews. Pilot Gomes had strategically left Guerra in command due to his Castilian lineage, and more importantly, his family relation with De Haro—the main private financier of the Armada of the Moluccas. The Casa solicited 53 of the 55 crewmen's depositions.

On May 12, Juan Recalde, accountant for the Casa, complained in a letter to Archbishop Juan Fonseca about the tedious and lengthy task of collecting and assimilating 53 varying accounts. He claimed it took half a day per testimony to record the complete events that transpired since leaving Seville. His complaining did him no good; the accounts were each taken in his presence.

The leading officers confessed they had entered a strait but could not confirm it led to a western sea beyond. The channel's depth, strong currents, and saltiness, however, did lead them to believe it to be so.

The mutineers had pre-planned a scathing attack against their former captain-general, all in a coordinated effort to deflect and obfuscate from their own misdeeds. They accused Fernão Magalhães as a Portuguese loyalist, and that he was bent on a mission to destroy the armada, thus depriving Spain access to the Moluccas, and thereby giving Dom Manuel of Portugal a resounding victory. They claimed he was secretive about the route and leveled a rather false testimony that he was unwilling to consult with his captains. The conspirators further insinuated he ordered brutal tortures and murder in Port San Julian. Deliberately they distorted and falsified the actual events by claiming the flagship and other vessels never returned to the rendezvous point. After a lengthy search without success, they decided to return to Spain, for their supplies were diminished greatly due to Magalhães' constant delays and poor leadership.

The officers then accused the captain-general's cousin, Captain Mesquita, of insubordination by refusing the unanimous decision to return to Spain, and that he stabbed Gomes in the leg, which Gomes answered by plunging a dagger into Mesquita's hand. But in fact, it was Gomes that initiated the mutiny.

Mesquita was alone in defending the honor of both himself and Magalhães. He immediately proclaimed his innocence and insisted to the Casa that he was tortured into making a formal statement in support of the mutineers. He presented them with a formal record of the proceedings in Port San Julian, over which he presided. The documents had been concealed on board the San Antonio, and now he offered them in his defense. But due to an anti-Portuguese sentiment instigated and stoked by the conspirators, he was not believed.

Later, Archbishop Fonseca summoned the leading officers to Burgos for additional questioning and were all held in custody. He was incensed when informed about the actions taken against his son, Captain Cartagena, and the priest, both marooned on the small island and left to their uncertain fate. Fonseca inquired why the commanders did not search and recover the marooned men. Gomes and Guerra concocted excuses. They claimed to have tried, but the vessel was swept out to sea by strong winds, and they could not return to search for the provisions on board were severely diminished.

Gomes had always been extremely antagonistic against the captain-general, for it was Magalhães that had secured the crown's approval of commanding the Armada of the Moluccas over his own proposed plans to the Spice Islands. Furthermore, Magalhães never trusted his loyalty and had twice passed him over for the captaincy of the Trinidad. Gomes, Guerra, and the other leading mutineers continued their combined testimony against Magalhães until they were finally released from captivity. Mesquita was the sole witness defending Magalhães and the actual events of the voyage, but Fonseca and the Casa refused to believe him, and he thus remained a prisoner.

While the events in Seville ran their course, the remaining two-ship fleet of Fernão Magalhães' grand expedition had sailed past Bohol and headed off to the southwest, by dead reckoning, the general direction toward Brunei. They continued past an island called Panilonghon (Panglao) where Pigafetta described the natives as black as the men in Ethiopia.

On board the flagship *Trinidad*, Captain-General Juan de Carvalho, and Master Giovanni Battista di Polcevera were discussing their sailing plan. Due to their vast experience as navigators, both officers shared the pilot duties.

Pigafetta climbed the stairs to the quarterdeck, then addressed them, 'I have the provisions report sir.'

'What is the status?' Carvalho asked.

'We estimate two weeks until we run out, even with rationing.'

'Two weeks?' Carvalho asked in dismay. 'That is all? Are you certain?'

'Yes sir.'

'It is a shame we had no time to take on supplies in Cebu,' Polcevera remarked with disdain. He never understood how Carvalho abandoned Juan Serrano and left without a fight.

'Yes, a shame,' the captain-general muttered. 'Polcevera, take us into the next suitable harbor.'

As supplies ran out, the ships finally anchored in Quibit, a port off the Mindanao Peninsula. Not long after the crews dropped anchor and secured the ships, a large proa rowed out from the shore to the flagship, *Trinidad*. As it came alongside, the crews lowered rope nets for the guests to climb on board. The commanders of both Spanish vessels were gathered on the main deck.

Once the guests climbed aboard the main deck, an ornately dressed man of their company addressed the officers through an interpreter.

'I am Rajah Calanao. Welcome to my land. What can I do for you? Do you wish to trade merchandise?'

'Yes, very much so,' Carvalho replied. 'We need provisions.'

'What do you offer in return?' Calanao asked.

Carvalho looked around the deck crowded with salvaged gear, and noticed the skiff salvaged from the scuttled *Concepción* taking up too much deck space. 'I can give you that,' he said.

Calanao's eyes opened wide. He smiled, and exclaimed, 'A good trade! Let us seal our peace with blood.'

The commanders looked at one another, puzzled. Calanao drew a dagger from his waist and sliced open his left hand. He smeared blood over his face, tongue, and all over his body. The officers opened their shirts and did likewise, in order to confirm the peace.

Calanao said, 'Please come and examine our foods and select what you desire. I would like to bring you to my home and provide a feast.'

After the events in Cebu there was not much enthusiasm for going ashore.

'You are captain-general of the fleet,' Cano said. 'Since it is your overall responsibility, perhaps you should be the one to go ashore.'

'No need for that,' Carvalho said. 'We will convey to the rajah's interpreters what kinds of foods we need, and his own men can bring them.'

'I would like to go ashore,' Pigafetta said. 'There is much to be observed here.'

'You are just as likely to wind up dead,' Carvalho replied. 'But that is fine, do as you wish.' He waved his hand toward Pigafetta and turned toward Rajah Calanao.

'I am afraid I must pass on your generous offer to visit your castle. We will need to proceed straightaway. Mr. Pigafetta shall accompany you as you procure our needs—if this is acceptable.'

'I understand,' Calanao said, his disappointment obvious. But he smiled at Pigafetta and gestured to his canoe where his men waited. 'Let us proceed then.'

Pigafetta was escorted into Calanao's canoe. The men put their oars to the water, and they skimmed away from the Trinidad across the bay to the mouth of a main tributary leading inland. As they proceeded up the river, the rajah and his leading men stripped off their loincloths and began singing merrily in time with their rowing. Pigafetta, having become accustomed to the uninhibited lifestyles of the natives, smiled, and nodded along with them. It was well after dark when they finally arrived at Rajah Calanao's house. Still, they feasted and drank, and before long the rajah indicated where Pigafetta should sleep for the night.

'In the morning we will load up with foods and return to the ship,' he explained.

I appreciate your hospitality,' Pigafetta said.

In the light of the following morning, Pigafetta noticed the rajah's house was decorated with an abundance of gold urns and bowls. He asked the interpreter, 'Where do you find the gold?'

'Come, I will show you,' the interpreter said.

Two guides escorted Pigafetta and the interpreter a short distance from the rajah's house to a steep hill overlooking several ridges. 'There,' the interpreter said as he pointed to a valley. 'More gold pieces than hairs on our heads. But we have no manner to extract it in great quantities. But there is so much of it. What we use is easy to get.'

Pigafetta wondered to himself as he mentally calculated the value.

'Here,' said the interpreter, reaching to the ground. He handed Pigafetta a small nugget. 'A souvenir for your long journey.'

'Thank you,' Pigafetta said. He smiled as he slipped it into his coat pocket.

They returned to Rajah Calanao's house where the rajah was busy dispatching his men to fetch supplies for his guests. Early in the afternoon, the proa was loaded and they were ready to depart. As Pigafetta climbed aboard he noticed the foodstuffs were mostly fruits, fowl, and fish. The fleet would need to stop again, more sooner than later.

The trip down river to the *Trinidad* went relatively quick, as they approached, Rajah Calanao was pleased to see the Spaniards had taken his boat off the deck and put it in the water. He directed his men to row up next to it.

As the proa pulled up to the ship, Pigafetta looked up to see Carvalho looking over the goods on board the proa. The commander frowned. 'Most of this is perishable. It will not last us long.'

'Sorry sir, this is what they have available,' Pigafetta said. They climbed aboard as Calanao's interpreter explained Carvalho's comment.

'I am sorry my brother,' Calanao said to Carvalho. He sulked for a moment. He looked at Pigafetta, then Carvalho, and said something to his interpreter. The interpreter addressed the ships' officers.

'If you sail west, you can find a place called Brunei. It has much gold, spices, and provisions.'

'I have heard of this place,' Carvalho said. 'Thank you, my brother, for the confirmation.'

Rajah Calanao bowed politely, then climbed over the railing. Once he had secured his prize and began heading back to the mouth of the river, the Spaniards prepared their ships to return to sea.

Carvalho ordered the expedition to weigh anchor, sailing toward the west, then changing course south and west. Even after only a couple days crossing the Sulu Sea, it was apparent the food supplies were being consumed quickly. The *Trinidad* and *Victoria* made for the next land mass they encountered.

Arriving at Cagayan Island, they encountered a community of Moors who had been banished from the island of Borneo. They had never seen Europeans and believed they were perhaps malevolent heavenly beings, and they were not very welcomed. Little food was obtainable here, but some natives informed the captains there was a large island to the north with a great quantity of provisions. The Spaniard ships were soon back at sea.

After consuming the perishables, the fleet now had only eight days of supply remaining, and not very much was good. Desperate with hunger, they sailed west by northwest for 25 leagues, finally arriving at Palawan Island where they found a warm welcome. The local ruler desired immediately to make a blood compact. He cut his chest, then marked his forehead with the blood as a sign of peace. The ship's officers did the same to seal the peace.

The island was abundant in pigs, goats, poultry, bananas, coconuts, sugarcanes, sweet potatoes, figs, and especially rice—a non-perishable item of crucial importance to life at sea. Finding such a bountiful island, the men called the place, *The Land of Promise*, for they had reached a stage of hunger at which they were willing to leave the ships and to remain in whatever land they found in order to survive.

The few days they were in port allowed the men some time ashore. Pigafetta wandered the shore and noted the people had many poison-tipped weapons, and a great love for betting on cock fights. One afternoon, as they were taking on provisions, a black man named Bastião came to the *Trinidad* and introduced himself in broken Portuguese. Surprised to hear their own language, some of the officers inquired how he had learned it. He claimed to have acquired a working knowledge of it in the Moluccas, where he had become a Christian. All the men who knew of Fernão Magalhães' friend murmured excitedly when he mentioned the name Francisco Serrão. Bastião said he had heard they were looking for a local navigator and insisted he could guide them to Brunei. The officers accepted his offer, although the ships were not ready to leave just yet, as they were still procuring supplies. The man said he would return, but when they were set to depart on June 21, he never appeared.

'What shall we do, captain-general?' Polcevera asked.

We cannot wait any longer,' Carvalho replied. 'The wind is favorable. Give the command to weigh anchor.'

The *Trinidad* and *Victoria* began making way, just as a junk made the entrance to the harbor. Carvalho and Polcevera looked at each other.

'Shall I signal Cano on the *Victoria*?' Polcevera asked.

'Send him on their left flank,' Carvalho said, then called down to the crew on deck. 'Prepare to board!'

The battle was decisive and quick. The Spaniard force commandeered the junk and captured three Muslim seamen, two of whom were pilots. The Spanish ships then sailed on, past the southern end of Palawan. They passed between the islands of Balábac and Banguey, and sometime later sighted the mountains of Borneo. The native pilots were able to assist in navigating the dangerous shoals along the coast. Pilot Albo had noted in his journal that they had to sail near land because of the reefs, and always had to use a sounding lead, because it was "a very vile coast." Brunei itself was also surrounded by dangerous shoals to the extent that without a native pilot they might have shipwrecked. They sailed along the length of the island a good distance before making the harbor, a bustling, crowded port, busy with commerce.

Not willing to appear hostile in this Islamic stronghold, the Muslim captives were released, but only on condition they would accompany one of the ships' men to deliver a message of greeting, from the emperor of the Christians to the Rajah of Brunei. The guides agreed to this and were sent ashore in a skiff with the messenger.

The following day of July 9, two fishing boats escorted a large proa toward the ships accompanied by the sound of drums on board. The proa was elaborately decorated in gold at the bow and stern. At the bow flew a white and blue banner with peacock's feathers attached to the top of the pole. A delegation of eight elderly statesmen, sent by the local rajah, boarded the *Trinidad*. Pigafetta recorded their visit in his journal:

> They seated themselves on a carpet in the stern, and they presented to us a painted wooden jar full of betel and areca, which are the fruits that they always chew, with orange flowers. The said jar was covered with a cloth of yellow silk. Also, they gave us two cages full of poultry, a pair of goats, three jars full of distilled rice wine, and some bundles of sugarcane. And they did likewise for the other ship. Then they embraced us, and we took leave. The said rice wine is clear as water, but so strong that some of our men became intoxicated, and they call it *Arach*.

The delegation included several of the city's elders, and one of them stepped forward, speaking through a translator. 'Rajah Siripada has heard of the sacking of Malacca by ships of the King of Portugal.

We have come to enquire if you are from that king, and the reason for your visit.'

The Spaniard and Portuguese crewmen looked at one another. Carvalho smiled wryly, and nodded at Gomez de Espinosa, as if he should go ahead and answer.

'We are servants of the King of Spain,' Espinosa replied. 'We only wish to trade in peace. As of now, we need to resupply with wood and water, and especially food, for a long voyage.'

Once this was conveyed to them, the dignitaries smiled, and relaxed. They indicated they would convey the visitors' greetings to Rajah Siripada and bring his answer to them.

Nearly a week went by before there was any news from the rajah, but on the sixth day, a great fanfare arose near the shore as three boats rowed toward the Spanish ships carrying a royal delegation. Drums and *tamborins* heralded their approach. Those aboard removed their head wear and donned it in a salute to the visitors. In response, the Spanish ships fired off a battery, without shot. The booming guns earned cheers from the shore, and another salute from the welcoming delegation.

Two of the boats came alongside the *Trinidad* and *Victoria*. The islanders passed across all manner of rice cake delicacies. From the third boat, the delegation reported that the rajah welcomed them to Brunei and had granted they should resupply whatever wood and water they needed, as well as come ashore at their liberty. In the meantime, they were prepared to escort a delegation from the Spanish expedition to the rajah's palace for an official audience. The ships' officers quickly met to discuss their response.

'I should not go, or any other Portuguese,' Carvalho said. 'Someone may recognize our dialect. Pigafetta, you are most practiced in matters of royalty. Perhaps you should lead the delegation.'

Pigafetta smiled. 'As you wish,' he said. 'I will do my best for the King of Spain,' he replied. It was agreed that Espinosa would accompany him, and several other Spaniards were quickly chosen. After selecting gifts from the storeroom to present the rajah and to the members of the welcome committee, Pigafetta led the entourage onto the rajah's boat. They were rowed to the shore, where they were to await an escort from the Palace.

Most of the housing in Brunei was built over salt water, with wood and bamboo houses, all constructed on tall beams over the shallow waters near the shore. As the entourage waited on the boat, Pigafetta learned from the locals that there were roughly 25,000 such family households. When the tide rose, the women went by boat to the shoreline to barter or purchase daily supplies for their families.

After waiting two hours on the boat, an escort of 12 men from the palace arrived with two elephants. The Spanish crew was invited to climb into the silk howdahs that were strapped to the elephant's backs. There were an additional 12 escorts to carry the gifts to the rajah, which they placed in large porcelain jars covered by silk cloth. They then led the procession to the governor's house for a fine meal and comfortable night's rest before making the further journey to the Palace.

The next day at noon, the gift bearers again escorted Pigafetta and his companions on the elephants to the Palace. The procession went along city streets which were lined with men who were armed with spears, swords, and shields. It was a spectacle meant to impress and deter.

The Palace itself was made of brick, with towers like a fortress, armed with 56 brass cannons, and 6 of iron. The elephants entered the courtyard and the guests dismounted. Following the governor and his entourage, they climbed a ladderway and entered a large hall, full of Brunei's nobility.

As they entered the hall, Pigafetta took in the expanse of the palace interior. At the far end of this large hall was another one, higher but not so large, hung with silk drapery. On either side were windows with red curtains, which were pulled back to let in light.

At the back of this hall were hundreds of warriors, naked, standing at the ready with swords and fighting stakes raised to protect the rajah. Beyond them was a wall with a window covered with a crimson curtain. As Pigafetta and the Spanish entourage were seated on a carpet with their gifts placed before them, the crimson curtain was pulled back. In a room beyond sat the rajah. He appeared to be about 40 years old. With him was one of his young sons, and they sat and chewed betel nut as a congregation of the wives of elders and royalty stood behind them.

One of the rajah's advisors approached Pigafetta. "When you are introduced to the rajah, you must put your hands together over your head, bow three times, and then raise each leg, blowing kisses to the rajah.'

Pigafetta explained this to his companions. Unlike him, they were not so used to the manners of court and scoffed at the notion. But all of them repeated the motions as the advisor performed it in front of them, and again when each was introduced.

'You cannot speak to the rajah, but if you wish to send a message, I will inform my superior, and he will then communicate it to one of the governor's brothers who is in the smaller hall. He will then speak through that tube inserted in that wall over there to another inside with the rajah.'

Tell him the King of Spain sends greetings and highest regards,' Pigafetta said. 'On behalf of this king we have come from the other side of the world to establish new trade routes. King Carlos further presents these gifts as a small tribute of respect and friendship to Rajah Siripada.' He gestured at the vases containing the gifts from the ship's store.

The host conveyed the message to his supervisor and was then passed up to the rajah. The escorts stood in front of the vases as the message was relayed to the rajah. When he nodded, the vases were opened one by one, with each escort holding up the contents and announcing what it was. At each mention, Rajah Siripada nodded once and appeared to be unimpressed. Nevertheless, when the presentation ended, the rajah grinned widely and spoke to his brother through the tube. The message soon came to the Spanish delegation.

'Rajah Siripada welcomes the emissaries of the King of Spain to Brunei. You are permitted to take wood and water and are welcome to stay as long as you deem necessary. So long as respect and warm regards remain between us, the ships and crews of the King of Spain will be welcome to Brunei and the shelter of our harbor. But should this trust be broken, the warriors before you, and in the street as you approached, and many more like them, will be ready to defend the city as they have done in the past. Please enjoy your time here. The Governor may assist you in procuring items for your journey.'

With this, servants of the rajah came up to the members of the fleet delegation and presented each of them with an assortment of crimson clothes, silk, and gold. The meeting was concluded, and the curtains were quickly drawn. The escorts led the delegation out of the palace and back down to the elephants, then they departed to the governor's house to feast for two more days before finally returning to the ships.

For three weeks, the fleet remained stationed in the harbor gathering supplies, including necessary items to repair the ships. But then, on the morning of July 28, the crew awoke to find four armed junks anchored between the fleet and the bar, potentially blocking any exit. It was uncertain to the ship's officers if they intended trade or were present in that location for some other purpose. After the events in Cebu, the men feared the latter. To compound the situation, three crewmen had not yet returned from their mission ashore to locate caulking materials, and Carvalho's young son, born in Brazil, had gone along with them. The delayed return further added to their concern. The Portuguese and Spanish crewmen eyed the junks suspiciously while they carried on ship repairs.

The next morning, July 29, a massive flotilla of 100 proas approached from the shore. Another 100 smaller vessels accompanied them. Carvalho called a council meeting with his officers on board the *Trinidad*, including Pigafetta as fleet recorder.

'As you can see, a sizeable force has been building against us,' Carvalho said. 'What shall we do gentlemen? Fight or run?'

'We all remember the massacre at Cebu,' Cano said. 'Is there any doubt this is a hostile action? They are blocking the harbor exit! If we do not act quickly, we are trapped and easy targets.' The other officers all supported this notion.

'Very well,' Carvalho replied. 'Let us weigh anchor and attack!'

Once they returned to their stations, the two ships moved toward the junks, then quickly came around to level broadsides at them. Two of the junks slipped anchors to escape the bombardment, but they grounded on the shoals. The Spanish guns thundered as they had for the salute, but this time cannon shot blasted across the decks of the remaining junks. The *Victoria* came alongside one and it was quickly boarded. After the devastating cannon bombardment, the remaining crew were unable to put up much resistance. The Spanish took most of them alive.

One of the prisoners was a prince, the son of a Rajah on Luzon, who was also the captain-general to the Rajah of Brunei. He had returned to repair his vessel after leading a punitive mission against another rajah who had changed fealty from Brunei to Java. In addition to the prince, 16 others, and three young virgin princesses of exceptional beauty were taken prisoner. The officers and crews watched as the prisoners were led on board the *Trinidad*.

Everyone took special notice of the prince and three beautiful women as they were escorted to Carvalho's quarters. Two sailors had followed them surreptitiously, then stationed themselves behind a crate situated near the cabin door. Through the cabin's iron-barred window, they saw Carvalho hand the prince a handful of gold coins and overheard him offer the prince his freedom on condition he, in turn, would ask the rajah for the release of their own hostages. The prince was soon released and escorted to shore, but the three ladies were confined to Carvalho's quarters to serve as his personal harem.

Later in the day, when the crew had resumed repairs on the ship, the two seamen approached Pigafetta on the main deck.

'Sir, can we have a word with you?' one of the sailors asked.

'What is it?'

'We just thought we should say something,' he replied. 'We believe the captain-general has been acting in a manner unbecoming his station.'

Pigafetta looked at them for a moment. 'You mean regarding the women?'

'Yes, but also making deals without consulting the other commanders.'

Pigafetta leaned forward, and said, quietly, 'You should be careful of your words. You know the penalties for sedition and mutiny.'

'Yes sir,' the other nearby replied. 'But we saw him pay gold to the prince in exchange for his release.'

Pigafetta stared at them. 'You will testify to this? In front of the other officers?'

'Yes sir,' they both replied.

'Very well. Keep this between yourselves. If I hear this from anyone else, I will come looking for you. In the meantime, I will bring this forward when the opportunity presents itself. Fair enough?'

'Yes, sir.' The men returned to their duties, and Pigafetta to his, though somewhat more disturbed than before. The fleet leadership had become unbearably tenuous, and they still had the other half of the world to traverse.

When Rajah Siripada learned about the flare up in the harbor, he sent a messenger to convey his outrage over the actions of the Spanish fleet. The messenger explained to the ship's officers that the flotilla of proas sent from shore were on a mission to subdue a region hostile to the rajah's rule. The messenger then displayed the heads of the rajah's enemies as proof.

The officers were astounded. Carvalho answered with a plea for Rajah Siripada to deliver the three crewman who had not yet returned from shore. But the rajah remained indignant over the actions of the Spanish fleet and refused their request.

They waited two more days for release of the hostages, but nobody returned. Another message was sent to the rajah, saying that the fleet would wait two more days. Two more days passed without even a reply. Carvalho abruptly ordered the expedition under way.

The *Trinidad* and *Victoria* left the harbor of Brunei, leaving an able seaman, a smith, and Carvalho's own son to their fate. In addition, two Greek seamen who had converted to Islam, were suspected of desertion. The fleet roster had been reduced another five men.

Pigafetta approached the pilot, Polcevera, on the quarterdeck when Carvalho was below, in his quarters.

'Antonio,' Polcevera said, when he saw Pigafetta come up on deck. 'Are you on watch so soon?'

'It is a serious matter, I'm afraid,' Pigafetta said.

'What is it?'

'The crew are shocked that we have left our men so soon,' Pigafetta replied. 'As am I, to be quite honest. It is unfathomable that our captain-general has left even his own son, Joãzito. He seems to have no remorse for anyone or anything.'

'Yes, I have witnessed these things also,' Polcevera said. 'Everyone has. There are no secrets at sea. He has developed a high opinion of himself.'

Pigafetta nodded. 'But, Giovanni, you should know of something else I have been burdened with.'

'What would that be?' Polcevera asked.

'Two of the crew came to me claiming to have witnessed an exchange of gold between the prince and the captain-general for the prince's release. Perhaps I am too used to the manner of Captain-General Magalhães. He always consulted his officers in important matters, especially regarding fleet funds.'

'You are serious?'

'Yes,' Pigafetta replied. 'I did not want to believe it myself. But they were adamant. I told them to hold their tongues and allow me to report the matter.'

'It is scandalous, especially considering his rash behavior lately,' Polcevera said. 'First, he abandons his long-time friend Juan Serrano in Cebu without a fight. Then he trades away a valuable skiff for perishable foods.' Polcevera shook his head. 'He abandons his men, even his own son! And now this.'

'Yes,' Pigafetta replied with a nod. 'His actions seem contrary to the good order of the fleet.'

'That's a good way to phrase it,' Polcevera said. 'I cannot believe this. He could have kept the prince for leverage to rescue the hostages. And he dares to pretend that prince we captured would act as a fair mediator. At least if he kept the ladies unsullied, they could have been additional leverage. He has no self-discipline.'

'Well, that is another story entirely,' Pigafetta said. 'The men are pretty upset the women are kept on board in his cabin. Fernão Magalhães never allowed women on board. It only causes strife among the crew. But there is little I can do about any of it. I am only here at the behest of the king to help protect his enterprise. I am not in the direct fleet chain of command.'

'Yes, this is a fair point,' Polcevera said. 'And it is true, Carvalho has traded every advantage for a little personal gain. I will bring up the matter in consultation with the other officers. Until then it is best if those men keep their mouths shut, so that morale does not become worse than it already is.'

'I'll speak to them,' Pigafetta said. 'Let me know when you want to bring them forward.'

'Aye,' Polcevera replied. 'It will be soon.'

The fleet retraced their route northwest along the Borneo coastline in search of a suitable place to repair the ships. The *Trinidad* had already been taking on water, and the shorthanded crew had trouble continuously manning the pumps. They were becoming exhausted. Furthermore, the *Victoria* was without an experienced pilot familiar with the dangerous reefs, and began tracking to the inside when she grounded, just off Bilabon Island. Many of the crew jumped off the side to try to get a foothold on the reef and push her up with the waves, but it was difficult. At last, a large enough wave swept her up and forward, and she was free of the shoal.

Not long afterward, off Cape Sampanmangio, the heavier *Trinidad* grounded on a shoal. No effort of the crew could help dislodge her, so she sat marooned for four hours, crews inside pumping furiously the whole time, before she was released by the change of tide.

On August 15, the fleet finally found a safe harbor, in a small island off the northern end of Borneo. Pigafetta called it *Cimbonbon* in his journal. The fleet officers agreed to remain here to complete the repairs they had begun in Brunei, mainly careening, and caulking the hulls. But they were still short of materials for repairs, so their stopover dragged on for 42 days. Each man, to the best of his ability, contributed to the several ongoing team efforts. But the most difficult tasks were not necessarily the repairs. At this point in the journey all their footwear was worn or shredded, so foraging for wood, barefoot among the briars and sharp thorn bushes, became the least favored task.

Dangerous wild boars also lived on the island. The crew killed one in the water as they passed between islands in their skiffs. Its head was measured at two and a half feet long, and it had large sharp teeth. They turned it over to the cooks.

Crocodiles also roamed the island and swam along the coast. Giant oysters abounded, with the flesh of one recorded at 25 pounds, and another at 44 pounds. Pigafetta discovered a tree with leaves that walked along the ground. He kept one leaf in a cage for nine days, and when he opened it up, the leaf danced about. Later, these creatures were identified as insects of the genus *phyllium orthoptera*.

During the sojourn on the island, two men died, one of infection, from wounds received in the battle of Mactan, and the other succumbed to an illness. But work on the ships continued unabated, and the repairs were eventually completed. The *Victoria* and *Trinidad* were both being outfitted to return to the open sea when Carvalho's leadership flaws were finally confronted.

On September 21, the two well-respected and veteran shipmasters- Giovanni Battista de Polcevera from the *Trinidad*, and Juan el Cano from the *Victoria*- were supported by their crews in the removal of the incompetent and self-serving Carvalho from his position of fleet commander. It was agreed Polcevera would take command of the fleet as the new captain-general for the two-ship fleet. Juan Cano continued to captain the *Victoria*, while Gomez de Espinosa was chosen to captain the *Trinidad*.

A week later, on September 27, the ships were prepared to depart. The crews made ready, and the fleet set sail on the final leg of their quest for the

Moluccas. Polcevera ordered a heading eastward through the Celebes Sea, until spotting a group of islands, situated off the southern coast of Mindanao. Coming into the islands, they encountered a large proa, whose occupants refused first to acknowledge, then answer, and finally surrender to, the larger vessels. In fact, they demanded both Spanish ships to retreat elsewhere.

On board the proa were 17 brave warriors armed with scimitars, kris daggers, and shields. They fought valiantly, until finally being overwhelmed. Seven of them were killed, and the remainder taken prisoner. In the interrogation, it was discovered they were all leading men of Mindanao, and one was a brother of the rajah. But the thing that stunned the officers of the Spanish fleet, was that the brother claimed to know Fernão Magalhães' old friend, Francisco Serrão, and in fact had visited his house in Ternate, which was one of the Spice Islands.

With this information, the fleet immediately changed course, southeast, in search of the Moluccas. For the crew, this news brought about a new sense of urgency and purpose to the impending completion of their long mission, and the relief that would come of it. But there was, as always, the task of getting there.

On October 26, a great storm arose at sea, tossing the ships about like corks and putting the fear of God and nature into the crew. Pigafetta recorded a moment of divine intervention in the midst of the storm:

> "Praying to God, we struck all the sails, and immediately our three saints appeared, dispelling all the darkness, namely St. Elmo, St. Nicholas, and St. Clara. St. Elmo remained almost two hours at the maintop, like a torch."

The fleet rode out the storm, soon making the island port of Saranghani, where gold and pearls were known to be found. They anchored in the harbor, and some of the men went ashore in the skiffs to learn more of the whereabouts of the Moluccas. After conversing with the locals, Pigafetta discovered an old man with two of his friends, who all claimed to know the way to the Moluccas. Initially, the trio agreed to guide them, but history repeated itself when the old man never appeared at the time of departure. The two younger men had shown up, however, but they also suddenly wished to leave. The pair were forced to remain and complete the job they had agreed to do.

Heading southward, the tiny Spanish fleet at last entered the Molucca Sea. As they sailed near Sangi Island, the prisoners; the captured brother of the Mindanao rajah, his son who had been with him, and one of the pilots from Saranghani Island, escaped overboard. It was quickly decided they were not a prize worth chasing, so the crew watched as the men swam for shore, the boy hanging onto his father's shoulders. They were soon swamped by a large wave, and the boy lost his grip, falling off his father's back, and disappearing into the deep.

A few days afterward, November 2, a gunner's accident on the *Trinidad* killed an armorer named Pedro Sanchez. Only two days after this, a powder explosion on the gundeck claimed the life of Gunner Juan Bautista. Finally, with great relief and little fanfare, on November 6, the fleet sighted four islands with mountain peaks. The remaining pilot from Saranghani confirmed these were four of the Spice Islands.

After losing almost half the crew in the 25 months of perilous journey, the men of the Spanish expedition had finally reached their destination. The ships cannon sounded in celebration, and the men gathered on the decks to give thanks to God, for delivering them from the perilous journey, and allowing them to cross an unknown sea to the edge of a world they had left two years before.

18

The Moluccas – November 8, 1521

Three hours before sunset, on November 8, 1521, the two-vessel Portuguese fleet anchored at a depth of 20 fathoms in the port of Tidore Island. An artillery salute was fired to announce their arrival. Tidore's volcanic peaks were much like all the Spice Islands, frequently enveloped in a misty cloud and surrounded by dense forests, all conducive to the abundance of quality cloves.

On the following day, an ornately decorated proa approached the ships. Pigafetta and some officers lowered a skiff and rowed out to greet them. A well-dressed man introduced himself in Spanish as Rajah Sultan Almanzor (Al Mansur). He was attired in a white linen shirt with the sleeve tops worked in gold and a white cloth from his waist to the ankles. On his head was a silk veil with a crown of flowers. The rajah was a Moor, 55 years old, well built, and eloquent.

Almanzor called out to the sailors in the skiff, 'Please, come on board and sit with me.'

The men clambered into the proa and seated themselves with the rajah under a silk canopy. Standing before the rajah was his son who held the royal scepter. Also standing nearby were two servants with gold basins for washing the hands and two others with gold vessels full of betel.

Almanzor addressed the men, 'I have dreamed that ships would arrive from a great distance. I have divined it by my astronomical observations of the moon.'

The officers looked at one another, unsure how to respond to his claim.

Pigafetta broke the silence, 'I am curious how you know the language of Castile?'

'I know of many things from my merchants who trade to the west, to Malacca, and India. I have known for a long time your people would arrive and thus prepared myself, learned of your kingdoms and your language.'

'Our captain-general invites you on board his ship,' Pigafetta said. 'Please do us the honor.'

The rajah nodded and the proa followed the skiff back to the *Trinidad*. Once on board. The officers dutifully kissed his hand according to the local protocol. They brought him up to the captain's quarters, but he could not enter, for he refused to ever bow or tilt his head. Thus, they climbed to the deck above, and then back down another stairway to a secondary entrance to complete the tour. Later, on the high-level poop deck, a red velvet chair was set for Almanzor and they dressed him in a robe of turquoise and yellow velvet. Captain-General Polcevera remained standing while the rest of the crew sat on the deck to do the rajah great honor.

'We have been searching for a friend in these parts,' Polcevera said. 'His name is Francisco Serrão. Have you heard of him or know where we can find him?'

The rajah scratched his chin a moment, then responded, 'Ahh, Serrão, the Portuguese captain. Yes, I heard he was trading in cloves.'

'Do you know of his location?' Pigafetta asked.

'I am uncertain, these men come and go,' he replied. 'I will inquire.'

Polcevera gave a nod to the rajah, for the moment satisfied with the answer.

'We wish to establish trade with your people,' Polcevera said.

'I know of your Spain,' Almanzor said. 'My people wish to become friends and vassals of your King Carlos.' He smiled. 'You are all welcome to my kingdom and your men will be as my children, and you will stay in our houses as if they were your own. And we shall no longer call our island Tidore, but Castile.'

The men responded to these fine words with gifts. In addition to the velvet chair and robe, they presented the rajah with exquisite clothes, caps, crystal glasses, knives, mirrors, and many other items.

'I have no ability to match such generosity,' Almanzor said. 'But I can pledge my life as a loyal servant of Spain. Please, bring your ships closer to the city. If anyone comes near, shoot them with your arquebuses.'

The ships followed the proa into the harbor near the city and then Almanzor departed to shore.

On the following day of November 10, Polcevera, along with Pigafetta and a small contingent of men, landed on shore. They were escorted by one of the rajah's advisors from just outside the city to a large timbered house with a thatched roof. They entered and saw Almanzor seated with a woman in an elevated room. On the ground floor was seated what appeared to be a harem of 200 women. The rajah noticed his foreign guests arrive and waved them to come to his table.

Once they were seated, Almanzor asked, 'I am curious, when did you depart Spain?'

'We departed on September 20, 1519,' Polcevera replied.

'The year 1519? Oh my, such a long journey. Such a long journey indeed.' Almanzor then asked about the wages promised to each crewman and other related questions pertaining to their mission. After numerous inquiries, he said, 'Please, let us pledge an alliance with your king's seal and banner.'

'We shall consider your proposal among our officers,' Polcevera cautiously replied.

'I must confess to you, captain-general, that for many years I have been at war with my neighbor, the Rajah of Ternate. But if you shall make an alliance with me, I can use my influence to bring them under Spanish rule.'

'Your proposal is appealing,' Polcevera said. 'But our main purpose here is to secure a trading arrangement for the market of cloves and other spices.'

'We have an abundance of cloves,' Almanzor said with a big smile. 'We have five islands producing them: Tidore, Ternate, Motir, Makian, and Batjan. Currently, my island has few cloves ready to harvest. But I know Batjan Island has many to harvest soon and I will visit there to arrange whatever you desire.'

'We appreciate your gracious assistance,' Polcevera said.

'Please stay for tea and a light meal before you depart.'

The officers accepted Almanzor's offer. Pigafetta spoke with the rajah's advisor during the meal and learned more of the local customs. He later entered the information in his log:

> Those kings have as many wives as they wish, but they have one wife whom all the others obey. The King of Tidore . . . can see all the others who are seated around, and to the one who pleases him most he sends word that she shall come to sleep with him that night. And after dinner, if he commands that these women eat together, they do so; if not, each of them retires and goes to eat in her own chamber. And no one may see them

without the leave and permission of the king. And if anyone is found by day or night near the king's house, he is killed. Each family and household are obliged to give to the king one or two daughters. And this king had 26 children, 8 of them sons and the rest daughters. Before this island is another very large one named Gilolo (Halmahera) inhabited by Moors and heathens. And there were (as the king told us) 2 kings among the Moors, one of them had 600 children, and the other 525. The heathens do not keep as many wives, and do not live so superstitiously as the Moors, but in the morning, as they leave the house, they worship the first thing that they see for the whole day.

On November 11, two proas approached and were accompanied by a steady beat of gongs. Assuming this to be a foreign delegation, a messenger was sent on shore to ask what should be done since they were in the jurisdiction of Tidore. Almanzor knew it was the son of the Rajah of Ternate but wishing to display his ability to be at peace with his neighbors, he gave them permission to do as they pleased.

With the delay in reception, the son of the Rajah of Ternate pulled back his proas. Pigafetta and some men rowed a skiff toward the entourage. They presented gifts to ease any mistrust due to the long delay. On board the prince's proa was an Indian who spoke Portuguese. Pigafetta noticed a Javanese woman with a young boy and girl—both fair-skinned mulattos. The Indian was requested to return with them on the skiff to the flagship.

On board the *Trinidad*, the Indian stood before the officers of both fleet vessels. Captain-General Polcevera was surrounded by the acting captains, Espinosa of the *Trinidad,* and Cano of the *Victoria*.

'Who are you?' Polcevera asked. 'How did you learn to speak Portuguese?'

'My name is Manuel and I have been baptized as a Christian. I was a servant of Pedro Afonso Lorosa and he taught me his language. My master was living in Banda but now resides in Ternate.'

'You know of a Captain Francisco Serrão?" Pigafetta asked.

'You seen the Javanese woman with her children on board the proa?' Manuel asked. 'That is the wife of Francisco Serrão and those are his children.'

The attention of all the officers were aroused. They all knew of the famed adventurer and best friend of Fernão Magalhães. It was he who was one of the great inspirations for the entire expedition to the Spice Islands.

'Where is Serrão?' Captain Espinosa asked.

'He died,' Manuel replied.

The crew gasped.

'When did he die?' Espinosa asked.

'The first week of March of this year.'

Pigafetta reflected on the date, and where they would have been on the journey. 'What a twist of fate. Fernão Magalhaes was so close to reuniting with his long-time friend, so close to achieving their goal to open a spicery enterprise. And they perished only seven weeks apart.'

The men contemplated the somber revelation.

'My lord, Pedro Afonso Lorosa, can give you a more detailed report of the captain,' Manuel said, then turned to the status in the region. Apparently, according to Manuel, the Moluccan chiefs were tired of their Portuguese overlords and were eager to ally with Spain.

'Please, ask your master, Pedro Lorosa to meet with us,' Polcevera said. 'I will write an official letter for you to deliver.'

'Yes sir,' Manuel said.

On November 12, Rajah Almanzor built a storage warehouse in just one day to accommodate the ship merchandise. Almost all the stores were brought on shore and three crewmen were posted to guard it.

The following day, the captains informed the rajah they had some Indian prisoners on board. He immediately replied they should be delivered up so that five of his leading men could parade them around the island to display the fame of Spain. The captains obliged his request and delivered over most of the prisoners, including the three beautiful ladies. The rajah then implored that they kill all the swine on board, and he would give them goats and poultry in exchange, for his island was Muslim. As per the rajah's direction, they slaughtered the pigs in an enclosed section under the deck so the people would not be offended by the sight or smell.

In the afternoon, Pedro Loroso paid a visit to the *Trinidad*. The officers sat him down in the captain's quarters. 'Your servant Manuel says you were living in Banda and have recently arrived in Ternate,' Polcevera said. 'Where did you come from before?'

'I have been stationed in India for 16 years and in Malacca for 10,' Lorosa replied.

'Manuel says you know of Captain Francisco Serrão,' Polcevera said.

'Yes. We sailed in the same fleet from Malacca 10 years ago to the Moluccas.'

'So, how did Serrão die?' Pigafetta asked.

'I may have to explain recent events. How long have you been away from Spain?'

'Two years now,' Cano replied. 'Why should that be relevant?'

'Well, many things have transpired since you left,' Larosa answered. 'I can relate some things I have heard which will help answer your question concerning your friend.'

Polcevera nodded to continue.

Larosa continued his account, 'A year ago, a large ship from Malacca visited Ternate. The captain of the vessel was Tristão de Meneses and he relayed some curious news from Iberia. A fleet of five ships had set out from Seville in search of the Moluccas and was commanded by an expatriated Portuguese named, Fernão Magalhães.'

The officers leaned forward.

Lorosa took notice of their heightened interest and continued, 'The King of Portugal was angered that Castile was set upon usurping his lucrative trade and had sent ships to blockade them, some to the Cape of Africa, and others to the Cape of St. Mary in the New World. But they all failed to locate the fleet.'

The captains sighed in relief.

'So, they have given up the search?' Cano asked.

'No. Later, King Dom Manuel was informed Magalhães had discovered a strait and had entered another great sea with intention of reaching the Moluccas.'

Cano clenched his fist and looked at Polcevera with concern.

Lorosa continued, 'Manuel wrote to Captain Diogo De Sequiera to dispatch six ships to the Spice Islands, but it was never fully implemented, for they were in a war-time engagement with the Turks in the Red Sea. Only one large galley could be employed. It had two tiers of artillery and was sent under the command of Francisco de Faria. But due to its

270

immense size, they could not navigate the dangerous reefs and currents around Malacca, and against the current headwinds, they were forced to turn back.

The commanders were again relieved at the failed search attempt.

'But I heard other news from Captain Meneses. He said that a caravel and two junks had visited Ternate to inquire about the fleet of Magalhães. They were also looking to arrest Captain Serrão.'

'Portuguese vessels in Ternate?' Cano asked with exasperation.

'Yes,' Manuel replied. 'But since finding no evidence of the fleet of Magalhães, they continued with their other mission, to secure a load of cloves. Seven Portuguese sailed the two junks to Batjan Island and left the caravel in Ternate. During their stay, the seven men abused the rajah's wives and people, although the ruler had repeatedly warned them to desist. Refusing to refrain from their lecherous and abusive behavior, they were swiftly put to death. When the crew on the caravel learned of their demise, they immediately departed for Malacca, and left the junks loaded with 400 bahar of cloves and enough merchandise to purchase 100 more bahar of cloves.'

The captains again sighed with relief at another failed attempt.

'You should know, Captain Meneses revealed to me of King Manuel's clandestine trading network in the spice trade from the Moluccas to Banda to Malacca. He never informed King Carlos of its existence.'

The officers considered this news.

'Why were they planning to arrest Serrão?' Pigafetta asked.

'Serrão loved Ternate and the islands. He wished to continue trading from here. But the Portuguese officials did not trust him and considered him a renegade, and in league with Magalhães and Spain.'

'What happened to him?' Polcevera asked.'

'First, I will tell you what has been said in public,' Larosa replied. 'Serrão had served as a mercenary and vizier to the ruler of Ternate—Rajah Boleyse (Abdul Hassan Al Buleis). In his service, he compelled the Rajah of Tidore, Almanzor, to give one of his daughters to the Rajah of Ternate, Boleyse, and to give most of the children of his leading men as hostages. A tenuous peace alliance was made, but with a simmering anger lingering in the heart of Almanzor. A reckoning was inevitable. One day Serrão returned to Tidor to purchase cloves, and during his stay was given poisoned betel. He suffered a slow death. After four days of torment, he succumbed to its effect.'

'You said what is known in public,' Polcevera said. 'Was he not poisoned?'

'He was poisoned, yes. But, I believe, from certain reliable sources, it was Captain Meneses, who hired a Malay girl of Rajah Almanzor's harem to poison him. An easy cover, since all knew of the animosity between the rajahs, and few would expect foreign involvement.' Larosa shook his head. 'I knew Serrão as a friend and have a strong distaste for those who betrayed him.'

'Remain with us Pedro,' Polcevera said. 'We will reward you with generous wages and an allotment of the profits if you return with us to Spain.'

'Your offer is tempting,' Lorosa said. 'I accept.'

With such welcome news, the captains ordered wine and food for them all.

Polcevera and the others toasted Lorosa.

The men cheered and clanked their cups together. They continued to drink and feast as they recounted stories until 3 a.m.

272

On November 15, Rajah Almanzor informed the officers he was going to Batjan for the cloves. While on the ship he curiously looked over the ship's small arms and requested a demonstration. Obliging his curiosity, they fired off rounds from arquebuses, crossbows, and culverins—which are larger than the arquebus. The rajah was ecstatic when he fired off three shots with the crossbow, which he favored over all the others.

Afterward, Polcevera pulled the rajah aside. 'You were not quite forthright in your knowledge of Captain Francisco Serrão.'

The rajah looked away quickly, but there was no way to escape the accusation, and he frowned. 'I am very sorry. I was ashamed that his death was from one of my own people, on my island.'

'Is there any other deception we should be aware of?'

'No, please be assured of this. When I realized he had a connection to you, I panicked, that is all. Please let us get on to Batjan. Your cloves will be ready, I assure you. All is well.

'Very well then,' Polcevera said, unsure if he was telling the truth about anything.

A little more than a week later, Almanzor approached the ships in his proa and accompanied by the thumping of brass drums. He announced the cloves were ready and would continue to arrive over the next four days.

It was the following day when the first load of cloves arrived as promised. The ships sounded off a salvo of cannon fire in celebration.

The rajah further confessed that he never left his island but had made an exception and came out to the ship for the love of the King of Castile. He exhorted the crew go to Spain and return with many ships so they could assist him in taking revenge upon the death of his father, who was slain on the island of Baru, and then thrown into the sea. Almanzor then declared it was customary to hold a feast to inaugurate the first load of cloves. He added that the city streets had been cleaned for the Rajah of Batjan and that one of his brothers was invited to attend. Almanzor implored the captains and men to attend the great feast.

But with the recent events at Cebu and the poisoning of Francisco Serrão, some of the men were justifiably concerned. Adding to their trepidation were the whispers between the locals and the remaining Indian prisoners they still held. Eventually, the suspicious crewmen convinced the captains to bring a counteroffer to the rajah and invite him to the ships.

Almanzor accepted the offer and boarded the *Trinidad*. The captains presented more gifts to the rajah. Polcevera gestured to four crewmen who stood nearby.

'Rajah Almanzor,' he said. 'Please accept these men into your land. They have volunteered to stay and manage our new trading enterprise. We plan to depart once the cloves are loaded.'

'So soon?' Almanzor asked in surprise. 'You should remain longer. It will take 30 days to properly load the ships. You should also be aware that the season for navigating the dangerous shoals has not yet arrived. And now, the risk of encountering Portuguese vessels is much greater.' Alamanzor first appeared agitated, then saddened that the captains would not reconsider. Exasperated, he tried one more tactic. 'If you insist on leaving now, I will be obliged to return all your merchandise that you have given me.'

The officers looked at one another, confused.

'Why is this?' Polcevera asked.

'All the other rajahs will think I betrayed you through some treachery and caused your early departure. They will believe I am a traitor.' Almanzor called to one of his servants, 'Bring me my crown.' His hands were shaking as he accepted it from the servant. He was almost to the point of weeping as he exclaimed, 'By Allah, I wish to be a loyal friend to the King of Spain.'

It was an act, and a convincing one. The captains were moved by the rajah's apparent devotion and sincerity, enough that they promised another 15 days before departing. Furthermore, they concluded by giving him the king's signature and royal banner.

The trading and the loading of cloves continued until the ship stores were bursting full.

On December 17, their departure now eminent, the captains gave the rajah a gift of some weaponry, including arquebuses, small cannons, and four barrels of powder. Also, at this time, Pedro Loroso and his family had boarded, as promised.

The next day, the Rajahs of Tidor, Gilolo, Batjan, and a son of the Rajah of Ternate, came to escort the fleet to the island of Mareh. The *Victoria* set out first and waited outside the harbor. The crew of the *Trinidad* could not weigh anchor due to a sudden leak in the hull. With the long delay, the *Victoria* returned to port to inquire about the matter. Water was gushing as if though a pipe, but nobody could ascertain the source. Men feverishly worked the pumps while others unloaded the cloves to lighten the load and spare the cargo.

Informed of the dire predicament, the rajah came to inspect the ship holds himself, but after some time without success locating the leak, he dispatched five good swimmers to dive and look for any hole. They searched under water for half an hour but found nothing. Almanzor appeared genuinely upset for the vessel was in grave danger. As water continued to gush in, the *Trinidad* began to list. Almanzor sent for three expert divers from the cape of his island, men who were known for their ability to remain under water for extended periods.

Early on December 20, three divers arrived. They immediately loosened their long hair, for any inrushing current would pull the hair toward the leak.

After an hour of fruitless searching, they had found nothing. Almanzor exclaimed with tears in his eyes, 'Who will go to Spain to give the king my lord news of me?'

A short time later, the captains convened to formulate their next course of action. Eventually, they came to a consensus. The *Victoria* would take advantage of the monsoon timing and sail with the southeast winds and attempt to steer south of Portuguese routes until reaching the Cape of Good Hope.

The *Trinidad* would remain in the islands to perform the needed repairs. By the estimated time to refurbish and reload, the captains knew the monsoon winds would prevent their return via the Indian Ocean. Therefore, rather than wait many months longer, they decided upon a daring plan. The *Trinidad* would sail north until they found westerly winds to carry them all the way across the Pacific to the Americas, at which time they would follow the coastline south to the Spanish colony in the Darién (Panama).

The rajah promised to loan 225 workers to assist the remaining crew of the *Trinidad* make needed repairs and a storage facility to hold their cargo of cloves and merchandise. He said the crews would only need to supervise the workers so as not to cause them harm in the heat, and all of them would be treated as his own children.

On last inspection before departure, the captains agreed that the *Victoria* was overloaded, and in endanger of splitting open the hull. They ordered the vessel lightened, and the surplus cloves stored in the warehouse.

On December 21, the rajah came to bid farewell to the crew of the *Victoria* and assigned two pilots to guide them through the islands as far as Timor. The *Trinidad* crewmen were given extra time to write last minute letters to their loved ones in Spain and thus delayed departure of *Victoria* until noon. It had been decided Espinosa, Polcevera, and Pancaldo would remain as leading officers for the *Trinidad*. The *Victoria* would be captained by Cano, piloted by Albo, and Pigafetta would join as supernumerary in his usual role to record events as ship chronicler.

With all the letters completed, the men embraced one another with tearful last words.

Pigafetta found his Norwegian friend on the shore. 'Hans!' he yelled as he approached. 'I heard you will stay with the *Trinidad*.'

'Yah,' Hans replied. 'They need me serve as master gunner.'

'I understand. Well, I pray the repairs go well and you arrive safely to your home. And if you ever visit Italy, bring me some salted cod. It is my favorite.'

'Sure, I will,' he said. 'You also have a safe journey.'

The two clasped arms, then parted ways.

The guns of the *Victoria* thundered a farewell salute. Some of the remaining skiffs followed them out of the harbor and shouted out blessings for a safe voyage, then watched as the *Victoria* sailed over the horizon.

19

Return to Spain – December 21, 1521 – September 6, 1522

The *Victoria* had left the harbor of Tidore with a full load of fresh cloves and crew of 60 men, made up of 47 Europeans and 13 natives. The ship made a brief stop at Mare Island to take on a load of firewood that had been precut for them and bundled per Sultan Almanzor's orders. After this, the *Victoria* sailed out into the open sea and took up a southwesterly course, bound for the Horn of Africa.

Near Motir, one of the five principal islands containing quality cloves, Pilot Albo took a reading of 191 degrees 45' longitude.

Pigafetta looked over Albo's shoulder as he recorded his reading. Pigafetta had taken to recording their daily position in his own journal. Albo seemed disturbed.

'What is it?' Pigafetta asked.

'According to this reading, the Spice Islands are in Portuguese domains, based on the Treaty of Tordesillas.'

'You are sure of this?'

'Yes,' Albo replied. 'I do not think the king will be happy.'

'Kingly problems,' Pigafetta said.

Albo smiled.

Pigafetta had also continued to build his working knowledge of the trading language of Malay. He was becoming proficient enough that he had begun conversing with one of the Moluccan pilots, an older man named Katipana. As they sailed past a group of small islands, namely Caioan, Laigoma, Giaggi, and

Caphi (Gafi), Katipana pointed at the latter and said, 'This island is inhabited by pygmies.'

'What is 'pygmy'?' Pigafetta asked.

They are people, very small,' Katipana said. 'They always happy.'

Sailing on a west by southwest course they neared another group of small islands, but the Moluccan pilots warned there were many dangerous shoals, so they altered their course southeasterly, until anchoring at an island called Sullach (Sula Besi). Pigafetta recorded that the people of this island had no king, were cannibals, and went about naked except for a piece of bark two fingers wide over their private parts.

The Moluccan pilots informed the ship's officers that many of the nearby islands were likewise inhabited by those who consumed human flesh. The *Victoria* soon returned to sea, taking up the original southwesterly course, being now clear of the shallows.

On December 27, they anchored at Buru Island, at a latitude of 3 1/2 degrees south and longitude of 194 degrees. In continuous need to replenish, Pigafetta itemized the procurement in his journal: "rice, swine goats, poultry, coconuts, sugarcanes, and sago—a food made from figs (bananas), almonds, and honey wrapped in leaves, dried in smoke, and made into fairly long pieces, and it is called canali (chiacare)."

After taking on as much as was available, they departed Buru Island and soon passed Ambon Island. The *Victoria* had entered the Banda Sea where there was no land before them, but they had a sure course for the Sunda Islands and their next resupply.

On January 8, 1522, Pigafetta was on the quarterdeck with Captain Cano and both pilots. As the *Victoria* approached the island of Mallua (Alor) at 8 1/2 degrees south, ominous clouds gathered ahead.

The winds quickly strengthened into a powerful gale and began to blow the *Victoria* toward the reefs.

El Cano began pulling on the whipstaff. 'Something is wrong!' he called. 'The rudder is not responding!'

The ship rolled and Pigafetta grabbed at the rails to catch himself, then saw the powerful current running into the hull. He looked off to the mountain side where overflowing rivers rolled into the sea. 'Captain, the currents from land are strong!'

'Albo!' Cano said. 'Help me on the whipstaff.'

The two men struggled to control the ship as the gale slammed them from the stern. After struggling against riptides for hours, the *Victoria* narrowly stayed clear of the dangerous reefs, and stood out to sea. After the storm abated, the crew inspected the hull and found significant damage. The hull was leaking, in immediate need of repair and caulking.

The crewmen took turns on the pumps, and it was still another day before they reached harbor at Alor. On January 10, Cano anchored the ship in the island bay. Pigafetta and a crew of armed men loaded the skiff with merchandise for trade. The two Moluccan pilots stood near watching.

'Will you join us, Katipana?' Pigafetta asked.

'No!' he replied. 'Dangerous place, man-eaters.'

Pigafetta and the men looked at them. Pigafetta looked at the men, and back at Katipana. 'Good to know. We will bring more weapons and gifts. Hopefully, only the latter will be necessary.'

Once on shore, the Portuguese were quickly confronted by a force of natives, men, and women, all armed with bows and arrows. They wore pieces of ox-hide which were all decorated with pig's teeth and small shells. They had goatskin tails attached on their front and backsides. The Portuguese stared in

282

amazement at the native men. They had their hair pushed up high, with bamboo pins holding it in place. Their beards were long, wrapped in leaves, and shoved into lengthy bamboo shoots. One of the crewmen standing alongside Pigafetta whispered, 'Of all the sights I have seen in my life, that is the most ridiculous of them all.'

Pigafetta chuckled and replied, 'I am certain they consider us the same and wonder how we taste in a stew.' He gestured for two crewmen to retrieve the merchandise.

The men laid out everything on the beach: trinkets of glass, silver, mirrors, and fine cloths. The women cautiously approached. They picked up the objects and smiled. The men finally lowered their weapons and beckoned the shore party to enter their village. The island was plentiful, so over the next 15 days, the Portuguese acquired what fresh provisions they could find and refurbished the vessel.

On January 25, the *Victoria* departed Mallua (Alor). Pigafetta was with Katipana on the main deck. The old pilot pointed in the distance.

'Over there is Aruchete Island,' he said. 'The people live in caves.' Katipana then pointed to his forearm. 'Tiny people.' He held his hand flat, about two and a half feet above the deck. 'Only this tall. They are all naked, hairless, and have shrill voices.' He then attempted to replicate the high pitch.

Pigafetta laughed.

'But you must know,' Katipana said. 'They have enormous ears and use one for a blanket, the other for a bed.'

Pigafetta touched Katipana's arm. 'I would probably not believe you, my friend. But having discovered giants in far off lands, who is to say there are not pygmies with giant ears?'

'Giants?' Katipana stuttered.

Pigafetta chuckled and nodded his head. 'Oh yes. There was one aboard the *San Antonio*. I wonder if he is in Spain now?'

'That would be a sight to see,' Katipana said. 'Both the giant, and Spain.'

The following day, the *Victoria* anchored off Amabau (Ambeno) on the northwestern coast of Timor, at a latitude of 9 degrees 15' south. Pigafetta went on shore alone to bargain for provisions, for what they had gathered in Mallua was perishable, and the crew was always at the edge of starvation. He met the leading chieftain who agreed to trade for oxen, pigs, and goats. But when the price for an ox was set at an exorbitant price, well beyond the reasonable norms, Pigafetta cancelled the transaction.

In the meantime, two crewmen deserted. Martín de Ayamonte, an apprentice seaman, and Bartolomé de Saldaña, a cabin boy. Both swam ashore in the cover of night and never returned. The consensus among the crew was the fear instilled by the recent storms combined with the bleak prospect of more starvation and sickness had driven them away.

With depleted provisions and the crewmen famished, the officers reasoned that more leverage was needed in their negotiations with the inflationary locals. The opportunity arose when a chieftain from a neighboring village called Balibo (Silabão), and his son, were visiting aboard the flagship and were seized as ransom. The chieftain of Amabau feared that his neighbor, who was an important ruler, would be killed, and that he would be held responsible for the outcome. He quickly acquiesced to the officer's demands to surrender 1 ox, 10 pigs, and 10 goats. In exchange, the men presented gifts in proper and reasonable trade value.

Timor had been known to abound with white sandalwood, which was found nowhere else, and so was exported throughout the Indies trade network. Pigafetta was informed by the locals that when they go to cut the sandalwood, a devil appears to them in various forms, and tells them if they have any need, they should request he fulfill it. They claimed the apparition often caused them to be sick for several days. It was also observed in all the islands of the Timor archipelago, a malady named "the disease of St. Job." Some claimed it to be syphilis, and others leprosy.

With fresh provisions, the *Victoria* continued to sail westward along the north side of Timor.

On the main deck, Pigafetta joined Katipana to continue his study of Malay and listen to the old man's stories.

The old pilot pointed out to sea. 'You know, there is an island far to the west called Ocoloro (Enggano). It is a colony of warriors, all women. They become pregnant by the wind.'

Pigafetta grinned. 'By the wind, you say?'

'Yes,' the old pilot seriously replied. 'If it is a male child, they kill it. But any girl will be raised as their own. And if any man visits the island, they are put to death.'

'Sounds like they are not very fond of men.'

Katipana pointed again to the sea. 'You know, in Java, the women love their men much more if they alter their manhood.'

Pigafetta gaped at him.

'It is true!' Katipana said. 'When a young man falls in love with a maiden, they will tie little bells, with thread, under their foreskin.'

Pigafetta winced, and immediately thought of the mutilation of Palang in Cebu.

Katapina continued, enthralled with his own tale. 'These young men stand below their loved one's window and pretend to urinate. As they shake their member, the bells ring. They continue ringing until the maiden hears the sound and come down. The couples unite, and the maidens take great delight in having the bells ring inside them.'

'That is the most preposterous thing I have ever heard,' Pigafetta said.

'It is their custom,' Katipana insisted.

'Would you do such a thing to your member, for a woman?' Pigafetta asked.

'Not on my life, never!' Katipana replied.

'After some of the things I have seen.' Pigafetta said. 'I don't know if I can doubt you.'

Katipana grinned broadly.

On February 8, the *Victoria* reached the western Cape of Timor. The two Moluccan pilots met Pigafetta on the main deck. 'We leave now in Timor,' Katipana said. 'Your captain plans to sail south of Java, into the great Indian Ocean. We do not know these waters and cannot help you anymore.'

'I understand,' Pigafetta said. 'We thank you. I thank you. And I shall miss your company.'

'I wish you safe travels,' Katipana said. The pilots disembarked at Timor.

Captain Cano brought the *Victoria* into the Lesser Sunda Island Chain. As expected, on February 13, Albo had them take up a course west-by-southwest, sailing well south of Java, but also well out of range of any Portuguese vessels. They had now entered the Indian Ocean on a course toward the Cape of Good Hope.

On March 18, a high island was sighted at 38 degrees south. But any hope of temporary shelter was quickly dashed. The winds made it difficult to anchor, and since the island appeared to be uninhabited and barren, there was little sustenance to be taken from it. The *Victoria* sailed on. The place would later be named Amsterdam Island.

As they sailed south, the lower latitudes meant lower temperatures. The crew, in tattered clothes and barefoot, shivered and cursed as they fought the sea and the winds with frigid waves washing the deck and no land in sight. On April 3, the hull began to leak. They were forced to strike the sails and repair what they could on the high seas. Meanwhile, the commanders plotted their next course of action. The skies had been too overcast, making readings difficult, and the spent crew was threatening mutiny. It was decided they would sail close to 42 degrees south latitude, closer to the African coast but still far enough out to sea to ensure a safe distance to round the Cape.

From April 7 to 16, the *Victoria* tacked back and forth into a prevailing west wind in heavy seas chilled by the Antarctic, on a westerly course, at 40-41 degrees south latitude. The skies remained overcast, but the officers on deck believed they had accurate readings. So, on April 17, believing they were beyond the Cape's longitude, Cano and Albo turned the vessel north.

They sailed for three weeks before spotting a long coastline off the port bow. Pigafetta and Albo were in the captain's cabin looking at a sea chart spread over a table.

'Have we rounded the Cape?' Captain Cano asked.

'The coast has been running N.E. and S.W. and a quarter east and west,' Albo replied. 'I am afraid we are still on the east coast of Africa.'

Cano punched a wooden beam, regretting it immediately. 'Dammit!' he exclaimed. 'How far are we from the Cape?'

Albo looked over the sea chart and placed his finger on a point. 'We are 8 leagues north of the River Del Infante and 160 leagues from the Cape.'

Cano cradled his fist in his left palm and looked at the chart. 'This is how days become months,' he said. 'We will either freeze or starve.' He sucked the blood off his knuckle. 'Pigafetta, what's the status on our rations?'

'The meat has all rotted,' Pigafetta replied.

Cano frowned.

'Spoiled, some maggots,' Pigafetta offered. 'We had very little salt to preserve it.

'Is anything left? Water?'

'We have water,' Pigafetta replied. 'And a little rice to go with it.'

Cano shivered and sighed. 'Very well,' he said. 'We will search for supplies along the coast.'

With the crew at the high edge of desperation, the *Victoria* sailed the coast, but there was never any suitable harbor. The men were weakened from malnourishment, and sick from exposure to the cold. Nevertheless, many of them had to take turns at the pumps to keep the vessel afloat, and most saw no chance of making it around the Cape in their present state.

Threats of mutiny again surfaced. Some of the men wished to sail to Mozambique to obtain provisions, and regardless of the risks of imprisonment or execution. They would plead for mercy to the Portuguese officials.

But many others, especially the Spaniards, stood firm, desiring to preserve their honor over their lives. They were determined to continue onward, no matter what the cost. Eventually their attitude won over the majority, and they made the bold decision to never surrender, no matter who they encountered. The ship turned back out to sea in search of a route around the Cape, the mood carrying them for some time. But as they approached the Cape, the seas rolled harder, and the winds howled.

On May 16, a storm battered the *Victoria*. Heavy seas sent the ship tottering sideways down canyons of waves while the winds ripped at the masts. Men were swept overboard; others were injured colliding with bulkheads. The foretopmast crashed, broke away, and sprung the foreyard. The *Victoria* was forced to turn back. But the survivors rallied, and repairs were made the following day.

On May 18, at 20 miles out, Cano and the pilots agreed to make another attempt. But once again, as they approached the Cape, rough seas pushed them back.

Finally, on May 19, the seas were rough, but not nearly the sight they were previously. The *Victoria* pushed through the crosswinds, rolled from wave to wave, and sailed past the recognized 20 degrees longitude mark on their chart. They had been at sea for five months and had lost nearly a third of the crew to get this far, but they could now head north, for home, as long as they could find food.

With some small sense of relief, Cano ordered a change of heading. They would sail up the coastline 70 miles north of modern Capetown to acquire water and firewood in Saldanha Bay.

When they arrived, a Portuguese ship was in the bay. Cano assumed it was en route to the Indies. Having little to fear, Cano saluted its captain, Pedro Cuaresma, and explained who they were, and whence they had come. Fortunately for Cano, the captain was

289

preoccupied with supplying his own vessel. He simply saluted without any inquiries.

The *Victoria* left Saldanha Bay on May 21 on a northwesterly course. With the winds in their favor, the crew sailed on for more than 2 weeks, the impetus to get home stronger than any hunger. The *Victoria* passed the equator on June 8, sailing on through the rest of the month. She finally halted on July 1. The men had been decimated from hunger, disease, exposure, and exhaustion by working the pumps. Twenty-one men had now been committed to the deep. Pigafetta curiously noted that when the Christians were buried at sea their faces turned upward toward heaven and the natives always downward.

Cano, Albo, and Pigafetta convened in the captain's quarters to discuss their next course of action. Cano began the meeting.

'Gentlemen, we have a dilemma,' he said. 'If we do not act now, we will all die at sea. Either we anchor in Cape Verde, or we starve to death.'

'Cape Verde is a Portuguese stronghold!' Albo exclaimed. 'They will seize our vessel, likely imprison us, or worse, execute us.'

'But maybe they do not have to know of our mission or where we have really been,' Cano said.

'How?' Pigafetta asked.

'I propose the following,' Cano said. 'We say that we have come from the Spanish islands in the West Indies. We inform the Portuguese authorities that on crossing the equator, we encountered a storm and were driven off course.'

Pigafetta began to see the captain's line of reasoning. 'The foremast is broken,' he said. 'We have evidence of that claim.'

'It would be a clever ruse,' Albo added.

'Precisely,' Cano said. 'We can claim we were separated from our other two vessels, and that they proceeded onward to Spain.'

The men smiled and nodded in approval of the ploy and went to inform the crew.

On July 9, the *Victoria* anchored off the Port of Ribeira on São Tiagu Island (Santiago Island, Cape Verde). A skiff was sent to shore for supplies, under the command of the ship's clerk, Martín Mendez.

The following day, Mendez and his detail returned, and he reported to the captain on the quarterdeck. Albo and Pigafetta were nearby.

'Mendez,' Cano said. 'What is the news?'

'Good news sir,' he replied. 'The officials believed our story. We have procured our first load of rice.'

'Excellent,' Cano said.

'There is something else, sir,' Mendez said.

'What is this?' Cano asked.

'Our logs say today is Wednesday July 5th, which is the date of the invoice. But the port officials laughed and insisted today is Thursday the 6th.'

'Thursday?' Albo asked. 'That is impossible. I have it entered as Wednesday in my logs?'

'It is Wednesday,' Pigafetta replied. 'I am certain of this. I have entered the date every day of our voyage in my journal.'

The officers, confused, looked at Mendez and each other for a moment.

'This is very strange,' Cano said. 'We will have to figure it out. But now we have starvation to attend to.' He looked at Mendez. 'Send the boat back for more supplies.'

'Yes sir,' Mendez said.

Over the next few days, the winds picked up. On July 13, the high winds threatened to drag the *Victoria* further into the harbor. Cano put out to sea to allow for an easy escape, if needed.

On the following day, Cano sent yet another boat into the port to obtain one last load of rice. The crew never returned, alarming the officers. Perhaps they had been found out. After waiting another day, Cano moved the vessel closer to the harbor to investigate. A Portuguese boat soon approached with a delegation of port officials.

'Surrender your vessel now,' one of the officials exclaimed. 'It is to be seized and your men will be sent to Lisbon on the next available ship.'

'We shall not!' Cano responded in defiance. 'I demand you return my men immediately.'

'Very well,' the official replied. 'Your message will be delivered to the governor, and we will return with his answer.'

As they waited outside the harbor, a lookout spotted four caravels in port loading armed men. With a weak and malnourished crew, Cano knew had no choice but to set sail. The boat crew of 13 men would have to be abandoned. The *Victoria* headed out to sea.

It was later found out by testimonies in Spanish court that the ruse had been compromised by a certain crewman named Simón de Burgos. He had signed on as a Castilian but was Portuguese by birth. He felt at ease among his countrymen and talked too much, revealing how they encroached into the Portuguese domain of the Spice Islands.

After they rounded the Cape Verde Islands, the *Victoria* took up a heading for the Azores, to catch the westerly winds from there. The sick and malnourished crew continuously labored at the pumps to keep the vessel from sinking. Headwinds eventually brought the ship's progress to a miserable pace, and more men were buried at sea. Finally, near the end of August, the winds became northwesterly and steady, and they were able to sail toward the Iberian Peninsula.

On September 4, the lookouts sighted Cape St. Vincent, on the southwestern corner of Portugal. The crew's spirits lifted as they passed the iconic landmark, knowing they were almost home.

Finally, on September 6, the dilapidated *Victoria* creaked into the harbor of San Lucar, Spain, with a remaining crew of only 18 Europeans and 4 Moluccans. The following day, the vessel was towed up the Guadalquivir River.

On September 8, 1522, the *Victoria* tied up in the harbor of Seville and fired off a final salute of artillery. Onlookers gasped at the gaunt and sickly crew with ribs clearly visible through their tattered clothing. Agents from Casa de la Contratación were quick to inventory and secure the valuable cargo of cloves.

By September 9, the news of the returning voyage to the Spice Islands had spread throughout Seville. Crowds thronged the streets to witness the mariners fulfill their vows of pilgrimage. The remaining crewmen summoned all their strength and formed a procession. They walked the city streets in tattered shirts, barefoot, and carried flaming torches. They arrived at Santa Maria de la Victoria, the very church where Fernão Magalhães received the royal standard for the Armada to the Moluccas. The men humbly knelt before the statue of the virgin, gave thanks for their safe return, and offered to fulfill their tithes to the church. The men then continued onward with their pilgrimage to the shrine of Santa Maria del Antigua in Seville Cathedral.

Crossing a wood bridge over the Guadalquivir River, Pigafetta walked up alongside Albo and put his hand on his shoulder. 'It is a miracle we are alive,' he said quietly.

'A miracle indeed,' Albo replied. 'I have figured we departed on September 20, 1519; and arrived home on September 6, 1522. It has been nearly three years to the date.'

'Yes. You realize we have completed a full circumnavigation of the earth, 60,000 miles, east to west? I cannot get over it.'

Albo stopped suddenly and turned to Pigafetta. 'Oh yes. Do you remember when the Portuguese informed us the day was Thursday, but our logs were recorded as Wednesday?'

'I do,' Pigafetta replied.

'You see, we have always traveled westward, around the entire world.'

'So, you are saying we should have lost 24 hours at some point,' Pigafetta reasoned. 'Of course. That's it. So, we must have, at some geographical point, a line of demarcation, to compensate for the logs in future voyages.'

'Precisely.'

The men smiled, nodding at the solution, and continued to the Seville Cathedral.

'Perhaps the Lord has just illumined us with this revelation,' Pigafetta said, as they approached the cathedral and went inside.

The next morning Pigafetta inquired with the Casa de la Contratación where he could find Magalhães' father-in-law, Diogo Barbosa. An agent directed him to the Alcazar. Pigafetta was granted entry by the guards at the fortress gate and was soon received by Diogo in the Ambassador's Hall.

'Diogo Barbosa?' Pigafetta asked.

Diogo nodded.

Pigafetta bowed. 'My name is Antonio Pigafetta. You do not know me sir, but I served as the fleet recorder under the command of your son-in-law Fernão de Magalhães in the armada to the Moluccas. It was an honor to serve under the great commander of the sea.'

Diogo noticed Pigafetta's gaunt appearance and waved at a servant. 'Bring some refreshments, now.' He turned again to Pigafetta. 'I heard the preliminary report from the Casa of what happened in Mactan. I will miss Fernão very much.'

Pigafetta nodded, then said, 'I wanted to inform his wife Beatriz of the journey.'

Diogo stared blankly for a moment, then responded, 'You have not heard then?'

'What sir?'

'My daughter has passed away.'

'I am very sorry,' Pigafetta said. 'Please accept my deepest condolences.'

'It should never have happened, her death you know,' Diogo said. 'It was the stress that killed her.'

'How do you mean, sir?' Pigafetta asked.

'Let me explain,' Diogo said. 'Fernão's cousin, Captain Mesquite has been held in prison by Fonseca and the Casa ever since the *San Antonio* arrived here, nearly a year and a half ago.'

'The *San Antonio* arrived?' Pigafetta asked in astonishment.

'Yes, and with mutineers. It was Gomes, Guerra and others who conspired among themselves to level false testimony against my son, Fernão. Mesquita tried to defend his honor, but his testimony alone carried no weight against the mutineers. He still rots in prison.'

'This is absurd. The captain-general was in the right for all his actions. I was there.'

Diogo nodded. 'But that is not all. The Casa sided with the mutineers and revoked all prior commitments. They refused to pay the 50,000 maravedis to Beatriz that was prior authorized by the king. They claimed the funds were not available and thus her means of living was denied. I could help little myself, for my savings were all invested in the expedition. We all suffered, but the mistreatment of Beatriz was unforgiving. She was placed under house arrest to prevent any escape to Portugal. Beatriz had already lost an unborn son and then she lost Rodrigo to sickness. She passed less than a year later, in March of 1522, just six months before your arrival.'

'This is unconscionable,' Pigafetta said. 'There must be a way to defend the captain-general's name.'

'I paid the price for trying and was ordered to forfeit Fernão's property which had been given him before the voyage. I was furious. Mesquita's testimony was valid. Fernão treated the mutineers in Port San Julian well and pardoned many who never deserved it. I even dared to warn the king to the effect that such poor treatment of the Magalhães' family would set a bad precedent and discourage those who sincerely wished to serve the crown and only encourage the malefactors who chose the contrary.'

'What did the king say?'

'My pleas went unheeded,' Diogo replied. 'Nobody in the court or the Casa would trust a sole witness until any further counter-testimony should come forth.'

'Sir, I will make sure all of the crew are informed of what has transpired. I assure you.'

'Thank you,' Diogo said with a smile. 'You are indeed a good friend to our family, and especially Fernão.'

Once Don Carlos heard the news of the *Victoria's* return, he immediately sent his congratulations, for not only had they discovered a new route to the Spice Islands, but had, according to Casa agents, acquired the highest quality of cloves ever seen. The value was estimated sufficient to return a profit for the armada. It was also proof the crown could attain much more, for the signed treaties were now secured among the Moluccan rajahs.

The Victoria's crew verified the veracity of Mesquita's testimony concerning the events in Port San Julian and orders from the king were given to release him from prison.

But, with the excitement of the first circumnavigation, and the lucrative cargo of cloves from the Moluccas, Don Carlos also chose to formally ignore the charges of mutiny and desertion against Gomes, Guerra, and all others. They were even paid their salaries due.

A few months after their arrival, Don Carlos intervened for the release of the 13 crewmen taken hostage by the Portuguese.

Eventually, all the surviving crew were summoned to the emperor's court in Valladolid to individually testify of the key events during the voyage. Pigafetta recounted his own experience in his final journal entry:

Departing from Seville, I went to Valladolid, where I presented to his Sacred Majesty Don Carlos, not gold or silver, but something to be prized by such a lord. And among other things I gave him a book written by my hand treating of all things that had occurred day by day on our voyage. Then I departed thence, and went to Portugal, where I spoke with the King, Dom João, of things which I had seen. And, passing through Spain, I came into France where I made a gift of some things from the other hemisphere to Madame the Regent, mother of the very Christian King François. Then I came into Italy, where I established my abode forever.

Epilogue: The "Trinidad"

After the *Victoria* had sailed out of Tidore in late December, the *Trinidad* remained to be careened and fully refurbished by the crewmen managing the local workers. It had also been decided to fortify the warehouse with the artillery and wooden beams saved from the scrapped vessels *Concepción* and *Santiago*. Five crewmen had volunteered to remain and manage the trading house.

On February 14, 1522, two months after the *Victoria* departed for Spain, former captain-general, Juan Carvalho, died of illness. The remaining officers would command the *Trinidad*. Gomez de Espinosa became captain, Giovanni Polcevera would continue to serve as pilot, León Pancaldo as co-pilot, and Diego Martín would serve as shipmaster. The commanders had formulated their plan to sail east, first to a latitude of between 38-40 degrees north, then catch westerly winds back across the Pacific, to turn southeast for landfall in the new Spanish colony of Daríen (Panama).

On April 6, 1522, the *Trinidad* was ready for departure. She was manned by 54 crew and loaded with 50 tons of cloves. An assortment of merchandise was also brought to trade for provisions. They sailed to Kau Bay on the northeast arm of Gilolo Island to pick up supplies which had been prearranged by the Rajahs of Tidore and Gilolo. They remained there nearly nine days to load water, wood, and foodstuffs.

On April 20, the *Trinidad* sailed east by 1/4 degree north. The westerly winds eventually changed, and they encountered the northeast trade winds, steering north.

On May 3, two small islands were sighted at 5 degrees north. These were part of the Sonsorol Group. Encountering headwinds, Polcevera directed them tack

299

on an east by north course. Between 10 and 20 degrees north they sighted 14 islands of the Marianas.

On June 11, they anchored in an island located just over 19 degrees north. The natives received them well, and one volunteered to join as a pilot. They continued to push ever northward in search of the expected westerlies. The commanders had believed the Asian mainland would appear on their port side but were sorely mistaken. The provisions were quickly depleted until only rice remained.

Sailing further north, the temperature began to drop. The men had been accustomed to the tropics for some time, and now they had no adequate clothing to endure the frigid winds. Scurvy and exposure set in upon them. Worse, a new and unfamiliar disease plagued them into a debilitating state. In search of an explanation, they performed an autopsy on the corpse of a diseased caulker, Juan Gonzalez. They discovered a parasite in his intestines but had no knowledge of how to treat the ailment or prevent its spread.

Adding to their misery, a typhoon off the coast of Hokkaido battered the *Trinidad* for five days with such force it carried away the main mast, then pummeled the forecastle and poop, which shattered into pieces. Now at 43 degrees north, Espinosa recognized the futility in pushing onward. He decided to retreat south to the warmer climates to find provisions and recover their health.

After sailing 20 days to the southwest, they arrived at an island called Mao (Maung Island of the Marianas). Here three men and their native pilot deserted. Their further journey from the Marianas to the Moluccas was a punishing 6 weeks of sickness and starvation. Of the 54 who sailed out of Tidore on the *Trinidad*, 33 had perished. The survivors were so weak that they could barely navigate the ship.

Sailing along the coast of Gilolo they encountered a proa of natives who they had known before and were informed of some disturbing recent events. Only 15 days after their departure from the Moluccas, a Portuguese armada of 7 vessels and 300 armed crewmen under the command of Antonio de Brita arrived in Ternate. He had learned in Java that two Spanish vessels had visited Tidore. Brito anchored off Ternate, and Brita sent a message to the Rajah of Tidore asking why there was a Spanish trading house on his island, for it was in Portuguese waters. Almanzor claimed he only allowed it because of threats from the Spaniards, but he would now obediently pledge allegiance to Portugal. Brito sent a squadron of men to dismantle the factory and confiscate everything therein.

Meanwhile, Espinosa's surviving men were so emaciated that only seven could do any work on the ship. In desperation, he decided to dispatch a letter via the ship clerk—Bartolome Sanchez, via a canoe manned by islanders, to Brito, pleading for assistance and requesting him to send provisions. Brito reacted without mercy by placing Sanchez in custody, then purposely waited some days to make sure the crews of the *Trinidad* had further weakened from their malaise.

Once Espinosa realized no assistance seemed forthcoming, he raised anchor to bring the vessel to a more secure location at Benaconora. Finally, Brito sent a squadron to investigate and arrived upon a ghastly spectacle. The stench of festering sores and men strewn about the decks in appalling conditions, and without the strength to move, shocked the Portuguese. Brito's men continued with their duties and confiscated everything, including charts, documents, nautical instruments, and even Magalhães' personal chest and papers. But they never recovered his private journal.

Espinosa was incensed and demanded a notarized list of everything taken, since it was the property of Spain. One of the Portuguese officers merely answered mockingly, 'Give him the list when he hangs from a yardarm!'

Those of the *Trinidad* who were able to walk were taken to Ternate, incarcerated, and put to work on the construction of a new factory on the island. The *Trinidad* was also brought to Ternate, but after unloading the cargo, a squall forced it into the rocky shore, where it broke into pieces. It would never sail again, and the materials were salvaged for use in the fortress construction. When Brito discovered that Pedro Lorosa had joined the Spanish fleet, he was publicly beheaded as a traitor.

The Portuguese mistreated their prisoners and forced them to live in squalor and privation. The remaining 22 survivors and the 5 men posted at the warehouse eventually suffered imprisonment in various distant lands, from the Moluccas, to Malacca, to Cochin. Only five would ever make it back to the Iberian Peninsula: Ginés de Mafra, León Pancalda, Gómez Espinosa, Juan Rodriguez, and lastly, Hans, the master gunner from Bergen, Norway. Hans perished while in a Lisbon jail. The others were eventually liberated and returned to Spain. All five may be included to the list of those who circumnavigated the globe in the Armada of the Moluccas and dared to sail off the edge of the earth. Fernão Magalhães was the one who proved the circumnavigation could be done. Many sailors followed in his wake, but it was more than a half a century before anyone succeeded.

The Magellan Chronicles:
Sources

Albuquerque, Afonso de. *The Commentaries of the Great Alfonso de Albuquerque.* Translated by Walter de Gray Birch. 4 vols. New York: Cambridge University Press, 2010. (London: Hakluyt Society, 1875).

Arciniegas, Germán. *Amerigo and the New World: The Life and Times of Amerigo Vespucci.* Translated by Harriet de Onís. New York: Alfred A Knoff, 1955.

Barbosa, Duarte. *A Description of the Coasts of East Africa and Malabar in the Beginning of the Sixteenth Century.* Translated by Henry E.J. Stanley. Kentucky: n.p., 2014.

Bergreen, Laurence. *Over the Edge of the World: Magellan's Terrifying Circumnavigation of the Globe.* New York: Harper Collins Publishers, 2003.

Blackburn, Graham. *The Overlook Illustrated Dictionary of Nautical Terms.* Woodstock, NY: The Overlook Press, 1981.

Bridgeman, Keith and Tahira Arsham, eds. *Magellan.* England: Viartis, 2008.

Camerota, Filippo, ed. *Museo Galileo: A Guide to the Treasures of the Collection.* Firenze, Italy: Gionti, 2010.

Caruncho, Daniel R. *Royal Alcazar of Seville: More than a Thousand Years of Art and Architecture.* Translated by Cerys Giordano Jones. Barcelona: Dos de Arte Ediciones, S.L., 2016.

Castanheda, Fernão Lopes de. *Historia do descobrimento e conquista de India pelos Portugueses.* 2 vols. Lisboa: Typographia Rollandiana, 1833.

Corrêa, Gaspar. *Lendas de India.* 2 vols. Lisboa: Academia Real das Sciencies de Lisboa, 1858.

Cliff, Nigel. *Holy War: How Vasco da Gama's Epic Voyages Turned the Tide in a Centuries-Old Clash of Civilizations.* New York: Harper Collins, 2011.

Cribb, Joe, Barrie Cook, and Ian Carradice. *A Comprehensive View of the Coins of the World Throughout History.* London: Little, Brown & Co., 1999.

Crowley, Roger. *Conquerors: How Portugal Forged the First Global Empire.* New York: Random House, 2015.

Danvers, Frederick Charles. *The Portuguese in India.* 2 vols. London: Elibron, 2007.

Delagado, Francisco Gil. *Seville Cathedral.* Spain: Escudo de Oro, n.d.

Diffie, Bailey W. and George D. Winius. *Foundations of the Portuguese Empire 1415-1580.* 10 vols.

Minneapolis, MN: University of Minnesota Press, 1977.

Edwards, Charles Lester and Amerigo Vespucci. *Amerigo Vespucci.* Edited by Keith Bridgeman and Tahira Arsham. England: Viartis, 2009.

Fernándo-Armesto, Felipe. *Amerigo: The Man Who Gave his Name to America.* New York: Random House Publishing Group, 2007.

Gibbons, Tony, ed. *The Encyclopedia of Ships: Over 1,500 Military and Civilian Ships from 5000 B.C. to the Present Day.* San Diego: Thunder Bay Press, 2001.

Góis, Damião de. *Lisbon in the Renaissance.* Translated by Jeffrey S. Ruth. New York: Italica Press, 1996.

Green, Toby. *Inquistion: The Reign of Fear.* New York: St. Martin's Press, 2007.

—. *The Rise of the Trans-Atlantic Slave trade in Western Africa, 1300-1589.* New York: Cambridge University Press, 2012.

Guillemard, Francis Henry Hill. *The Life of Ferdinand Magellan and the First Circumnavigation of the Globe: 1480-1521.* London: George Philip & Son, 1890.

Hargrave, Catherine Perry. *A History of Playing Cards.* New York: Dover Publications Inc., 2014.

Hazard, Henry W. and Kenneth Setton, eds. *A History of the Crusades: Volume III: The Fourteenth and Fifteenth Centuries.* 6 vols. Madison, WI: The University of Wisconsin Press, 1975.

Johnson, Donald S., Tapio Markkanen Juha Nurminen, and Pär-Henrik Sjöström. *The History of Seafaring: Navigating the World's Oceans.* London: Conway Maritime Press, 2007.

Joyner, Tim. *Magellan.* Camden, ME: International marine Publishing, 1992.

Kemp, Peter, ed. *The Oxford Companion to Ships and the Sea.* Oxford: Oxford University Press, 1988.

Konstam, Angus. *Historical Atlas of Exploration 1492-1600.* London: Mercury Books, 2006.

Krondl, Michael. *The Taste of Conquest: The Rise and Fall of the Three Great Cities of Spice.* New York: Balantine Books, 2007.

Lavery, Brian. *Ship: The Epic Story of Maritime Adventure.* New York: DK Publishing, 2010.

Major, Richard Henry, ed. *India in the Fifteenth Century.* New York: Cambridge University Press, 2010. (London: Hakluyt Societ, 1857).

Mandeville, Sir John. *The Book of Marvels and Travels.* Translated by Anthony Bale. Oxford: Oxford University Press, 2012.

Martyr, Peter. *The Discovery of the new World in the Writings of Peter Martyr of Anghiera*. Edited by Ernesto Lunari, Elisa Magioncalda, and Rosanna Mazzacane. Rome: Istituto Poligrafica, 1992.

Menzies, Gavin. *1421 The Year China Discovered America*. New York: Harper Collins Publishers, 2003.

Monteiro, Saturnino. *Portuguese Sea Battles Volume I: The First World Sea Power 1139-1521*. 8 vols. Translated by Maria do Céu Barreto. Oeiras, Portugal: Saturnino Monteiro, 2014.

Morris, John Gottlieb. *Martin Behaim the German Astronomer and Cosmographer of the Times of Columbus*. Baltimore: John Murphy and Co., 1855.

Morrison, Samuel Eliot. *Admiral of the Ocean Sea: A Life of Christopher Columbus*. Toronto: Little, Brown & Co., 1970.

Newitt, Malyn, ed. *The Portuguese in West Africa, 1415-1670*. New York: Cambridge University Press, 2010.

Nicolle, David. *The Portuguese in the Age of Discovery c. 1340-1665*. Oxford: Osprey Publishing Ltd., 2012.

Nielsen Jr., Niels C., Norvin Hein, Frank E. Reynolds, Alan L. Miller, Samuel E. Karff, Alice C. Cochran, and Paul McClean, eds. *Religions of the World*. New York: St. Martin's Press, Inc., 1983.

O'Bryan, John. *A History of Weapons*. San Francisco: Chronicle Books, 2013.

Passos, John Dos. *The Portugal Story: Three Centuries of Exploration and Discovery.* Lexington: Doubleday, 1969.

Pearsen, Michael. *Port Cities and Invaders: The Swahili oast, India, and Portugal in the Early Modern Era.* Baltimore: The John Hopkins University Press, 1998.

Perreira, Duarte Pacheco. *Esmeraldo de Situ Orbis.* Translated and Edited by Geroge H.T. Kimble. New York: Routledge, 2016.

Pigafetta, Antonio. *Magellan's Voyage: A Narrative Account of the First Circumnavigation.* Translated and edited by R.A. Skelton. New York: Dover Publications Inc., 1969.

—. *The First Voyage Round the World by Magellan.* Edited by Henry John Stanly. New York: Cambridge University Press, 2010.

Pires, Tomé. *The Summa Oriental of Tomé Pires.* 2 vols. Surrey, UK: Ashgate Publishing Ltd., 2010.

Preto, Luis. *Jogo do Pau: The Ancient Art and Modern Science of Portuguese Stick Fighting.* n.p. 2013.

Rossfelder, André. *In Pursuit of Longitude: Magellan and the Antimeridian.* La Jolla, CA: Starboard Books, 2010.

Sanceau, Elaine. *The Reign of the Fortunate King 1495-1521*. USA: Archon Books, 1970.

Stephens, H. Morse. *Albuquerque*. Oxford: Clarendon Press, 1897.

Theal, George McCall. *History and Ethnography of Africa South of the Zambesi 1505-1795*. 3 vols. New York: Cambridge University Press, 2010. (London: Swan Sonnenschein & Co., 1910).

Thomas, Hugh. *The Slave Trade: The Story of the Atlantic Slave Trade 1440-1870*. New York: Simon and Schuster, 1997.

Webster, Roderick and Marjorie. *Western Astrolabes: Historic Scientific Instruments of the Adler Planetarium & Astronomy Museum*. 2 vols. Chicago: Adler Planetarium & Astronomy Museum, 1998.

Weinstein, Donald. *Ambassador from Venice: Pietro Pasqualigo in Lisbon, 1501*. Minneapolis, MN: University of Minnesota Press, 1960.

Whiteway, Richard Stephen. *The Rise of Portuguese Power in India. A.D. 1497-A.D. 1550*. Columbia, SC: n.p., 2018.

Varthema, Ludovico di. *The Travels of Ludovico di Varthema in Egypt, Syria, Arabia Deserta and Arabia Felix in Persia, India, and Ethiopia, 1503 to 1508*. Lexington, KY: Forgotten Books, 2014. (London: Hakluyt Society, 1863).

Vicente, Gil. *Four Plays of Gil Vicente.* Translated by Aubrey F. G. Bell. San Bernardino, CA: Forgotten Books, 2015.

Zweig, Stefen. *Magellan.* London: Pushkin Press, 2011.

About the Author

Brett Stortroen has authored the biographical novel, *Night of the Dragon: The Saga of Saint George* and the non-fiction book, now sold in over thirty countries, *Mecca, Muhammad & the Moon God: A Candid Investigation into the Origins of Islam*. With a BA and MA in Theological and Historical Studies, he also publishes articles on his web site, bigfaithministries.com. Traveling the world as a telecommunication engineer in the cruise industry, he has been able to incorporate his maritime experiences and historical research into the latest biographical novel series, *The Magellan Chronicles*.